BLOOD
OF
BRIMSTONE

Copyright © 2023 By Sydney J Austin

Cover designed by **MiblArt**

ISBN: 979-8-218-16221-4

realsydneyjaustin@gmail.com
https://www.facebook.com/sydneyjaustin

CHAPTER ONE

Here lies my tomb—a vast and gray abyss of foreverness.

I take in the limitless horizon of blue and white. The waves that crash alongside the cliff beckon me to jump off the edge. The rocks below crave my blood. And upon my jump, any evidence of my death will be cleansed away by the deep blue. Almost as if I had never existed.

There is a more peaceful way to go. Many times I've fantasized walking into the water and letting the giant waves hold me down, the seaweed clasping onto me, till the last breath escapes my lungs. But, even after my death, I will still hear the muffling sounds of the ocean crashing above and the pressure of the water embracing me like a lost friend or my parents, who now no longer roam this earth.

Every time I approach the cliff, something tugs me back. I can't manipulate my legs to move any further. What is stopping me? I welcome death with open arms, yet it rejects me every time. Is this not the fate that is destined for me? And if it is not, then where does my destiny lie?

Just one peek. Just one look at the tomb that awaits me. One dive, and I can end it all. End this suffering. End me.

As I wander away from the windy cliff, my muscles loosen. My subconscious keeps me from making the final jump because it knows I don't want to die. I don't want to live this life of loneliness anymore. A life where I am not wanted. A life where I am a prisoner in my mind.

Another day. It will come.

I walk back towards the village, hoping for a better day than the last, although my hopes are never high. The sun is out, and the wind breezes past my face, sending goosebumps down my cold cheeks. I pull my cloak tightly against my body, preserving every ounce of warmth left in me. If I walk fast enough, I'll work up a sweat and keep myself warm.

"Morana, finally, your shift started five minutes ago," The tavern keeper shouts.

The wind catches the door and slams it shut behind me. Irritated eyes stare as the vibrations rumble through the room. The snow sweeps across the floor like an icy mist. Quickly melting from the burning fire in the fireplace.

"I apologize, sir." I hang my cloak on the hook, careful not to rip it since my last one had so many holes. I used my last pay for a new cloak for the winter. Unfortunately, good fabric is scarce in Rhemus.

Mr. Jack stands behind the bar, handling a rusty mug with a towel over his shoulder. His lousy mood reflects on his workers. Any of his customers can bring a smile to his face. They may pay to keep his business open, but everyone knows the workers are the ones who keep this place running. All for very terrible pay.

"Don't be late again, or I'll throw you out just like the last one."

I chuckle to myself, trying to conceal my smile. The last woman who worked here left on her own accord, only because the men he allows in this joint harass women. Sadly, I've grown used to the harassment and sexism by now. I force a smile on my face and pretend I don't hear the cruel things that spew from their mouths.

"Get to work," He orders as he disappears into the back room, shuffling his feet behind him.

I look at a table of malodorous men who just sat down, laughing and rustling each other up before the night's end.

This is not how I want to spend my day.

I would do anything to serve the lone wench with her face in a book or the silent man who warms his hands around a cup of hot tea. But, instead, I drag myself to the loud commotion the men have brought in. I hold my breath.

"What can I get for you?" I ask.

The tallest turns to me.

"A smile on that pretty face of yours." Draven and his clan laugh obnoxiously.

Draven is a woodworker. His crew are the ones who make most of our wood furniture in the village, even the chairs they sit on in the tavern. His talent is impeccable, but his personality isn't so pleasing. It's repulsive. He works hard, there is no denying it, but he has the mouth of a pirate. And I have the pleasure of serving him.

To avoid encouraging his disgusting behavior, I keep my face neutral. Any emotion I reveal to him is a chance for him to talk and make a fool out of anyone and himself. His voice makes my ears hurt. I can already feel a headache coming on.

"Sorry, we don't serve that here," I cross my arms. "Now, what will it be, or are you going to sit there without buying anything?"

The smiles dissipate from their faces. Draven does not look so amused. It's almost hilarious. He can't comprehend the back talk of a woman of lesser rank than him.

He lightly strokes his beard.

"Ales for all."

I walk away, noting the order in my head. The men snicker behind me, but I try everything to tune it out. Reacting would only give them the satisfaction they crave. They thrive off attention, whether it be negative or positive.

If I could send them to an eternity in Tenebris, I would not hesitate. For his crimes against women, I imagine a vampire would drain him of his blood, leaving a single drop to the wandering werewolves. But, alas, his crimes do not call for banishment from Rhemus. And in this cruel and unjust kingdom, it never will.

The light realm is many things, but fair is not one of them. Only one thing can send you to Tenebris, which is the most unforgivable act. Murder. The King and Queen could care less about the thieves and other criminals in the realm. A slap on the wrist is all they ever give for petty crimes. A few weeks in jail and community service is all they will serve.

People claim the light realm is the best place to be. But every business has its flaws and secrets. We still have the thieves, rioters, and sexist men running about. Everyone turns an eye. The King is corrupt and brainwashes his people into believing we are a perfect kingdom. If by kingdom, he means his castle.

I pour the drinks into the biggest mugs we have. The bigger, the better, and the fewer times I'd have to refill them. Anything to avoid them and their comments. I peek around the corner. They laugh menacingly, smearing their dirty hands all over the table, and the mud from their shoes sticks to the floor. None of them sit still, and the chairs scratch across the floor.

"Keep your cool, Morana. I cannot have any more violence in this place." Mr. Jack whispers in my ear. His rancid breath hits my nose, and I almost gag.

I swiftly turn to him, creating a space between us.

"You can't be serious. So, you are blaming me?"

I reach around him to grab a stained rag and fling it over my shoulder, wetting my dry clothes.

"They are men. What do you expect after a hard day's work?"

I shoot him a disgusted look, "No, we are not having this conversation. I am here to do a job. Not to make men happy."

Mr. Jack shakes his head and leaves. He knows I'm right, and he turns away in defeat. No point in arguing with someone who has never experienced a man's harsh tones and unwanted touch.

I return to the men's table with a tray of ale. Quickly placing each one in front of them without a word or batting an eye in their direction.

"You are strong for a woman. Carrying all those mugs in one run. You know I wrestled with a basilisk once? Came over the border slithering around aimlessly. The poor thing didn't even know where it was." His face lowers. "So, I put it out of its misery."

"What a shame," I mumble. "Killing off such an innocent creature. Surprised you didn't wet yourself from pure fear."

Draven's eyes widen. Then, he smirks, "Sounds to me like you support the night realm. Filthy creatures they are. Sickening to the eye."

"Excuse me?" I tuck my tray under my arm and ready myself for the argument brewing. I know what Mr. Jack said but I'm not letting this go down so easily.

"They are vile and cruel and a disgrace to the entire kingdom. They kill without reason, and they are ugly to look at. Therefore, I damn them to the Inferno."

"With all the money you make at the castle, you think you would bathe more often."

Draven's eyes turn black. His jaw clenches. I want to laugh. I'm trying everything to keep my lips from twitching. I love to see men crumble before a woman.

"And I'm damn sure you could never please a woman as beautiful as the sirens that haunt the sea. You are pathetic." I say as I watch him squirm.

Without hesitation, the man lifts his hand. I stand my ground, chest out and chin high, ready for this fight. I don't move a muscle. I can't let him intimidate me. I've gone this far. Let him take the first hit.

"As far as I'm concerned, you are a criminal."

"On what grounds? Don't accuse me of being something without proper evidence." I growl.

"Anyone who advocates for Tenebris is a criminal. You might as well walk over the border and become one of them. Let them decide if you live or die."

Draven and his group take gulps of their drinks before slamming them to the table and spilling the leftovers everywhere. Draven spits next to my shoe, then wipes the corner of his mouth.

"I'd love to see your dead body in the mouth of one of those creatures." He shows a smile with yellow teeth.

I keep eye contact with him until he's entirely out of the building. As soon as he shuts the door, I let out my breath. My heart races from the adrenaline. The energy flowing through makes me want to have an ale myself. It would be well deserved.

"Morana!"

I break from my trance and hurry to the back, hoping Mr. Jack didn't witness the whole ordeal. Mr. Jack stands in the doorway with his arms crossed. His nose pointed upwards. The tapping of his foot makes me believe he did witness the conversation. It makes no difference. He will never stand by my side on the matter. He only cares about his business and money, like every other man in the damn village.

"Didn't we just talk about this? Stay quiet and do your job."

"With all due respect, Mr. Jack, Since starting here, there hasn't been one day I've gone without being harassed. You claim these are hardworking men. But they have wives at home, and their behavior is disgusting and disrespectful to all women."

"If you want a job, you will lower your tone with me."

Mr. Jack disappears around the corner again. I am curious to know how much more of this I can take from everyone. He is right, though. I need a job. I cannot go back to the life I had before this. I can finally afford to feed myself, but only barely enough. I don't have it in me to fight anymore. This might have been my breaking point.

The night simmers down, and only a few people still linger in the dining hall. I finally catch up with my cleaning and finish the last of the dishes.

I'm surprised to see so many dishes with food still in them. Just recently, Mr. Jack has come up with a new soup recipe. If I hadn't gotten into it with him earlier, I might have told him that people don't like the soup. That would only make him angrier. He'd probably find a reason to blame me for his soup tasting horrible.

Barnabas, the oldest man in the village, sits with his head lowered to the table and his arms at his sides, and a bowl full of Mr. Jack's soup. This is a regular thing for him. He comes in twice a week, demands the finest ale in all the land, and drinks to his heart's desire. He passes out before closing, but we usually let him rest until we close. He stirs in his sleep.

"Excuse me, Barnabas," I nudge his arm.

"What?" He stutters.

"We are closing for the night. Do you need help walking home?"

I raise my voice at him because his hearing has decreased over the years. Others say he fell victim to the siren's songs, which caused his deafness. It won't surprise anyone if it's the truth. The old man has some crazy adventurous stories from his younger days. However, we aren't sure how accurate those stories are. Years of drinking can change ones memory.

"No, I can do it. Thank you, sweet child."

He lifts his head and looks around. He wipes the drool off his mouth and pats me on the back before shuffling out the door. He almost falls on his face but catches himself on the door frame.

I clean the table off before moving to the next one.

"Morana, my lovely girl." a tiny voice echoes behind me.

I turn to see tiny flashes of light following a small creature. Raisel, my only friend, and the fairy that has shown me kindness. I can't hug her; she's as small as a butterfly. Yet, despite her size, she always knows how to put a smile on my face.

"I heard Draven and his group talking about you today. Well, they didn't say it was you. They talked about the woman who worked here, and you are the only woman who works here. They were making a ruckus, talking about a useless girl and–"

"Raisel, slow down."

She smiles and flutters before my face.

"I had to see if you were okay."

I fold the rag into fours as she hovers before my face. Glimmers of light pulse around her.

I've always wanted to touch her blonde hair. It resembles golden silk in the sunlight. I can't even tell what color her eyes are. They are so tiny. If I were as little as a butterfly, I'd fly far away from here. There would be no need to worry about life when your size can't compare to human problems.

"Yes, I am fine. It was only a little misunderstanding." I wipe the table in front of me.

"They are going around calling you a criminal. Did you do something?"

With no emotion, I say, "No. Not a damn thing."

Raisel sits on my shoulder to rest her wings. I always feel at peace when she does, even when she weighs little to nothing.

I tell her the whole story, and she has no words to say once I explain. Stillness is always a sign of worry. I didn't want her to judge me. That's why I would have rather said nothing.

"You're not worried they will go to the King's court about it?"

"No. Why should I be? Besides, they were drinking. Probably were already drunk as they walked in."

Raisel fiddles with her fingers and hovers in the air again. Unable to keep still. This is her thing, though. Once she has a thought, she focuses on it until it ends.

"You said the basilisk was an innocent creature. Who knows what that thing was trying to do over here? They always cause trouble."

"Do you agree with Draven that I am a criminal?" I ask.

"No, I'm not saying that, but–"

"But nothing. I did nothing wrong. Call me a criminal or not. No creature or human should be slaughtered for something they cannot control. Everyone has their own demons."

Raisel backs down. Her flutters become softer. She apologizes, and I gladly forgive her. I can't lose a friend like her. Not when she's been the only one there for me since my parent's deaths.

On chilly nights like this, I crave nothing more than to come home to my family, a fire burning in the fireplace, and a warm meal sitting on the table. That is how it is supposed to be. That's what a perfect life looks like to me.

The last time I experienced something like that was when I was twelve. It was right before my parents disappeared. I could still smell the fresh chicken right out of the oven. Chicken was rare, so it was a treat for us. Freshly cooked vegetables were beside it, and a cup of fruit juice was on the side. Fresh bread was served before dinner. Since then, I haven't had a meal like that. My stomach rumbles just thinking about it.

Most of the shops have closed and put out their lanterns. Open signs are now switched to closed, and the sound of crickets bounces off the building walls. Finally, some peace. Alone with my thoughts and not a worry in the world. At least for a moment.

I walk in the middle of the street. During the day, the streets are crowded with horses, carriages, and wagons hauling lumber and crops. It's nice to feel like I own the road.

"Hey."

I turn around. All is dark and quiet. I know I heard something. And I know that it was not some boy out after dark. This is a man's voice.

The sound goes off again. Next time, louder. I look to the alleyway beside me, and a figure of a man creeps around the corner.

The black silhouette comes running towards me in full force. The moonlight suddenly disappears, and pressure lays over my eyes and mouth. I lose my balance, but I am picked up just before I hit the ground. My feet drag across the ground.

I try to scream, but the pressure on my mouth is too much for me to make any noise. There are no cracks for me to breathe through. I struggle to pry the hands off me.

My feet leave the ground. Something hard digs into my stomach. I'm over someone's shoulder now.

I can't free myself to grab my dagger. I'm entirely helpless.

The figure sits me down and moves away from me. A single lantern lights the room. A window. There's a window I can jump from. If I could just run to the window, I'll be okay.

"I'm so sorry." The man cries. His sobs are low.

I rub my eyes so they can adjust to the light. Finally, his face comes into view. He stands back. He holds his arms crossed against his chest, sweat rolling down his face.

"Draven? What do you think you are doing?" I say.

He paces from one end of the room to the other. He's shaking. This frantic behavior is not normal for him. This is not the drunkard man I saw earlier today.

"I know how this looks."

"What do you want? Why did you —"

"Listen carefully, Morana." He comes to me, face in front of mine. "You need to kill me."

I blink.

"What are you talking about? I'm not doing that." I pant.

He grabs my hands and takes me to the balcony. Seeing him in the moonlight, I've never seen him so worried. Something is scaring him. After how he treated me today, I don't know if he's being honest or just trying another way to anger me.

"You must kill me. I can't —"

"You are drunk. Draven. Go home."

I usher him to the door that leads into the building. He halts. I reach for the dagger in my cloak pocket. He's gone mad.

He planned this. He waited till the shops closed and when people went into their homes for the night. No witnesses. Only he and I. I can't help but think, did he decide before or after our quarrel in the tavern?

"Listen, about earlier. I just wanted to apologize. It was a failed attempt to show off to my friends."

"You called me a criminal. Then waited till everyone was gone to kidnap me. You can't apologize for that."

He steps forward. I freeze with my hand hovering over my dagger, ready to charge if needed. I don't want to, but I'll do anything to protect myself. This dagger has yet to fail me.

I lean onto the railing of the balcony. My back is harshly pressing against it. I steady myself. I don't want to hurt him. I can't hurt him. I'm silently begging him to stop creeping closer.

"I'll take it back if you only give me something in return." His rough hands slither up to my chest and open my cloak. Everything in me turns in a split second. Now I don't want to die. A swarm of energy consumes me. This isn't the way to die, and I am damn sure I'll let no one take advantage of me.

"There is nothing I have to offer. So, get your filthy hands off me."

I use every ounce of strength and rip myself from his grasp. I duck under his legs and kick him with all the force I have in me. But it isn't till he disappears; I realize I've pushed him over the balcony's edge.

His body thumps as his back meets the ground. His head slams on the rocky road. My heart drops. I peer over the edge. All I see is a black silhouette of a man lying on the dirt road.

What have I done? Is he dead? He is dead.

CHAPTER TWO

The chains on my hands tighten with every move. Digging into my skin, scraping against it, and reminding me of all my wrongs. Reminding me of the man I killed.

I can't move the hair out of my face without scratching myself. I can't stretch my back and can hardly move a few inches from the carriage wall.

I think about what I will say, but nothing sounds right. Nothing sounds convincing enough. I was notified that I'd only have a minute to speak. Given the time, I'm not confident enough to convince King Alaric I'm not guilty. I was only trying to protect myself. Surely, King Alaric could understand the need to defend myself from such horror. If not him, then I'm hopeful of Queen Inina.

The carriage is crowded with local offenders waiting for their trial. The town drunkard, which causes fights, the thief trying to feed his family, and the lone harlot who makes her money in the alleyway late at night. However, I don't blame her. Had she worked in a brothel, the king would heavily tax her earnings.

Those are minor offenses. But mine is unforgivable in the eyes of the court, more so the King. My crime will not only get me sent to Tenebris but also to the Inferno if I become fortunate enough to die. I don't know how I can pull out of this.

"Are you the one who killed Draven?" the harlot asks.

I keep my head pointed to my shoes. The curiosity of how she could know such a thing goes through my mind. It had only happened the night before. Words travels fast in this small village.

"If you did, there is nothing wrong with that. Too many times, he's come to me. The man can't take no for an answer. I don't believe his wife ever knew about his infidelity."

Yeah, but did he ever beg you to kill him?

I think of his wife. The pure torment she must be going through hearing the news of his death. A guard most likely visited her house late last night, woke her from her slumber, and told her of the horrifying news that another citizen of Rhemus killed had him. The story will be twisted, making it seem like I killed him in cold blood.

I never intended to kill him. I wanted him off me. As would any other woman. But I also wanted him to feel pain. Nobody should be treated so poorly. No woman should experience a man's unwanted touch and desperate behavior.

"Does he have kids?" I mutter.

"I don't believe so. His wife hasn't been able to bless him with a child. That could be why he's gone to so many women. Men will do anything to have a son to take on the name."

The carriage stops, and the horses huff. A prison guard swings open the door. The light of the sun blinds us all as we shield our eyes.

"Get out one at a time." He barks.

The thief is the first one to go. Then the drunkard, then the harlot, and next, me. Even the prison guard helps the harlot out of the carriage. Not a single eye is pointed at me when I emerge. I'm being treated like a criminal and haven't even spoken.

The light of the morning sun burns my eyes. I've been kept in a cell all night—Fed with only a piece of stale bread and murky water from the bog. Not enough to sufficiently live, but enough to survive. That's all they care about.

As I look up, King Alaric's castle stands tall. Centaurs stand guard at the iron castle gates. Their spears in hand, ready to strike if one of us acts out of line or those who try to run from their sentence. Or perhaps if one was to invade the castle grounds.

We form a line in the order we came out of the carriage. I follow closely behind the harlot. She's been to the castle plenty of times. She knows the drill, and she needs no directions. The castle has become second nature to her. We all head to the throne room to state our plea to King Alaric and Queen Inina.

"Line up against the wall." The guard points. "You will be called in one by one. The King will give you one minute to state your plea. Then, both the King and Queen will decide your fate."

This is not fair. Only one minute, or even less if the King is bored. The same people who rule the land cannot oversee the justice system. There has to be a reformation of this unfair system.

I wait patiently in a long hallway covered in ornate rugs. A beautiful chandelier hangs from the top, too high for any average human to get there. But, of course, the dragons might have helped with that.

The harlot disappears into the throne room. Her body language suggests she isn't worried about the outcome. The king will see her offense as minor. However, she is likely to be sent to community service or pay the King in bags of gold coins. Whatever her sentence, the King is probably tired of seeing her in the castle.

Time goes by so slowly. Thoughts race through my head. I can't process a single thought. My fate is in the hands of a ruthless king. My hands are sweaty, but the chains prevent me from rubbing them in my dress. In these conditions, I am not even capable of presenting myself properly.

The harlot exits in the throne room with a smile on her face. The outcome is exactly what I thought it to be. She got off easy.

They take her back to the carriage unchained.

I am going to be eaten alive.

"Morana, you may enter." A guard pokes at my back.

Entering the throne room, I am greeted by minotaur's wielding spears. Surely, they don't need this many guards for this many people. Or am I the only one they see as a threat? It surprises me they don't have an ogre guarding the castle gates, but something much worse could be lurking in the dungeons.

The room is bigger than the courtyard. Much bigger than any room I have ever seen. Walls dressed in gold and decorated with portraits of our history. Past rulers, to be exact. Tables are adorned with ornate vases filled with the flowers the fairies plant yearly. Raisel planted the ones that brighten the castle. As much as I don't want to be here, this place is stunning.

The guard places me many feet away from the King and Queen. I have yet to make eye contact with them, but I notice their unique attire as I enter the room.

They stare at me with concerned eyes. I can't run away. I'll be struck with a spear the minute I'd escape through the doors.

"Morana of the east village. I have summoned you here under the claim that you have murdered Draven of the east village. State your plea."

This is it.

"Your majesty, I was acting out of self-defense. Draven had pushed himself on me. I made it clear that I did not want him to touch me. I had no intention of hurting him. He was aggressive and –"

"Enough." King Alaric cuts me off. "Do you or do you not plead guilty in the murder of Draven of the east village?"

This feeling is unreal. The slightest ounce of hope I had has now vanished. I don't know why I thought he'd let me tell my full story. I have so much more to say. But first, I must convince him this was all an accident.

"Your majesty, it was self-defense."

King Alaric sits up straight. I stiffen just as he does. I don't dare tell him what Draven said to me before his death. I can't tell the King that Draven practically begged me to kill him. If I tell the king that, I'd be sentencing myself. His death will look intentional, and he will have my head at the guillotine.

"Tell me, Morana, where were you when your encounter with Draven began?"

"I was leaving the tavern. He blindfolded me and dragged me into the upstairs loft in the floral shop."

Queen Inina has a look in her eyes that only a mother could have. She has no children, or at least any of which the east village is aware of. Maybe I can have her on my side. She can't be that ignorant to believe the King, even if she is his wife. Her being queen gives her some authority.

"And what did he do then?"

Telling him what happened is horrifyingly embarrassing. I inform the king of my assault, and he doesn't bat an eye with concern. His face lacks disgust at Draven's actions. His face is like that of someone with no emotion, heart, or conscience. A monster with no soul.

"I released his grip from my hair, then slid under his legs, and he fell forward over the railing."

Oh, my god. I just lied to the King and Queen.

"He fell forward? That is not what our witness has informed us of."

Of course, there's a witness. There is always something. I'm surprised that the King has asked as many questions as he has. Usually, he would be done by now. Instead, he is bored with my case because, in his mind, he already knows where he is sending me. I know where my fate lies.

"I did not see anyone else around. It was incredibly dark, your Majesty. The lanterns were out for the night. So how could they know it was me?"

"Morana, are you questioning your King?" Queen Inina speaks. She hadn't made a sound this entire time. Hearing her voice sends chills down my spine.

"No, your grace, but –"

"Tell me, Morana. Do you carry any weapons on you?" King Alaric mumbles.

I cannot lie—no more lying.

"Yes, Your Majesty."

"From what? This is the light realm. There is nothing to fear here. "A flicker in his eyes glimmers wickedly.

"I protect myself from men like Draven who prey on women for fun."

Queen Inina shoots her eyes at the King; his eyes turn down. I say all I can say to convince him. My fate awaits in the hands of the cruel king. He is prolonging my sentence that I've been dreading to hear.

Queen Inina leans over to the King and whispers something in his ear. As she was doing this, she kept her eyes on me. King Alaric's eyebrows stiffen. He mutters something to her, and she sits up straight, fear in her eyes.

"Right." King Alaric strokes his beard. "The witness also informed us of an argument between you two that evening. Something about you defending Tenebris. Care to elaborate?"

I recount the night as if it was happening all over again. The King's face never shows compassion, once, or even a flinch of horror. My hands are cold and sweaty, and my heart is racing. What else can I possibly say to prove I am innocent?

"You sure know how to stir things up, don't you, Morana?" He pinches the bridge of his nose. "I remember now. The death of your parents. Tragic."

I remember it all. I remember waiting for them to come hom, it was getting late. Food was turning cold on the table. I thought they had been caught up in the fields. I remember the guard that came to my house to tell me the news.

All he told me was that their bodies were found near the border. I assumed it was a night realm creature. And since then, I never once blamed the creature. I blamed myself for not being there with them, so I could have left this world with them. Because a life without them would not be worth living.

He sighs, releasing the bothersome tension in his shoulders as if my presence is causing him any stress.

"Your parents. Do you imagine seeing them again?"

My stomach drops. How did this become the conversation?

"More than anything, your majesty."

His words strike me in the heart like lightning and makes my heart skips a beat. My eyes burn from the need to cry. I try to slow my breathing to stop myself from becoming emotional. This is not the time for tears. I've spent enough of my days weeping over the loss of my parents. Just a few months ago, I thought I was done grieving. Instead, he's opening the wound again.

"All right then. Enough of that." King Alaric waves his hand, and the guards rush in, taking each wrist and guiding me out of the throne room.

"What does that mean?"

I struggle against the hold of the guards. Does he intend to kill me so that I may meet my parents in the afterlife? As much as I'd love to see their faces again, this can't happen. Not this way. I want to die on my terms.

"I'm doing you a favor," he says.

The guards grip tighter on my wrists as if the chains weren't already tight enough. I trip on my dress, and they pull me up again. I don't have it in me to fight. How could I fight this treachery alone?

Tears roll down my face and block my vision. I know we're outside now. The light of the day creeps in between the tears.

"We are taking you home." A guard says in hushed tones. "Your parents will be waiting for you."

"Impossible."

They bring me to a different carriage this time. Bigger than the one before. I struggle to wipe the hair from my face. I look up, and men of all sizes surround me. The carriage is cramped, and there is almost no room to move a finger. It reeks of dead fish and unwashed bodies. The guard slams the door behind me. And at the click of the lock, everything becomes real.

The men stare at me with hungry eyes. None of them look familiar, though. All of them strangers and criminals of Rhemus.

I notice a man with a hood up and his face to the ground. He creeps into the corner like a shadow figure. His hands are resting in his lap, avoiding my touch at all costs.

"Where are we going?" I whisper.

"Where all murderers go."

No. I am not a murderer. I cannot go to Tenebris. There has to be a way out. There are enough men in the carriage to break the door easily. But all of them look defeated, like they've given up.

"I can't go there. They said they would bring me to my parents."

"I'm going to say this only because you are a woman. We are all murderers. King Alaric doesn't care about us. So, keep your head down and be quiet. Don't trust anyone."

I lean against the wall. I don't want anyone touching me. I hold on to my stomach; it growls. The bread and water weren't enough. It is unclear when my next meal will be.

Hours pass on, and I drift off to sleep many times. Each time the carriage rocks or a man coughs, I wake up. My nerves alarm me when we come to a complete stop. Heads rise, and the men sit straight and tighten their fists. I don't want to get out of the carriage. I don't want to see it.

"Ladies first." A guard opens the carriage door and waits for me.

The men watch with dull eyes as I hurry past them. I had been treated poorly since boarding the carriage, and they suddenly care about politeness and let me out first.

The guard grips my chains as I step out of the carriage. It is dark now, and the only lights come from the carriage lanterns and the moon. But out there, this dark is the deadliest. The dark is where the monsters hide. The dark is where our souls die.

The rest of the men follow behind me. All of them stand feet taller than I. In comparison with them, I feel so vulnerable. Despite this, I cannot show fear. We are all here for the same crime. They may think I am no threat because I am a woman, but underestimating a woman may be a crime all on its own.

"King Alaric has deemed you all murderers of the Light Realm of Rhemus. Your punishment lies within Tenebris." The guard walks up and down the line of criminals. "Once your chains are undone, your enchantment will activate."

The blood they had extracted from us earlier was used in a ritual. Witches from Rhemus used our blood to bind us to Tenebris forever. They say there is no spell to break it. Perhaps maybe they haven't found the proper witch for the job.

People have tried walking back into Rhemus. But, once they reach the border, their skin sets afire and then burns into ash. I once roamed too far near the border and could still smell the burning flesh swimming in the air.

Others immediately drop dead once crossing the border. Others try to live by Rhemus right outside the border and end up killed by the creatures of the forest.

"You can no longer step foot in the light realm for *all* eternity. Some of you may die." The guard stares me down. "And others may live a very lonely life."

One guard unlocks our chains. Even in the moonlight, I notice the redness the chains have caused.

"I have informed Tenebris of your arrival. So don't be surprised if you encounter savage beasts along the way."

"Why are you telling us all of this?"

Heads turn to me, and the man eyes me with surprise.

"Never in my years of transporting prisoners has anyone ever spoken out of turn, let alone a woman."

"There is a first for everything." I smile.

"King Alaric is many things, but he is not cruel, little girl. He makes sure criminals like you have no business in Rhemus. We must keep our land pure." The guard stands face-to-face with me. He towers over me. His armor shines in the moonlight.

"Yet he sentences us all to the most dangerous realm in the continent without the chance of a fair trial. He is a wicked king."

The guard grabs me by my cheeks. His nails dig into my jaw. He stares into the depths of my soul with his dark eyes. Then, he takes my hands and unlocks the chains, all while keeping eye contact.

"I know about you, Morana. Kicked poor Draven of the East Village right off the balcony. Should have just given him what he wanted."

My arms drop to the side. Relief soars over me as the chains free my wrists.

"And I'll do it all again. If it means I can save another woman from a man's harmful hands."

The men snicker to themselves and chuckle.

"It's time to go."

The guard walks off to the carriage. The horses kick the dirt, eager to leave this evil place. The energy drives the horses mad, but they are well-controlled.

The men and I face the darkness that is our fate. Each of us hesitant to take the first step. We can't turn back. Our bodies won't allow us to step foot off Tenebris territory after this. Never in my life had I ever imagined I'd be this close to the border. It gives me an eerie feeling along my spine. Like something is attaching itself to me.

I can't stand here all night. I have to find food and shelter. The sun has only just set. Nobody will survive the night. We will either be killed by natural causes or the things that lurk in the shadows.

I take a step forward.

"Wait!" The hooded man interrupts.

I turn to him as he breaks from the line.

"Most of us are from the north village. I'm sure the guards didn't give you a dagger." The man reaches inside his pocket and takes out a dagger. "Here. The guards of the North don't leave us empty-handed."

"Aren't you lucky? They confiscated mine when I was taken into custody. Guess a woman isn't fit to defend herself."

I look at the rusted dagger. The pointed edge barely secured in with the grip.

"Never said they were impressive weapons."

Despite the hood covering his face, I gaze at him.

"Show me your face. I ask. "I don't want the last face I see to be his face." I turn to the guards down the trail.

The man hesitates. My stomach builds with suspense as he pulls his hood back. It reveals a younger man around the young age of twenty. His unkempt hair falls over his face, but his dark eyes peek through the strands of hair. A single scar lines his face from his eyebrow down to his cheek. We keep our eyes locked on each other.

"What is your name?"

"Sora, of the North."

I walk towards the trees, leaving the dagger in his hand. No one stops me. I don't want to be stopped. I can't go back to my old life. Everything I know is gone. My parents. Gone. Raisel. Gone. Did she even know what happened to me? Surely, she does. I'll never see her again. And if I survive, I'll have to live with their absence for the rest of my life.

I venture further into the dark depth of trees. I don't hear the men walking. I hear nothing but the chirping of the crickets and the growling of a creature in the distance. Maybe it can smell me, find me, and eat me so fast I won't feel a thing. It isn't a dive off the cliff, but it will do.

I don't know how far I've walked, but I know I am far from the border. I want to go back and see if the other men are still there or if Sora is still there. He seems too intelligent to hang around the border.

My pace quickens. I often trip over rocks and small branches from a fallen tree. I've scraped my knees on thorny bushes too many times to count. Some may have called me crazy, but death is calling to me. I am desperate to leave this world with nothing but a faint memory of whom I killed. My name will always be spoken from the mouths of those who despise me. I will always be known as the girl who killed Draven of the East. How could I go on living with that thought invading my mind? I am a prisoner of Tenebris now. My life was over the minute Draven fell to his death.

CHAPTER THREE

A crackling fire jolts me awake. The heat of it washes over my body. I don't want to move from my position. The warmth of the fire is numbing my skin against the cold air. I must be in a dream because it's been so long since I have been able to sleep by a thriving fire.

I sit up in a hurry. I sway side to side from the blood rushing. I rub my eyes so they can adjust to the light. A familiar man sits in front of me. Sora tends to the small fire.

"Glad to see you up." He pokes the fire with a stick. Sending sparks outward. He keeps his eyes focused on the burning wood.

"Where are we?"

"Still in the night realm."

My stomach rumbles. I notice my mouth is dry. Sora offers me a leaf with a charred frog on it. The smell of it reeks, but how can I reject his offer?

"How did you find this? Why are you even here? I thought you'd be dead by now."

He chuckles. "I saved you. I found you sleeping, and luckily, I found you when I did. A pack of wolves was preying in the area."

"You should have left me to die."

He puts the other frog on a leaf similar to mine.

"Nobody wants to die. They don't want to live the life they've been given. Besides, you don't strike me as someone who wants to end their life. Mouthing off to a guard like that. You're fighting for something."

He takes a single bite of the frog. I instantly become uninterested in taking one nibble. I force myself to eat it.

His words hit me in the chest. I don't want to admit it, but maybe he is right. I fought for my freedom. I fought to be heard. And since my parents were killed, nobody has been sympathetic. He doesn't know my struggles, but he talks as if he does. I've just met the man, yet he's tried to help me survive. And for what? What does he gain from it? Is he only acting like this so that maybe when his soul passes, he will be taken to the Otherworld? The only place benevolent souls can go after death. He is a murderer too. We both are. That is the most unforgivable thing anyone can do.

The fire crackles through the silence. Should I even thank him? I don't want this. I was hoping I'd be devoured by the wolves to end my agony. This is no way to live.

"Where are the others?"

Sora coughs. "Dead. I tripped on a body. Bloody and half his insides hanging out."

I choke on the piece of frog meat and try to force the image from my mind. I notice the blood smeared on his pants.

"That was quick." I dust off my dress. "How are you still alive?"

"I had two daggers when you wouldn't take one." He mumbles, irritated with my endless questions and doubts.

"So, the guards in the north village gave you two daggers? Highly unbelievable."

"I offered you the only one I had. So, I made the other one."

It's hard to believe he'd do these things out of goodwill. We live in a society where women are seen as weak and useless anywhere outside the home. This man has shown me compassion. From the moment I met him, he made me feel seen and heard and less invisible than anyone I've known besides Raisel. He wouldn't be acting like this if he wanted something in return.

"You don't even know me. Why do that for a stranger?"

He stays silent for a moment. Part of me wishes I had said nothing.

"Something about you seems all too familiar. You remind me of myself back in the village. The others see you as a threat, but I don't. In fact, I was almost frightened when you mouthed off to that guard."

I crumple the leaf and toss it behind me. The taste of unwashed frog lingers in my mouth, and bits of it stick between my teeth. I need something to wash it down with, but the water here could be tainted with evil magic.

"What was your life like in the north village?" I whisper.

Sora looks around. We both hear the howling in the distance, but it is too far for us to be a threat. It creates an ambiance for the atmosphere—an omen for our future.

"My parents died when I was thirteen. I've been on my own ever since. I was on the streets, always looking for food and shelter. Nobody trusted me. Like there was something they knew about me that I didn't."

Thoughts of my deceased parents flood my mind. This sounds too familiar.

"One day, a faun by the name of Stornyn, took me in. He taught me to be a blacksmith. He cared for me and taught me to fend for myself, all while being my friend too. He changed me for the better. I used to hate the world and everyone in it until he came along."

I warm my hands by the fire. "So, how did it happen. Tell me what happened that got you sent here."

He takes a shaky breath, wondering if he should delve into such topics this early in the conversation. But what do we have to lose now? All we have is each other and our thoughts.

"I'm not proud of it. I went into the brothel on the outskirts of town, where the nymphs are." He scratches the back of his head. "I was lonely, and I was looking for a companion."

I raise my hand, stopping him. "No need to elaborate."

"Well, I felt so much regret and shame. The nymph wouldn't take no for an answer. I had already paid her. I didn't care about the money. She used her magic to paralyze me. Something in me broke through the magic, and I snapped. I pushed her off me, and she hit her head on the corner of the table. Next I knew, the place was swarmed with minotaurs and I was in chains."

Nymphs are notorious for taking things too far. She was already paid, so what made her push anymore?

How can this be? Two people from different villages tried for the same crime, in similar situations. The murders were not because of hatred but because we defended ourselves from being taken advantage of.

I can't help but feel bad for him, though. He seems so distraught and ridden with guilt. He didn't have any intention to kill, but he did. My mind wanders through the endless possibilities of how this could have turned out. If only the wicked King could have given us another chance. We are good people. Good people don't deserve this kind of life.

Now that I am in night realm territory, my heart is growing colder and blacker than before. The essence of this territory changes us every second of being here.

"Enough about me, though. Didn't you kick someone off the balcony?"

I raise my hands near the fire. The warmth travels up my arms and to my chest. He will never believe me. Our stories are far too similar.

"Well, the thing is—"

The bushes rustle behind us. Growling echoes through the dead trees. We both freeze. Sora grips his dagger, ready to charge at any moment. He slides me the other dagger, and I grab it for dear life, hoping this rusty thing will give me a fighting chance.

"What is that?" I whisper.

Sora raises his finger to his lips. "It's not a wolf."

My heart skips a beat. This is it. I am going to die. There is no way I can defend myself against anything. The creatures of Tenebris are far more terrifying than the ones in the light realm. All the creatures carry the ability to make a death a gruesome one.

The growling grows louder, and next time with more viciousness than before. A snarl so deep it rattles the tree limbs.

"We need to run."

Sora stands up and grabs my hand. I jerk my hand away. I'm tired of running. We can't possibly live a life here if we continue to run. We can only go so far. If we hit a village, they won't hesitate to tear us apart. Or worse, torture us for fun for eternity.

"You are out of your mind." He takes my hand and pulls me upwards. My dress makes me trip, but I grab a handful of fabric and pull it up off the ground while trying to carry the dagger close to me.

We sprint our way through the dark. He has a firm grip on my hand, and there is no prying it away.

We dodge through trees and jump over rocks. Barely any moonlight comes in through the treetops. Blindly, we run through the forbidden forest, full of fears and nightmares.

The growling creeps behind us. Whatever is following us has caught up to us. I can't see anything. I don't want to look. I fear that if I turn, ill see the eyes of a beast that Ill never be able to erase from my memory.

Before I can speak, I am thrown to the ground and pinned down. I squirm under the pressure of the unknown creature. It seems to have two hands with deadly claws. The scraping of my skin pierces my ears. Its all I can focus on. Pain shoots through me.

"Sora!"

That's it; he's left me to die. I knew something odd was going on.

The creature stops and falls off me. It gurgles as its soul slowly escapes its body.

"Sora, where are you?"

A rough hand falls on my shoulder, and I jump. I bring my elbow to the figure behind me, fearing it may be another unknown creature of the same strength.

"Damn, Morana."

I feel around me. "Sora, oh my gods, I am so sorry."

"It's just me." A lantern ignites my face. The heat of it burns my skin. He's holding his nose and wiping a streak of blood from it.

I look up and notice how tall the trees tower over us. I've never seen trees so massive. It makes sense that these are the trees that separate the two realms. They are too tall for anyone to climb, and the trunks are too wide to wrap their arms around.

All of them are capable of making anyone lose their way.

We follow the bloody mess on the ground. A black silhouette of a creature sprawls beneath our feet. Sora edges closer to it. Keeping his guard up, his dagger to his chest, hoping the creature doesn't lunge forward.

"What are you doing? It could still be alive."

He reaches down and pulls over the cloak to reveal the bloody mess. A woman, no more than my age, lay dead on the ground. Blood covers her face, and her eyes still lie open with a glaze-like opal over her eyes. Her skin is gray in the lantern light, almost like it's rotted for weeks. Rigor mortis takes over the body.

"What is it?" I ask.

He grabs my arms and observes them. Blood drips from the sides. Nothing too deep, but deep enough to hurt and leave a trail of blood behind us. Enough blood to alert all the vampires and werewolves in the area.

"Are you okay?" He takes the ends of his cloak and rips two pieces off, wrapping them around my arms. "Are you in a lot pain?"

"I'm okay. How did you kill that thing?"

He smooths over the fabric.

"I didn't kill it. I thought you did."

"My arms were tied down. I felt teeth dig into my skin. The next thing I heard was a gurgling sound like it was choking on blood."

We look at each other perplexed. If neither of us killed the creature, what could have done it? Who could have done it?

"Must have been a vampire."

"Aren't those things immortal?" I ask, wiping my hands on my dress. I follow Sora as he moves forward.

"Supposed to be. But it still makes little sense that it dropped dead without a steak in its heart. Those things are tricky to kill."

None of it makes sense. The vampires are immortal. It tried to drink my blood. Blood gives them energy and keeps them looking youthful. So, it should have become stronger when it drank from me, not drop dead. Instead, it looked as if the life was sucked out of it.

"We need to move from this area." Sora sighs. He's out of breath, just as I am.

"We don't even know where to go. This lantern doesn't give off much light."

Sora hangs the lantern in front of him. He looks left and right. We are lost. I don't know which way is which, and the stars hide behind the treetops. So, there is no way to decipher where North and South are.

"There's got to be a village close to here. I found the lantern just a few feet away."

He is so confident. I can't help but thank him for it. I wanted to die hours ago, and now all I want to do is survive. Maybe it's the fact that we were so similar. I never met someone else like me. I feel at home with him, but I could never tell him that.

We walk further into the dark abyss. Creatures call around us. I am sure we would have been crushed by a cyclopse or eaten by a goblin. This has me thinking. Is the night realm as evil as the King tells it to be?

My legs are tired, and the wound on my arms stung. It's sore and stiff to the touch, swollen most likely, but I haven't looked at them in a while. My muscles are weak from the blood loss. The bleeding stopped a while ago. Without Sora's quick thinking, I'd probably be dead. A heavy breath escapes my lungs. I want to stop, but we have to keep going. I look at Sora; his face is unbothered.

"I think I see lights ahead." Sora points.

I push my muscles to walk faster. Every ounce of energy I have left, I put into the last few footsteps. The pain becomes worse with each move, but we are so close.

"Wait, Sora, if someone sees us." I snatch his arm. "They will kill us without a second thought of it."

He turns to me and holds the lantern to the side. "We just have to play by their game. Put your hood up."

I nod my head and do as he says. The lights become brighter as we edge the village. In Rhemus, there would be no people lining the streets at dark. This is the night realm, so the creatures only came out at night. It means we would have to rest during the day and survive at night.

We kneel behind the bushes. Tiny huts and buildings line the outside of the village. Goblins waddle down the street with their teeth barred, and gorgons slither away with a basket full of something bloody. I don't want to think of what it might have been. I swallow hard. This is a death trap.

This is nothing like the east village; it's worse. village fresh produce markets, but there are jewelry markets, all run by devilish goblins trying to con someone out of their money.

"We shouldn't be here," I whisper.

Sora continues to observe the area. He is dead set on entering the village as we are. I don't trust the plan entirely. We will get caught the minute we step foot in the fire's light. We are either turned to stone at the glimpse of a gorgon, drained of blood by a hungry vampire, or lured to the water caves by the sirens.

"I got an idea. But I'm not sure you're going to like it."

I twist my head at him.

"Pretend you are dead."

"Are you crazy? How am I supposed to pull that off?"

He looks me up and down. Conjuring a grand plan in his head.

"The vampire left blood on you. It will mask the smell of your human blood. No one will know you're human. I'll carry you into the inn over there."

He points to the rickety wooden building that sits only twenty feet ahead. Creatures of all sorts lurk around it. No clear point to make our way ahead unseen.

"There's no way we can fool such ravenous creatures."

Sora stares at me like he completely ignores what I say.

"Whatever," I say. "But if a gorgon turns me to stone, please destroy me before you die."

I pull my hood up and wipe the blood off my cloak and onto my face. The coldness of it makes me gag. He picks me up into his arms with no effort. I guess the years of malnourishment are paying off. I am lighter than a fairy.

"If you can hold your breath too, that might make it more believable."

I tilt my head upright. "Are you serious?"

"Morana, make it believable." He yanks the hood over my face until I see nothing but a black void.

I hear the rustling of the bushes. Slight light from the lanterns comes through the threads of the cloak. I can only make out silhouettes at that point. Sora grips me tighter.

"It's okay. We are almost there." He whispers in my ear.

I relax my body more. *Make it believable.* I release the tension in my body.

He stops. I take a long, deep breath. My lungs burn with fiery rage.

"One room for the night." Sora's breath shakes. I hear his heart racing through his chest.

A rattling cough frightens me. I almost jump, but I stay still. Feet shuffle on the floor in front of us or next to us. I can't tell. I lost all sense of direction.

"Just one, for you and your... lady." The creature hesitates. It has such a low tone that I can't tell what it is—Vampire, gorgon, or even worse. I don't know what Sora is up against, but the increase in his heart rate isn't anything good.

"Yes, she's, uh, very exhausted." He breathes. His hands tremble.

"Certainly." It's quiet for a moment, then the sound of keys clattering. "Room six. Up the stairs, third door on your right."

The creature lays the keys on top of me. I almost shudder in horror. The hands are so close to me. So close to being discovered. I beg Sora to hurry to the room. I can't handle the suspense any longer.

I ease my breath lightly as he walks up the stairs. He is struggling to breathe. If we could only get upstairs out of sight, I will free myself from him and let him rest.

"It's clear, Morana. I'm going to put you down now."

I lift my hood over my head and came face to face with Sora. He gently sits me down, careful not to let me go so suddenly so I can catch my balance.

"Are you okay?" he asks.

I brush myself off and touch the dried blood on my face. It crunches with the creases of my skin.

"I'm fine, but are you okay? What was that thing?"

He fumbles with the keys, trying to get in quickly. He struggles to get the key inside the lock. I move him aside gently and unlock the door. He stands next to me with his head down.

We rush in and hurry to shut the door behind us. My expectations were low when I thought of staying in an Inn in Tenebris. I figured nothing would be sanitary, dusty, and rotted. But to both of our surprise, it is the complete opposite. Clean and swept wooden floors without a crack in them. The bed is neatly made with many ornate pillows of varying colors. The window is clear of any damage. The curtain is stainless. A small bedside table, clean with a single lantern. We hurried to light it.

"Sora, what was it?"

I hurry to close the curtains.

He finishes lighting the lantern, and the room ignites in an orange glow. He sits on the bed with his head lowered and his elbows on his knees.

"You won't believe me."

I sit next to him.

"What was it? A goblin? Another vampire?"

"No, worse. It was a gorgon."

I look at the door in horror. My breathing becomes uneasy. My stomach feels like I've jumped off a cliff.

"How did you—"

"I know." He swallows. "When a human encounters a gorgon, they immediately turn to stone. How it didn't happen to me leaves me clueless."

I rub my sweaty hands together.

"She didn't wear eye protection. I didn't know what she was until she came around — slithered around the counter."

Sora takes off his cloak. Bruises and scars line his arms, leaving not an inch of skin uncovered. I try to steer my eyes away.

"The only way we got past her was the scent of vampire blood."

I agree.

I never would have thought I'd smear vampire blood on my face for survival. But I also never thought I'd be in a small room with a man I had just met. We are both criminals. Who's to say he won't kill me in my sleep?

"So, we need to leave by sunrise. When everyone sleeps here. We only have a few more hours left of nighttime."

I stand up and look at myself in the mirror. That, too, is clean. My hair emerges from its braid, and tiny black hairs stick to my head. The dark bags under my eyes are darker than a few days ago. I am not how I used to be. I used to be so vibrant and awake. Now, I am fighting for my life in Tenebris.

I look at Sora in the mirror, careful to avoid his eyes. He takes off his torn vest. He uncovers the bed and searches the sheets for any bugs or anything suspicious.

I turn to him.

"Don't worry. I'll sleep on the floor." He laughs.

"Oh, no. It's okay. You don't have to. If we are going to get any rest at all, you need to be comfortable."

He stops. We focus on each other from across the bed.

"Yes, I'm sure. Just stay on your side of the bed." I laugh. "If I feel a hand on me, you might lose a limb."

The smile disappears from his face.

I can only imagine what my parents would think. I'm in a small room, with one bed, with a man I'd only met a few hours prior for the same crime I committed. I'd joke and tell Father I got myself a keeper. Mother wouldn't be so happy with the joke. I had no time to think of anything else but surviving.

"We leave at sunset and find some food. I know you must be hungry."

He lays in the bed first. I sit on the edge of the other side.

"I'm used to hunger. I've grown accustomed to it."

I slide into the bed and lay on the edge of it, careful not to invade his space. He does the same. This is awkward for both of us. We don't move. We don't speak. We listen to each other breathing. Slow and steady.

He turns out the light with a simple blow of breath. The room is quiet, and no leak of light shines through the curtains. No sound from outside. Nothing. Just emptiness.

The beating of my heart helps me relax and fall into a deep meditative state. My surroundings become nothing but foreign to me. I lay here, wondering what the next day holds—wondering if I'll survive to see another day.

CHAPTER FOUR

Rumbling sounds outside the door.

"Morana, wake up. We have to go. Now."

My eyes burst open. The fear in Sora's eyes sends chills down my spine. I'm barely awake before throwing on my shoes and cloak and quickly fastening the clasps. Sleep still claims me, so I can't exactly tell if I'm having a nightmare or if this is real.

"You can't hide from us, humans!" voices call outside the door.

"Who is that? How did they find us?"

Sora struggles to put his shoes on. He's fumbling with the strings. I kneel and help him as he rushes to put his vest and cloak on.

"What do we do?" I whisper, unsure if they can hear us or not.

We both search around. The sun is barely rising. There isn't enough light to run outside without getting lost or caught by the guards surrounding the building.

"They've got this place surrounded. We can't escape through the window."

I toss my hair into a bundle to keep it from my face. Whatever we're up against, it doesn't sound pleasant. They continue to bang on the door and rattle the doorknob. The lock won't hold much longer.

"Do you have your dagger on you?" He pants.

"Of course."

"Grab it and keep it at the ready."

The banging grows louder. Any moment they will be in here, and I will be dead. We will be dead. Taken by the very people we fear. It was foolish of us to think we could hide out here.

The door bursts off the hinges and lands right before us. We hold our daggers outward to protect ourselves, but I don't think they'd be useful in this fight. Gargoyles of every height swarm the room, swords on their belts and dangerous hands of stone. Their eyes are red like rubies and fury, nothing as I've seen before.

More gargoyles enter the room. We are surrounded at all angles. I grip the dagger tighter as if it would save me. Sora etches closer, almost shielding me. It's no use, though. We have lost this battle and haven't even lifted a finger.

A pair of hard stone hands grab me by my arms and flip me towards its face. Its entire body is made of stone. Horns jut out of its head and blood-red glowing eyes that could stare into the deepest part of my soul. I close my eyes and turn my head away.

"Sora," I call out.

I turn to see him with a piece of fabric tied around his mouth. Horror fills his eyes. The veins around his head become noticeable with every breath he takes. They quickly drag him out of the room. I try to go after him, but the harshness of the stone pulls me back.

They chain my hands together with iron cuffs. The old, worn fabric fits tightly around my mouth. I try so hard not to breathe in its musty scent. Their grip gets tighter by the minute. I'm so sure my hands will fall off. There is no getting out of their hold.

They take me under the arms and drag me to the hallway. I can still hear Sora's screams. I kick and scream, but it isn't useful. I have to save my energy for whatever is to come.

The gorgon slithers from behind the desk and hisses. A tall gargoyle drops a bag of coins on the desk. She turned us in without a doubt. I look behind me, and she smiles a wicked smile I'll never forget.

Outside, horses surround the place. Massive black horses. Surely, they didn't come riding in on them. The horses could never support the weight of a gargoyle. I feel a change of pressure on my arms—something like flesh. I whip my head to the side, and the gargoyles turn to their human forms. Each of them has normal hair and skin. Hair colors range from black to purest blonde. No more red eyes and horns.

"Up you go." one shouts.

They lift me onto a black horse. It huffs at the sudden pressure. The man who held me pushes himself onto the saddle and sits behind me. This feels so wrong. If I kick or make any sudden movements, I'll spook the horse, and we'd both be injured.

In the distance, a herd of horses rambles on. All with human-looking men riding them. I see Sora riding on a horse. They are taking him away too. I wonder if I'll ever see him again or if we are bound to the same prison.

Tears roll down my face, so much I can barely see what is around me. The man behind me sits so close I can barely move a muscle. I feel the magic in the chains. If I make a move, I know it will not end well.

The horse storms off in the same direction as the others. The icy wind pushes past my face, making me gasp for air. The saddle shifts, and I worry I'll fall off. Although, it may be a good thing. It's hard to tell how fast a gargoyle can run. Surely, their wings of stone could get them anywhere in a matter of time.

I stop struggling but work to stay on top of the horse. I grab the horse's mane and brace myself. I tighten my thighs around its broad shoulders. My muscles ache with all the tension I put on my body.

The dirt road is uneven. Dead trees scatter across the horizon, and cliffs drop off right at the corner of the trail. One wrong move, one slip, and we won't live to see another day.

An ice-covered mountain carves through the horizon. The jagged edges remind me of the sea stacks from the cliff I once stood over. The castle that occupies it gives me an uneasy feeling in my stomach. Like an invisible snake wrapping around my body, suffocating me. That's where I am going to die. I'm sure of it.

I've lost track of time. It feels like hours when it's probably been minutes. The pain in my body is excruciating. All I want is a hot bath and food to eat, but I don't think they are taking us to a luxury inn.

We near a cliff, and on the other side sits the dark castle. Birds of different species fly around it like it was protecting something. As we tread closer, I realize they aren't birds, but bats. Enormous bats with gnarly fangs sharp enough to kill someone with one puncture. How they haven't swooped down on us yet is a mystery to me. The men are unfazed by the monsters that surround us.

Ahead, is the same group that took Sora. I can't see him, but I can feel his presence. I can't risk running after him. I'd never survive out in the cold. I'd never survive the deadly bats and whatever lurks in the forest below.

The castle is much bigger than I had imagined when I first saw it atop the mountain. It shines with a dark stone I've never seen before, almost like an obsidian. The entire thing is made of it. The darkness of it fills the air with an unpleasant taste in my mouth.

Coming to the main entrance, I meet with more gargoyles. They are taller than the ones I've seen and deadlier too. Their red eyes beam at me, but their horns are longer and thicker. They are decorated in rubies and obsidian to match the castle.

I look around, and Sora is out of sight. He must have been taken inside already. I can't imagine the horrible things they're doing to him. What if they crush his bones to dust with the sheer force of their stone hands? They could cut his eyes out with their horns or, worse, leave him in a dungeon to rot and die a slow and painful death.

We enter the castle. The walls are like raw garnet, shining in the light of the lanterns that line the hallway. Marble statues of gory creatures and dying humans decorate the halls. The rumors are true. This is the night realm. They hate humans.

We round the corner to an open room similar to the hallway. Vast flames of blue and orange ignite the thrones and the jewels that adorn it. The heat is so intense but better than the icy winter chill outside.

Ahead, a body kneels facing the golden thrones. It's Sora.

I whimper to gain his attention. He turns to me swiftly, and his eyes light up as I approach him. They push me down next to him. Blood runs down his forehead. He must have put up a good fight to have such a gash like that.

The men release us from the fabric that binds our mouths. We gasp as we let the air into our lungs. I was right about the taste. It's sulfur-like.

The men transform into their gargoyle form. The horns grow out of the heads with a crack, and their eyes fade to red as if angry. They stand surrounding us to the point where there is no escape. We are in their territory now.

"Where are we?" I whisper.

"No doubt the King's castle."

My heart skips a beat. Why would the soldiers take us here and not let us die in the dungeons? Why were we chosen to kneel before the night king?

The gargoyles kneel around us, facing the golden thrones ahead. Their heads bow in compliance. I lower my head as they do, careful not to lift my head before I'm told. Careful to avoid the corrupt royals of the night realm.

"Ahh, you finally found them. About damn time, if you ask me."

I keep my head lowered. His heavy footsteps tread closer to us. He stops suddenly.

"You were ordered to bring them back unharmed," he says sternly.

A gargoyle steps forward. "Your majesty, they would not have come willingly if we had simply asked them."

The man treads closer. "I said, unharmed. Look, the man has blood running down his face." The man clocks his tongue. "And what of the woman?"

Sora and I keep our heads down. I don't want to look to see his face. I don't want his face to be the last one I'd see before my death. His shoes are right before me—black leather boots with silver buckles and one simple garnet on the side.

"My lady, please let me have a look at you." He gently grabs my hand and helps me to rise. I try to avoid his gaze, but his voice convinces me otherwise. His dark eyes penetrate my soul. The fire gleams on his pale youthful face in the firelight. And his long dark hair lays over his shoulders. Vampire, no doubt.

"She appears disheveled. Bruises on her neck are already forming." He takes my face with one hand and gently observes my skin. His fingers are cold to the touch.

At any moment, I expect him to drain me of blood and leave me dead on this beautiful floor.

"I should kill all of you for disrespecting a woman like this." He backs away from me gracefully. "Leave us."

He circles us. I see him through the corner of my eye. I focus on the thrones, but I sense his eyes resting on me. This burning sensation is unreal. It fills my cheeks and makes my knees wobbly. Is this magic, or is it the adrenaline coursing through me from pure fear?

"You must be wondering how you ended up in the castle," He says.

"Your majesty, we beg you to spare us. Kill me and spare Morana's life."

How did this king know Sora's name? And Sora didn't even mention it. I want to hit him for even suggesting he'd die for me. I refuse to let it happen. This isn't a time to act like a noble gentleman.

"No need for the nonsense, Sora of the north."

"Bellamy. Enough of *your* nonsense. Leave them alone. You will have your turn." A woman's voice rings off the walls.

A man and a woman enter the room. They match the aesthetic of the castle. Both are adorned in deep crimson and black with flecks of silver and gold. The woman's dress fit her body entirely too well, showing off the curves of her body. The plunging neckline exposes her breasts. I try to divert my eyes. Regal in the fire's light, there seems to be something off about them.

Their eyes are red, but not red like the gargoyles. A deep red, like blood. Their skin is just as pale as the man who stood before us. All of them are alluring, but something isn't right about them— something about their humanity that is no longer there. There humanity long gone, and the darkness ahs taken over.

"Oh dear, what happened to them?" She gasps.

"The gargoyles thought it would be fun to play rough." Bellamy folds his hands together. "Don't worry, your majesty. They will be dealt with accordingly."

Sora and I stare at each other in disbelief. They aren't angry people, or at least they don't appear as such. And they show no intention of harming us or that we've committed any crime in Tenebris.

"Your majesty. If it is something that we have done, we apologize to the fullest." Sora takes a knee.

The woman approaches him and lifts him with her hand on his cheek. He shutters. I'm shaking in my cloak, wondering if she will do the same to me. The tall, burly man stands in the back. I hope he won't come an inch closer to us.

"You did nothing wrong. We will talk over dinner. I'm sure you both are hungry. I am Davina, and this is Lazarus." she points to the man behind her. He lightly bows his head.

"We are the Queen and King of Tenebris."

Her eyes glisten with tears in her side profile. She tries so hard to conceal it. Wiping one just before it drops on the tip of her finger as if dust got in her eye.

Bellamy takes a stride towards me. His dark eyes gaze into mine. "It's an honor to meet such a lovely woman."

My stomach turns, and my heart races. I need air. The room is spinning. I'm balancing on my toes, just hoping I don't fall over from shock.

A woman much taller than me leads me to a set of double doors. I hesitate to enter. Stepping one foot in, pausing, then entering. The amount of light that fills the room shocks me. Not light from a lantern, but the light from the sun. Its golden hue washes over everything, making the room seem bigger and less doleful than the others.

A queen-sized bed sits in the middle of it. White sheets and a gold frame make the room shine with color. An oversized vanity adorned with a variety of gemstones sits diagonally from it. The window is the best part. It lets in the most beautiful picture of Tenebris. One in which I thought to be nonexistent due to that constant hate this kingdom gets. But this is a true beauty—a hidden treasure within the dark.

"The bath is ready for you, Miss, whenever you are ready. Then, I'll find you the perfect dress for dinner."

I look over at the woman. She's shuffling in the dresser drawers picking out garments for me to wear. I stand awkwardly in the middle of the room. This has never happened before. I don't know what to do with myself.

"I'm sorry, I didn't get your name."

"Greer, my lady." She bows.

"Don't bow. Please." My gaze fixes on the outside scenery. "What is going on?" I ask.

She stops rummaging through the dresser. Her face turns down. She wants to say something, but she swallows.

"Your majesty has forbidden me to speak of it."

I trace the dresser with my fingertips, smooth to the touch. Immaculately clean. No speck of dust on it, almost as if they had prepared for guests. It's an eerie thought.

"Please, call me Morana. I'm having enough trouble trying to figure out what is going on."

"Yes, Morana." she bows again.

I peer into the washroom. A tub made of porcelain, steaming and ready for me. It's intriguing. I want to get this dried blood off my face and into something more comfortable. I'm afraid, though, if I let my guard down, they'd strike me at my weakest. I'd have died a fool.

The steam of the water stings my body. I relax deeper into the tub, letting my body sink. I let the water wash off the dirt and blood. The bite mark pulses with pain as the water touches it. The blood looks like smoke underwater. I keep eyeing the door, thinking they'd come in any moment with swords drawn.

Greer had put out an entire ensemble for me to wear. Similar to the Queen's attire from earlier, but more modest. It's a black dress with a more modest neckline, but still too far from my liking. She combs through my hair gently, and I have to admit it felt so good that I could fall asleep in the chair. She decorates my hair with gold beads. When I look at myself in the mirror, an entirely different person stares back at me.

Upon looking deeper into the mirror. I don't recognize myself anymore. How did I end up from rags to wearing the most exquisite ensembles in the kingdom? This is unreal.

A knock on the door startles me. Greer smiles and puts down the accessories, and hustles to the door. She curtsies upon realizing who is at the door.

"Good evening, your grace."

"Is my guest ready?" Bellamy asks.

"Certainly." Greer turns to me. I nervously walk over to her.

"Lovely" He smiles. His dark eyes gaze over my body. I'm compelled to say something, but he quickly turns his head down. Greer stands in the hallway for a moment more before shutting the door. Her small footsteps ring behind us.

He holds out his arm for me to take, and I do so without hesitation. If I am going to die, I might as well enjoy the last moments, even with a strange, handsome man who looks like he's killed a few people.

We walk in silence the rest of the way until he breaks it with a question. "Are you alright? Those bruises. I ordered them not to hurt you. Sometimes they can get a little rough."

"I can't say they were gentle," I say. "But the guard wasn't wrong. I wouldn't have come here of my own free will."

I want to avoid any conversation until I get the truth, but Bellamy seems like the type of guy to get what he wants when he wants. And I'm not ready to be around that type of person, not after what Draven tried to do to me. A wave of nausea comes over me at the thought.

"It won't happen again." He assures.

We round the corner to a big room with a long table. Platters of food cover a black tablecloth. My stomach rumbles at the sight of it. Even more so, my nose is delighted with the scent. I take in the presence of all the foreign meats and vegetables, and none of it appears rotten. Fresh.

The King and Queen rise from their seats. Sora does the same but with a look of embarrassment. I bow my head out of respect.

"Morana, you look lovely."

"Thank you, your majesty." I nod.

Bellamy leads me to a chair across the table from Sora. The blood from his head has been cleaned, and the wound on his head is bandaged. He wears a black button-up tunic that shows his chest a little too much, but his eyes light up when we lock eyes. We find comfort in each other's presence.

I sit down and admire the set up of the dining table. There are so many things I have never seen before, and things I haven't seen since I was a child.

The meat doesn't look so appetizing, but the potatoes and onions look rather delightful.

I'm hesitant o even gather the food. I've never had so many options before, let alone fresh food. Everything seems too good to be true. Hopefully the food is just as good as it looks. Perhaps I can get a few bites in before I'm poisoned.

Bellamy leans over to me. "Care for some wine?" he asks.

I nod. As he pours it into my goblet, its scent of fresh berries washes over me.

I remember the last time I enjoyed a meal similar to this. I was with my parents after a long hard day. Mother had cooked the entire meal. I can almost smell the pine scent of the house after she finished cleaning it.

Dinner is uneventful. Conversations of politics and people I have no knowledge about. Sora and I share glances, wondering when they will tell us why they have brought us here. Curiosity is brewing in the air, and I'm becoming impatient. I am beginning to believe that this news won't be pleasant in the slightest. Why would the king and queen of another kingdom bring us to the castle to have dinner? My thoughts torment me.

Sora keeps his head down while eating. I note the exits in the dining room in case things turn quickly. Although, I'm still determining if I'd make it far, considering the gargoyles are patrolling the grounds.

"Now that everyone has gotten the chance to eat, I'd like to say a few words." The Queen stands up with her husband, the King, beside her. "Morana and Sora. Thank you for accepting our invitation to dinner tonight. However, there are things you must know. Things that may come as a shock to you."

Sora and I glance at each other.

"I apologize for not telling you when you entered the castle. I wanted your journey back to be welcoming." The King and Queen look at each other with worrisome eyes.

"You are the twins of Tenebris, and *we* are your parents."

CHAPTER FIVE

I choke on my wine. "Excuse me."

Sora's eyes turn down. And by the look of his posture, he's just as terrified as I am. My hand trembles over my glass of wine. I gently put it down to avoid breaking it. Although, I would like to smash something right about now.

It's impossible. It just can't be true. And when I first laid eyes on Davina, I compared myself to her, unknowingly, now that I think of it. Everything is the same. Down to the very strand of hair. The color of our skin. The aura of our souls. But I can't bring myself to believe it.

"No. There is no way. It's impossible." I tremble.

Queen Davina and King Lazarus glance at each other. The tears in her eyes drip down her cheek. More noticeable than the last time. I won't fall for her pity. I'd rather reach over this table and strangle them if only I knew I had a chance.

"I was born in the east village. My parents died when I was twelve. Your claims are untrue."

Queen Davina sits down along with her husband. She pats her face with a handkerchief. Careful not to ruin her red lipstick and eye makeup.

"If you are our parents, how did we end up in Rhemus?" Sora adds.

King Lazarus clears his throat.

"It was not a decision that was made lightly. There are things you don't understand. Hopefully, soon, we may inform you of those things."

Sora slams his glass down, red wine splattering on the tablecloth. Guards come into the dining hall, gargoyles, by the looks of it. My chance of running is no longer possible. They surround us from the darkness.

"Do you intend to keep us here? We aren't your children." I say. "You are sadly mistaken."

Davina sighs. "Oh, you can leave whenever you want. Only after you hear me. Don't you want to know what happened to Orna and Kai?" Her voice becomes dark.

She knows their names. I feel sick at the thought od it. Had she been spying on us our entire life? I don't know what is going on, but I intend to get every answer out of them. Even if it costs me my life.

"What do you know of their deaths?" I ask.

Davina takes a drink of wine, licking her lips after. "I will tell you, but first there are other matters that need to be cleared first."

I grip my fork as tight as possible to keep myself from saying or doing anything I may regret later. This is her kingdom. I don't know what she is capable of.

"All my life I've felt this unnerving darkness follow me. I felt as if I never fit in. Many times, the thought has crossed my mind that my parents were never mine." Sora says.

"Sora, you can't be serious. They had us bound by rags and chains, and you have the nerve to believe them. You aren't thinking straight."

Bellamy sits back in his chair and smiles as if he's having too much fun listening to this. Quarrel. Watching it all unravel before his eyes. Perhaps, he, too, is part of this ruse.

"Don't deny it, Morana. You felt different from your parents in some way. I could sense your doubts the minute I met you. You were told you would meet your parents again. This is what they meant. The light realm knew of this. They know who we are. The only uncertainty in all of this is why it happened."

"How do you know they told me I'd see my parents again?" I whisper trying to choke back the tears.

"Because King Alaric told me that I'd see mine. I knew it was impossible. I saw their dead bodies. I buried them myself."

The room becomes quiet. Sora keeps his head down, but his fists are full of rage.

"May I say something?" Bellamy asks.

"Who even are you? The Queen's whore?" Sora shouts.

Bellamy and King Lazarus lock eyes. Lazarus shakes his head. As if not to give more information than needed. This place reeks of secrets.

"How did you even know that we came into the kingdom?" I ask.

"The gorgon, Verena, who owns the Inn. She smelled your brimstone blood." Davina coughs. She's irritated at my lack of acceptance. If only I could wrap my hands around her throat and make her spit everything out at once.

"That vampire blood did nothing to mask your scent. Our guards went searching for human bodies and found the dead vampire."

I take a few deep breaths to slow my breathing. I need to relax. I wish they would have just killed us to get it over with. Anything is better than enduring this pain, this uncertainty. Nothing seems real. Like I've lost myself. I can't trust anyone.

"If I may be excused. I need to rest." I stand up and straighten my dress. I will not bow, curtsey, or whatever people do to respect their Kings and Queens. I refuse to participate in a life that was not mine to forge.

Pushing my chair in, I give Sora one last look, hoping he will follow me. He doesn't move or bat an eye.

The table sits in silence as I leave. No one says a word. The sound of my heels clicking against the marble floor echoes behind me. I don't turn to look at them. I want them to feel how angry I am.

I rip out the beads from my hair and the gold necklace that weighs me down. This isn't me. I am not royalty. I am not a child of Tenebris. I am

Morana of the light realm. My parents loved me. That is the truth. That is what I know to be true. I refuse to accept anything different.

I change out of the dress to find a simple gown I can sleep in. Everything is the same color. Shades of red, black, gold, and silver. All the same. I can't stomach looking at it anymore. I find a simple white gown that looks somewhat normal. It's sheer in the light of the sun, showing everything underneath.

I close the curtains to block out the light. I need the dark. I need to feel somewhat at home. In Rhemus. Where I belong. I want to feel the light on my skin and relive the feeling Raisel had given me during our last conversation. But that will never happen again. I just wish I could have told her goodbye.

Who they truly are remains a mystery. That remains a mystery. They look different from the vampire I encountered in the forest. Their skin is pale but still has some hint of life, pinkish in the cheeks. Their eyes are a deep red, like blood, but Bellamy's aren't. Maybe he's different. One thing I know is that they aren't human.

CHAPTER SIX

A knock on the door wakes me. I open my eyes, surrounded by darkness. It's hard to tell if I am in a dream or still in Tenebris. I don't know what time it is or how long I slept. My eyes hang heavily.

"Miss Morana. It's me, Greer."

I stretch before opening the door to her. Her dress is the same as yesterday. A plain black collared dress with a white apron. Simple but pleasant to the eye. Her blonde hair is neatly tucked in a low bun behind her neck. Nothing seems off about her. Surely, she can't be human. But it would come as no surprise if the king and queen kept human servants for their pleasure.

"I know you aren't used to the time here. It's nighttime now. Everyone is getting up. Would you like to stay in bed?"

I rub my eyes, blurring my vision for a short moment.

"No. I'll get dressed. Thank you."

Greer comes in with a towel in hand. She opens the big curtain and reveals the nighttime sky. But it looks different from what I saw the other night.

More stars line the sky, brighter this time. A hue of purple and green smoke swims through the sky.

Breathtaking. All my life, I was told Tenebris was ugly, dark and everything that nightmares are made of. To see this is a true masterpiece. Seeing this makes me realize that I have been lied to. So many people have been lied to.

"What is that?" I point to the sky.

Greer looks up from the wardrobe in the corner of the room. She holds out a red dress like the one I wore yesterday. She smiles.

"That is our realm's most treasured sight. It's called the Lights of Serderis. It lives right over the Sea of Serderis It's a reminder of the night realm's history."

"Care to tell me about it?" I ask.

"The story is for another day. But in shorter terms, it means there is always light in the dark, good in the bad, and love in hatred. That none of those cannot exist without the other."

Everything I had once known about Tenebris has diminished. The rulers of Rhemus believed that Tenebris was a place of horror and unruly people. But, that has been far from the truth. There is so much beauty to be seen in this realm. It's a place I can possibly call home one day.

"Queen Davina has requested your presence at breakfast."

I hold onto the dress she laid out for me. Soft, like the one from yesterday. Softer than any other garment of clothing I have worn in the light realm. Although I cannot be compelled, I still cannot let things pass so easily. Things are handed to me, and I feel less than deserving of it.

I stroll down the hallway slowly, admiring the art and decor that line it. Each is placed intricately, and each one with its own dark history to tell. And while I admire the creativity of the artist, I cannot help but wonder why they have chosen such things to place in their home.

Some statues portray a woman and her daughter, and others a half-dead human clinging to life under the foot of a gargoyle with its fangs protruding. Maybe it all tells a story. A story I am going to get to the bottom of.

When I arrive, everyone is sitting and enjoying their meals, including Sora. He looks well-rested and livelier than yesterday. I find myself shivering at the thought that we slept in the same bed, not knowing that we potential siblings. I still cant bring myself to believe it.

"Hello, Morana. Glad to see you on this fine night." Queen Davina stands alongside King Lazarus.

Looking at them sends shivers down my spine. Their red eyes, her overly cheerful personality. King Lazarus has yet to say more than a few words to me. Even if they are my parents, I cant blame Davina for wanting a relationship with her daughter. It will be a long time before such thing can happen. If at all.

I take my place next to Sora, whose plate contains bread and various fruits.

"Morning to you, Sora."

He nods his head, mouth full of food.

I fill my plate with mostly fruit. Some I have never seen in Rhemus. The light realm always had fruit, but a lot of it went bad quickly. Some had flies, and some had brown spots, making it hard to eat. But food is energy for the poor, so I couldn't be picky then. It feels wrong to overindulge myself with people who mean nothing to me, but they are the only ones who have shown us kindness since entering the night realm.

"Morana, I hope you find your room to be okay. We gave you the best view in the castle." Davina smiles.

Her smile seems genuine. But the teeth behind her lips scream deceit. Perhaps this is all a lie to get me to her side. I can't be cross with her if I want to be on their good side. If they even have one.

"It's amazing. Greer told me about the Lights of Serderis, well, not in full. I'd like to learn more about it."

"Of course, Dear." She pats her mouth. "Hundreds of years ago a pirate named Serderis crossed the sea from Kiveha to Tenebris. Amongst his travels he came in contact with a sea monster that is still unknown to this day. All we know of it if from the massive teeth that still wash up on our land and Kiveha's. He and his crew battled the monster and Serderis was the only one to live. But upon surviving, the monster left its magic at the sight. It's such a powerful type of magic. No one knows what it is or what it is capable of doing. No one in a hundred years has tried to use the magic to their benefit."

I twiddle the fork in my hand.

"But if you are looking for more history on Tenebris, I grant you access to the library we have in the west wing."

A library full of books. I can't be drawn in too easily, but it may have just done the trick.

The library in the light realm isn't so much a library but a single shop with only a few shelves of boring books. Most of it talks about the horrors of each deadly being that roams the border, much like the basilisk that Draven claimed he killed. Many of the books are through one person's eyes.

"Thank you" I examine the foreign fruit.

"Good night to all. Sorry, I am late."

Bellamy walks in, his chest exposed and his hair falling over his shoulders as if he didn't brush it. His eyes are black as they were yesterday, but he has much more stride in his step as if something happened last night when I left dinner.

"Pardon me for sleeping in so late." Bellamy looks over to me and notices me sitting by Sora. "Morana, lovely to see you joining us again. I apologize if last night caused you any distress." He picks my hand up and kisses the top of my hand.

I jerk my hand away. Sora chuckles next to me. I kick his foot slightly.

"Thank you for joining us, Bellamy. We are taking Sora and Morana to the Blood Reader." King Lazarus exclaims.

"Right, of course. Perhaps I could take her to the gardens tomorrow. We have the most spectacular garden, filled with flowers from all over the regions, even that of the —"

I swallow my food. "The blood reader? Who is that?"

Queen Davina pats her mouth as she finishes her bite of food. "He is like a shaman of sorts. He performs rituals as needed by this court. He's also very clever and an ancient old man. He will prove to you we are who we say we are."

She tells us that he is neither good nor bad. He does as he pleases for a small price. And if he's as old as she claims, then gold coins don't seem like the price to pay when preforming such rituals. They pay in blood.

"How are you so sure of this blood reader?" I ask.

"He has always been. And whatever he predicts, it comes true not long after. He's been here for many queens and kings throughout history."

Sora and I exchange looks of hesitation. No one says a thing.

"It's up to Morana."

I glance at Sora. His eyes are serious. They could burn a hole in the marble floor. His words hit with such a force that my heart skips a beat.

"I will do it. But if the ritual proves that I am not your daughter, I want to leave this castle."

Davina said the Blood Reader isn't far from the castle. He lives in a cave near the Sea of Serderis. A stormy sea full of leviathans and unknown sea creatures. He is a lonesome man with no family and no heirs. He is the only one of his kind, and his origin is unknown. However, Davina was adamant that we visit him as soon as possible; any day could be his last.

We were informed of the mountain's harsh weather is cruel to those who don't prepare. Greer set out on a black velvet long-sleeved dress. Decorated with a single gold belt.

Davina, Lazarus, Sora, and I take a carriage to the eastern part of the continent, far away from the border of the Light Realm.

The journey there is brutal. Rocky paths and uneven trails. It is entirely too bouncy. The scenery outside is magical to look at. The light of the moon lights our way and ignites everything in our path. There is almost no need for lanterns to guide us.

King Lazarus seems more enthusiastic today, talking more than usual. He'd been eyeing me more often. I catch glimpses of him every few seconds. I'm trying to see the similarities between us. I have dark hair. My eyes are brown, and theirs are deep red. Our skin complexion may be the same. Most are simple similarities. Even a commoner could look like them.

Once we reach the Blood Reader, I expect him to tell us we aren't related. I fear the worst for Sora and me. We have been treated like royalty since arriving at the night realm. For all of that to be washed away by some ritual frightens me. Will they attack on sight? Will they let us go? I feel in my pocket for the dagger Sora has given me.

We pass the foot of the mountain, and in the distance, stars glimmer on the land. They move in flutters, like a heartbeat, and flow across the ground. It isn't until I look closer that I realize it is the ocean. It is a sea of stars, reflective of the sky above.

"In the village of the east, we were only a few miles away from the coastline. Nothing compares to this." Sora says.

We are both mesmerized by the sheer wonder of the sea. Nothing in the light realm is as magnificent as this. It makes me wonder why the light realm has never looked like this. And if it has, what cruel king took all the beauty out of it?

We come to a sudden halt. I brace my feet against the floor.

"We have to walk the rest of the way." Queen Davina says.

The terrain is nothing but rocks. Some wet from the ocean spray and moss. Some are so slippery that I hold on to Sora as we jump from rock to rock. It's a dangerous maze, and I now know why few people make the effort. The nearest village is some miles away.

We come to a dark cave by the sea. We are so close to it that I can feel the ocean mist on my face. Memories of my time on the cliff haunt me. The dark waters splash on the rocks, leading us inside the cave.

We follow Davina and Lazarus into the dark cave. They disappear into the void. I grab hold of Sora's wrist and follow behind them. I feel with my feet for the rocks, hoping I don't trip and impale myself on one.

Davina laughs in the dark. "Oh dear, I forgot. You do not have eyes as we do. Yet."

Her red eyes must give her some ability. No human has eyes like theirs. It gives them the ability to see in the dark. As one should when living in Tenebris when everything is dark and arcane. No one knows if something lurks in the shadows.

"Take my hand, dear," Davina calls out. Her hands find mine, and she pulls me deeper into the abyss, guiding me through the unknown.

Sora must be with Lazarus. I hear nothing but the crumble of the rocks and the clicks of our shoes on the terrain. Every step is made cautiously, in fear I'll step on something and fall over. The stones are made to divert the weak. I am breathing heavily to keep myself from falling to my knees.

We come to a halt. Davina's hand is still wrapped around my wrist. I can't see anything. No glimmer of light. Absolutely nothing.

A door opens before us in a moment, letting in an orange hue of light. It's blinding, so I cover my eyes till they can adjust.

This is it. Just a few more moments, and I'll finally get the answers I've been wanting to hear. And once I get those answers. I'll run as fast as I can, maybe killing myself along the way. And if that doesn't happen, I'll leap into the ocean and never return. I won't give them the satisfaction of killing me.

"Blood Reader, we have come for your wisdom. We come not as king and queen, but Davina and Lazarus."

Davina calls out, and her voice echoes off the cave walls. The sound is ringing in my ears.

The cave is ignited by lanterns and candles on all sides, leaving no wall untouched by the fiery light. The rocks have been cleared on the walkway, and I now feel safer walking alone. I pry my hand away from Davina. She doesn't protest.

I stand next to Sora. Both of us take in the view around us. A makeshift altar stands before us, decorated with chalices, inhuman bones, and skulls. Feathers from a bird so large I've never seen before. Teeth and other trinkets are scattered along the table. Crumpled parchment and spilled ink. This is the work of a madman.

"Blood Reader, come before us," Lazarus says.

Around the corner is a small hallway. Shuffling echoes from it. The Blood Reader emerges from the hallway, covering his face with a raggedy hood. He hunches over, making small strides to the altar.

"I'm coming. I'm coming. These feet don't work like they used to." he laughs.

He's not at all like I had pictured him to be. Instead, he's a scrawny old man with bony fingers and an elongated nose that droops too far over his lips. His gray skin peeks under his sleeve, and his yellow fingernails remain untrimmed. He doesn't seem like the type of person to be feared. But then again, even the most beautiful things can be ugly.

"I haven't seen you since— well, that one thing. Years ago. My, have you grown?" He comes to me, resting his wrinkly hand on my face. His eyes squint at me like he can't quite see right. His gray eyes barely peek through.

"Blood Reader, we request your help in reading the blood of these two people."

"And what will you be giving me in return?" The Blood Reader asks, eyeing Sora and me.

"Gold for the next month and all the corpses of the humans found at the border." King Lazarus speaks.

That explains the awful smell from behind our carriage in the wagon. Those had to be the same men Sora, and I traveled with us to the border—the murderers. Soon to be devoured by the Blood Reader.

"Good. Good."

The Blood Reader shuffles to the altar. He straightens everything to a particular spot. By doing so, he creates more of a mess than before.

"Come here, children."

He takes our hands and wraps them around each other, so we hold onto one another's forearms. Sora's firm hands grasp my arm, but not too tight. But tight enough if something goes wrong, he could pull me out of the cave.

"Now, your majesties, place your hands on their arms." The Blood Reader directs.

Queen Davina takes hold of me and Lazarus to Sora. After that, I never leave Sora's eyes.

The Blood Reader takes out a silver knife. Clean, by the looks of it.

"What are you doing with that?" Sora asks.

The Blood Reader stands before us. "We need a little blood from all four of you."

"You haven't exactly told us what is going on. And we are supposed to trust you?"

The Blood Reader laughs. "No one trusts me, child."

The Blood Reader stands over Sora first. Taking the knife and sliding it across his skin a few inches. A few inches more than I think he needs. Sora hisses, and blood drips from his arm. Next, he comes to me with the blade in hand. I squeeze Sora's arm tighter to brace myself for the pain that is to come. Then, with a single swipe down my arm, blood flows.

Next, with the same knife, Davina and Lazarus give their blood with the same unclean knife.

We bleed together as one. I steer my eyes away from the it, as it sets my stomach uneasy. This is too much blood—more blood than should be coming from one person.

"When your blood meets each other, if you are not of relation, the blood will turn black as tar. If you are of such relation, the blood will burn and boil, and retreat into your body. Your wounds will heal from your brimstone blood."

I still don't understand what brimstone blood is.

The Blood Reader turns to me. His eyes look into mine as if trying to read me. To see into my soul. I glance at him once more, pushing him out of my head. I don't know how I did it, but even he looks surprised.

"Is this going to hurt?" I ask.

"Mentally or physically, child?"

The blood travels to the center of where our skin meets. It moves as if it's trying to find something. Something that won't be there. My heart races, not from the suspense, but from the continuous blood flowing out of my body. I'm scared I'll pass out at any moment.

The Blood Reader mumbles something under his breath. An ancient language I've never heard in my life. I can't make out anything he's trying to say, but he keeps it hidden.

Our blood meets, and it mingles with each other. Getting to know the person, smelling its scent, like it's alive. It merges to form a bigger pool of blood on our hands. Its warmth is that of a lava pool.

Just as I expected, the mans predictions do not come to perdition. The blood doesn't turn black, but it doesn't boil or burn. Perhaps he's just an old man who likes to put on a show for others, all for gold and bodies. I knew this would happen. I knew nothing would come of this. This was all a joke to bring us out here—

It burns. The blood burns. It is burning me like hot coal.

"It hurts," I say.

Sora struggles to release the bond. But there is no breaking it. We try to pull away from each other.

The blood is burning hotter. "Make it stop," I shout.

The blood is boiling just as he said. The blood pools and bubbles to no end. The boiling no longer burns, but maybe my skin has lost all feeling.

"No." I pull away. "This can't be happening."

The bond is still there. I can't let go.

Tears run down Sora's face. Queen Davina's eyes look down at the blood. A small smile twitches on her mouth like she's glad this is happening. I wish I could tear out her throat.

The bond is broken in a minute. Blood drips from our arms but slowly stops as the blood retreats into our bodies. The dizziness I felt earlier is gone, but my heart still races with adrenaline. Soon, our blood is nowhere to be found, like nothing had ever happened. No trace of anything. Out of existence.

"You have your answer, your majesty. They are your son and daughter. Princess Morana, and Prince Sora."

CHAPTER SEVEN

I lock myself in the bedroom after we arrive back at the castle. The journey back was quiet. Uncomfortably quiet. I'm still shaking from the very fear of who I am. My whole life is a lie played out by the most ruthless rulers in all the kingdom of Rhemus. My life was hidden from me for years. Nobody thought of the consequences this would bring to the future. I no longer know myself.

Who are the people who raised me? The people I truly love. Orna and Kai. Not Davina and Lazarus. What deal did they strike to make such a thing happen? I was a baby, a helpless baby. And so was Sora. Why were we separated? Could they not have done us any justice by keeping us together?

Knowing I've had a brother all along shakes me to the core. I'm angry I hadn't found out sooner. If we had each other, life wouldn't have been so against us. We could have led a better life. The both of us fighting for a life we both deserve.

I stare out into the night sky. The colors from the Lights of Serderis swirl in my mind, warping everything until now. Like I'm seeing everything happen from another body that is not mine.

Greer frequently comes to check on me. I know she's sent here by Queen Davina to make sure I am okay. I say nothing when she arrives. I want to keep to myself. Except, I need someone to share my feelings with. Someone I can fully trust.

I leave my room to find Sora. He said little when we came back. He retired to his room too. We both needed to escape from the emotions and hype.

I knock.

"Lachin, if that's you again, please leave."

Lachin must be another servant in the castle. I have yet to see him around. I haven't seen Greer outside of my room once. The servants know how to stay well hidden.

"It's Morana. Can I come in?"

"Yeah."

His room is like mine, except he doesn't have the mountain view as I do. His window towers like mine, but his peers are down the front of the mountain. Just in the distance, if I squint your eyes enough, you can see the lights from the village below. Not such a great view, but it's unique, nonetheless.

Sora sits on his silk sheets with a book in hand. He must have gone to the library. A spark of joy comes over me, knowing we enjoy the same escape. We both enjoy a good book when things are too messy to deal with. Instead, we'd rather be taken to other worlds and experience life much less morose than this one.

"I guess asking how you are is out of the question?"

He chuckles and sits the book down. The skin around his eyes is red and swollen like he's been crying. I don't blame him, though. The past few hours have been devastating in every measure. We are going through something we don't know how to handle.

"If we had known we were siblings, do you think our life in the village would have been better?" I ask.

He traces the spine of the book.

"Better? Probably not. But if we had each other, I don't think we would have suffered as much as we did." He sighs and runs his hand through his hair. "Maybe if we had known, we could have made better decisions that wouldn't have led us to this place."

"I can't look at the King and Queen and see them as our parents. I heard stories of Tenebris when I was a child. I was so frightened I'd be sent there for no reason because that's how the King is. I was scared I'd endure a long life in exile or suffer a painful death. Maybe that's why I had wanted to die in the east village, so nothing like that could happen. So, I could decide my own fate."

I run my fingers along the hem of my sleeve.

I look behind me to the window. Peering down at the village. The twinkling lanterns shine like those of fairy wings. It reminds me of Raisel.

"The creatures here are horrifying. But, they seemed content when we arrived. Even the goblins and the gorgons. How can life here seem so much better than in the light realm? I can't help but think maybe we were on the wrong side of history. The ones we feared were the ones we needed all along."

Sora turns to me. "Did you notice that the King and Queen looked almost upset when we arrived here? Happy, but yet distraught to see us."

I nod.

"I think they are hiding something deeper than this," Sora says.

I don't doubt it. The minute we arrived, nothing added up. To the gargoyles coming to take us, to them bringing us to the castle. To meeting Bellamy, whom we still can't figure out why he stays here and not in Kiveha. Much is left unsaid. There are still secrets within these walls.

"Bellamy is a cocky bastard," Sora exclaims.

"I don't mind him so much." I say. "The King barely speaks. He follows Davina around like a puppy."

King Lazarus acts like a king when Davina allows him. She is entirely in charge. For most courts, it would be the opposite. No king would allow their consort to behave in such a way. It's backwards in this realm. Queen Davina has made it clear that she oversees everything. What is spoken and when it is said. The women rule this realm.

"I'm going to the library later. Maybe I'll find something there." I stand up.

"Well, good luck. The library is massive. Hope you find what you are looking for."

I meet Davina in the east wing. She has a ring with old keys stacked together. All are unique in their make. Each one is a key to opening hidden secrets.

"Thank you for meeting me, Morana. I can't wait for you to see this."

She unlocks the enormous door, and it creaks when it opens. The sound echoes down the hallway. A cool breeze washes over us as we enter it like it had been abandoned for years, except when Sora was able to get in.

"I've been collecting books for many years. We have books of all kinds. History, romance, poetry. Books on magic and faraway places. I might have a problem with hoarding books." Davina laughs nervously.

The library is full of light from the lanterns and a chandelier above. Books are stacked on the floor, and most are neatly stacked inside towering shelves that reach the ceiling. No telling how many years she's collected all these books. Some look older than time.

A desk sits in the middle of the library. It's covered in dust and old papers, with ink that looks hardened over the years from lack of use. Gold trinkets decorate the table. Gold feathered pens, gold beads, similar to the ones my hair is decorated with, and gold cubes for show.

It's a mess of curiosity.

"The history books line that wall over there." Davina points to the left. "And the story books are to the right. Some might be misplaced. There has been no one to clean it for years now. So, pardon the dust."

I look around, taking in all the books and their adventures that await me. I want all of them. There will never be enough time in this world to finish every last book on these shelves.

"Where are the ones in the history of Tenebris?" I ask.

Davina freezes, trying to decide whether to answer. She walks to the left, and I follow her.

"This shelf has most of the history of the night realm. Some are left in the forbidden section, locked away from others' eyes. Things like old rituals, forbidden spells, and long-lost creatures that once roamed."

She's hiding something. I can sense it. She fumbles with the keys.

"I'll leave you these keys, dear. Keep them for as long as you would like." The rusty keys scrape my skin.

Her voice shakes as if she wants to say more, but she's holding back.

"Wait, before you go." I stop her. She swiftly turns. "I am humbled by your kindness. And I apologize if I am distant. Its like my world has crashed down on me and I'm barely breathing."

She relaxes her shoulders.

"All my life, I've known Orna to be my mother. And to find out who my real parents are is a huge adjustment. I wanted to run when the Blood ritual didn't go as I hoped it would. Even finding out Sora and I committed the same crime, and later find we are brother and sister. It's very different. So please, give us some time to adjust to this new life."

Tears swell in her eyes. I can tell she wants to hug me. I'm not ready for that. I can't picture her as my mother. I see her as a brokenhearted woman with two distant children who don't know who she is. So much is yet to be discovered, and I don't trust anyone, not even Sora. I need to keep my heart guarded at all times.

"I appreciate you being honest with me." She wipes a single tear from her face. "When I heard of your arrival, I was sick. There are things I regret, and I want to tell you everything, but I fear that would be too much for you. So, I will give you as much time as you need—the same for Sora. And your father— King Lazarus, I mean, he is here too. We thought we would never see you two again."

"What exactly happened?" The words spill from my mouth before I can think.

My hand twitches as if it wants to comfort her. I freeze.

"That is a conversation that needs to be held with Sora present. Soon enough."

She leaves in a hurry, her muffled cries echo down the hallway like a lonely ghost. I didn't mean to upset her. She's shown us nothing but kindness in our time here. But things like this cannot be forced. It's hard to change ways after living a certain way for years.

I lay the keys on the desk and admire the books around me. So many to choose from, and I'm still trying to figure out where to start. History would be a wise choice, but fantasy novels and classics taunt me to read them.

I search the history shelf for anything that may catch my eye. Spellbooks and magic of the old ages, agriculture, and politics. None of it sparks my attention until I see a book labeled: The Night Realm of Tenebris.

It's an easy choice, considering I know nothing of this realm I'm exiled to. I might as well read about the many wonders of this land and put that information to good use.

Dust lingers on the pages from years of neglect. I can see why it would be useless to those who live here. They already know everything there is to know about this place. They've experienced the worst of it.

An index of creatures that live here form the first few pages. It's like they keep track of every monster, and every race, down to the plants and crystals here. Nothing is left out.

Vampires and gargoyles and gorgons are some that I have already experienced. As I look further down the list, more deadly creatures are listed. Ogres, basilisks, sirens, and cyclops. All malicious in their ways, and rightfully so. Poorly mistreated creatures fight back when threatened.

A dybbuk catches my eye. This is the first I have heard of one before my time here. So, I read more into it.

A dybbuk is a disembodied human spirit, mostly malicious, that searches for a human body to take over. And once it accomplishes its goal, it leaves, often leaving the host very ill or dead. Only ones who deal with spirits can drive them out.

It sounds insanely dangerous. They lurk here in the forests of the night realm, searching for a living human body to occupy. I don't know how they were driven out of the light realm years ago. Maybe a witch, someone who works for the light realm, placed wards on the land. To make sure they never get in.

A depiction of a siren draws my attention. Her hypnotizing eyes, and her even deadlier voice. I've always wondered why the villages were placed miles off the shoreline.

Their songs of sorrow will lure anyone into their territory, destroying their mind from the inside and making them completely unaware of what is happening. Then the last minute before their death, they seal it with a kiss and devour their victims with their razor-sharp teeth, leaving no evidence of a murder.

It is not a lie that Tenebris is filled with deadly creatures. The ones that I've come in contact with haven't been savage like, as Rhemus makes them out to be. Perhaps I am not looking in the right direction for the more threatening ones.

I find the family tree of the monarchy system. It dates back hundreds of years before I was even a thought. This is the information I need.

I rummage through the pages looking for a timeline closer to this one. Finally, I reach it. I see Queen Davina's name and King Lazarus's name side by side, with a simple sketch of their bust. Stemming from them are Davina's parents before her, Queen Aurore and King Lonac. The tree goes on and on. Forming a long tree of life and many reigns.

I look deeper into King Lazarus's tree. His family comes from no royalty at all. His mother is Vespera of Rhemus and Tiecand of Rhemus. No information is on them other than their names and a small sketch of their faces—no king or queen titles.

I look above Queen Davina and King Lazarus. Three lines stem above it. It lists Sora, me, and one other name. The ink is smeared, but not enough to cover the name completely.

Astrid is the name. Only the name is there. No picture. No information on her. Nothing.

She is between my name and Sora's as if she's listed as another offspring of Davina and Lazarus. I haven't seen a girl anywhere near my age here. I've seen maids walking around but no other girl. Davina has yet to mention another one of us.

It is foolish of her to leave this book out if she's so filled with secrets of her own. Maybe they had intended for me to find this. Perhaps she lost a child, and I will never blame her if that's the case.

Curiosity runs thick in my veins. I can't let this go so quickly. If I have a sister, I want to know who and where she is. And why Davina hasn't mentioned her existence.

CHAPTER EIGHT

It is the biggest celebration of the century. That is what King Lazarus told us. Sora and I are the guests of honor at tonight's ball. They expect us to wear full Tenebrisean attire and have smiles on our faces, even if we are not so.

I never had the opportunity to attend a party while living in the light Realm. The commoners were never allowed in the castle. Only criminals during their trials. We could never afford elaborate dresses and shiny jewelry. Our rags and muddy boots were strictly prohibited. No one could get through the front gates if they looked lesser than.

Greer is rummaging through the wardrobe again. Her hands are moving so fast it's all a blur. She doesn't stop for a moment to take a breath.

"It has to be perfect." She mumbles.

I look at myself in the vanity mirror, wrapped in a black silk robe. My pale skin glows. I'd rather attend looking like this than something I am not. I was never one to go above the standards for beauty.

"Ahh. Perfect."

I turn around to see a dress so beautiful even I am impressed. A black chiffon dress decorated with flecks of gold on the hemline. Lace sleeves and a gold cape to match. More beautiful than anything I've seen in the light Realm. Of course, I never had the pleasure of affording such things.

Everything I've seen in Rhemus was always the same dull red, green, and blue colors. Nothing vibrant. Only the royals wear silver and gold.

"Wow. I like it." I smile.

"You will be surprised. Once you live here a while, you become accustomed to the everyday attire of the night court."

Live here. That's what I'm doing. I'm not dying. And I'm not simply surviving. I'm living here, thriving, well, and alive. The thought of spending the rest of my life here sends me chills. When I arrived, I wasn't open to staying here. I'd rather the king and queen throw me to the wolves to be devoured. Instead, I'm attending a royal ball dressed in gold and beauty to honor Sora and me.

Greer does the last touches on my hair. The hair is always the last. Getting into the dresses requires work, and she starts all over if one thing is ruined. I've noticed that about her. She takes nothing less than perfect as acceptable.

I wish I'd feel as confident as I look. I'm out of my comfort zone but also relaxed. I was so used to wearing ragged clothes that were always too short for me. Never thick enough to keep me warm. I never thought I'd be able to impress men with such a homeless look. And now, I feel like a woman that might have a chance to meet someone one day.

Walking down the dark hallway, my confidence decreases. Every step sends me into a state of anxiety. I've never shown my face in front of so many people, let alone looking like I can rule a kingdom. I know all eyes will be on Sora and me, and I don't know how well that will turn out.

I hear the rumbling of a big crowd. Voices echo off the walls, and it isn't easy to decipher each conversation and who is talking. Or what is speaking?

"Hey there."

I swiftly turn.

"Glad I caught you." Bellamy comes out from behind the corner. "Don't go that way. The King and Queen want you to enter through another way."

"Bellamy. Nice to see you." I observe him.

He's dressed flashier than I've seen him before. Still subtle but has more color. He wears a black jerkin with a plain shirt underneath to cover his arms. Gold buttons decorate his leather belt. His dark hair is nicely pulled back and away from his face, leaving his dark eyes the center of attention. Nice to see him look somewhat presentable tonight.

"You look lovely tonight." He smiles. His arm grabs mine without warning.

"As do you."

We walk in silence up a set of stairs. I find myself breathing hard to catch my breath. My lungs burn, and my legs shake. I haven't used muscles like this in a while.

"Your mortal lungs will do no good here." He says.

I roll my eyes at him.

"Well, some of us didn't have the pleasure of growing up in such a mysterious kingdom. My village didn't have stairs this high."

He pats my hand.

"I'm not from here. But where I am from, immortals are still a thing."

"What are you? You're not exactly human."

I've thought of many things he could be. Vampire is possible, but he's able to eat real food. And I have yet to see him drink blood unless he does it in hiding. Werewolf or shapeshifter, I don't know. He is something more ancient than the mind can comprehend.

"I am from Kiveha." He replies, ignoring the actual question.

"Where is that? I have never heard of it."

He takes a breath as if he's annoyed with my constant questions.

"A land a little smaller than this one just north of Tenebris. Have they taught you nothing in that filthy land you came from?"

We round the corner to a balcony that leads into the ballroom. King Lazarus and Queen Davina are waiting for us. Sora stands by the entrance with his arms crossed. We are both dressed in the same colors, almost matching each other identically.

"Morana. You look stunning." Davina takes my hands in her and twirls me. I never noticed how loud this dress is until now. The different textures rub against each other, sounding like a crackling fire.

Bellamy and Sora roll their eyes. I shook a look back at them.

"I hope you both enjoy this night. It's all for you and Sora."

I have to find the right time to ask her about Astrid. Tonight may not be the appropriate time to do so, but curiosity is killing me. If there is another sibling, I need to know.

"Who is Astrid?" I ask.

Davina and Lazarus's eyes shoot at me. I should have left it till the end of the party. Now I regret the words spilling from my mouth.

Davina faces me and gently grabs onto my shoulders. She breathes in. Lazarus eyes her intently like he's waiting for what she will say.

"She was your sister. She died as a baby. She would have been your older sister. I was hoping to have that conversation another time. How do you know her name?" Her voice shakes.

"I found it in the family tree book in the library. I'm sorry, it was just there. I saw the name, and I was curious."

Davina nods. "Well, I'm glad you came to me. I'm sorry I didn't tell you before. I didn't want to delve into so much information after all the events of the past few days."

"I'm sorry for your loss," I mutter.

Lazarus relaxes his shoulders. Sora is unfazed by the news.

"It was a loss for the entire kingdom."

I still have high suspicions. I still need to know more. I know others would tell me to drop it. But I want to know more about where I come from and everything I've missed out on, even if I'm still in denial about my birth parents.

"Thank You, dear." Davina wipes her eyes. "But let's move on. We are giving you a grand entrance to celebrate your homecoming," King Lazarus exclaims.

Sora's eyes go wide. He's just as nervous as I am.

"I hardly find that appropriate," Sora says. "Of course, given all of this is new to us. We have barely had time to accept it."

Davina's head turns to him, teeth clenched. I swear I see a flame in her eye.

"Can't we just enjoy the party and talk with the others?" I ask.

"I see it as an opportunity to help you. Maybe if you see the court and our people, it may change your mind." Davina says softly.

I cross my arms. I think of the ways this could cause harm. Do we make ourselves known and become a widely sought-after target? Or do we accept our role as the King and Queen's children? A symbol of their nation. A symbol of secrets.

The King and Queen have retreated to their thrones. Sora and I stand shoulder to shoulder. We wait patiently behind towering double doors. I'm shaking, and maybe he is too. But that could be because of me.

"If I fall, please fall with me," I mutter.

"Seriously? And have the eyes fall on me as well? Pathetic."

We freeze and burst out laughing in a second. With him, I can be myself and not feel guilty about it. Being here with him is the only way I can be here tonight. Had I come here alone, I'd have already been eaten alive.

The double doors open. I cling to Sora's hand, and we walk together. My dress flows behind me with such heaviness that I feel like I would fall over any minute. Part of me wishes it would happen so that I don't have to go on any further.

"Presenting, Sora and Morana of the Night Realm." A loud voice calls ahead.

Sora and I glance at each other in awe of our titles. The night realm. Not the light realm. This is our origin. I'm not fond of taking on the name in such a short amount of time. It's not like I have no choice, but no one had asked us in the first palace.

We reach the King and Queen. Both are smiling at us, proud of us for returning to Tenebris. It's hard not to be suspicious when you look at their red eyes.

The ballroom overflows with people that look like us and those who don't. Vampires dress in their finest wardrobe, skin no longer gray from the lack of blood, hair combed, and teeth cleaned of their prey. Snakes slither across our feet, greeting us with a warm and somewhat slimy welcome. The goblins and gorgons scatter throughout the crowd. The gorgons wear eye protection not to turn anyone into stone.

In their full-stone form, the gargoyles stand guard by each exit. Horns out, wings alert, and their hands ready to stop anyone who would harm us.

I didn't expect this—so much unity in one place. Everyone is well-behaved, and no one is trying to kill one another. This isn't how King Alaric made the night realm out to be.

Lazarus takes my hand as we take a step near the throne.

Two chairs are decorated with red jasper and obsidian, fit for the King and Queen. Two chairs smaller than the thrones sit next to the kings, and one other small chair is next to the Queens. Five chairs and one person is missing.

"My darling, children."

Sora and I nod our heads with hesitation. Her smile lights up her face.

Davina looks to Lazarus to call him forth. Eyes are still on us.

"We would like to ask you," Davina rubs her hands. "If we could crown you, publicly, Prince and Princess of Tenebris tonight?"

My jaw drops, and so does Sora's. I Release my grip from Sora's arm. My hands droop to my sides.

"I know we should have asked you sooner and not in front of hundreds of people. We would like to celebrate our family reuniting."

I curl my toes, trying to keep my tears in. The pain in my throat grows.

"It's only fitting. To be crowned Prince and Princess of the night court is an honor. We know there are many things still left unknown to you both. And in due time, those will be revealed. Please trust us. We haven't given you any reason not to trust us."

Except for the fact that we know nothing of how we ended up in the light realm.

"I'll do it. You have treated us so kindly since our arrival. And since we are no longer welcomed in the light realm. It would be my honor to take the crown." Sora bows his head.

Words can't come out of my mouth fast enough to object to such insanity. To give in so quickly is maddening.

"Morana, dear, I know we still have a lot to discuss. Will you please, along with your brother, take your rightful crown tonight? And if you are not satisfied at the end of the night, I'll be happy to take the crown back, and you may still live here. No duties."

I'm already a princess by blood, and Sora is a prince. If we publicly claim the throne, we could have many more opportunities. I'd be heavily watched, but I would have access to the forbidden section in the library. I will only take the throne not because of the title but the secrets I could potentially unfold. I could find out what happened to my mother and father.

"If Sora will, I will."

CHAPTER NINE

Sora and I stand as one and face the crowd. Being coronated a princess is something the old me would have frowned upon and fought so hard to avoid. I never wanted attention like this. I never wanted an entire kingdom to fall on my shoulders. Diplomacies, politics, wars, and parties are not my thing. They never were. I feel like an entirely different person than the little girl I used to be.

A priest stands before us, and a small boy about half my size holds a pillow with two crowns. One fitted for Sora and one for me. I try not to look at it for too long, in fear I may start hearing it talk, warping my mind and begging me to wear it.

The small boy's fangs peek from his lips as he smiles up at me. I force a smile in return.

Sora repeats after the priest word for word. With him, there is no hesitation. The words flow freely from his mouth. He is willingly becoming prince of a kingdom we've only just entered.

As Sora kneels to the ground, the priest places the crown on his head—a perfect fit.

"I give you, Prince Sora of the night realm."

The crowd bows in his presence. As he stands back up to face his people, our people, he looks stronger, more fearsome in his eyes.

The priest turns to me, and Sora sits on his throne next to Queen Davina. My hands are forming a cold sweat between my fingers. I wish he hadn't left me alone up here.

"Repeat after me." He says.

"I, Morana of the Night realm."

I can't believe I am doing this.

"Swear to uphold the law and rule with a kind heart, passion, and mercy."

It's happening.

"I swear to protect this land at all costs and protect all creatures alike."

No, going back,

"I will rule alongside my mother and father for all eternity."

What?

For all eternity. The words spill from my mouth without warning or hesitation of objection. Everything is spoken. Set in stone. I'm cursed to rule a kingdom I know nothing about.

The priest raises the crown over my head as I kneel with my head down. He places it gently on me, and it fits suspiciously well.

"I give you, Princess Morana of the night realm."

All goes silent, and the crowd bows before me. Eyes down. All I can think of is an eternity of this. An eternity of ruling over a place I fought so hard to avoid. Now, I'm in the heart of it.

I take a seat next to King Lazarus. He smiles with a mouthful of teeth. I can only think, how many people has he devoured with those teeth?

I look over to the empty seat next to me. Abandoned. Poor Astrid. She will never see this.

"All hail Queen Davina. All hail King Lazarus. All hail Prince Sora. All hail Princess Morana. Rest in peace, Princess Astrid."

I look over to Bellamy, who has joined in the chanting. He claps and cheers with the crowd. Never losing eye contact with me. He knows I know something isn't right with this court. I can see it glimmer in his dark eyes.

Music sounds around us. The most beautiful music I've ever heard. Nothing like what is played in the light realm. It's joyous, and people bounce to the beat, losing themselves in the harmonies reverberating off the walls.

King Lazarus rests his hand upon mine as I sit next to him. I'm unsure of what to do next. Do I sit here all night, watching my people enjoy themselves with food, laughter, and music? Is this what a princess is about?

"I think someone would like to dance with you," Lazarus says.

Bellamy walks up the steps and kneels before me, hand out.

"Would the crowned princess like to dance?"

I look over to Lazarus and Davina. Sora is nowhere to be found. He must be in the crowd enjoying this party more than I am. Who knew this would be a coronation?

Davina smiles as she ushers me to dance.

I take Bellamy's hand, and he kisses it ever so lightly. He takes me to a spot on the dance floor, and the crowd forms a circle around us. Gorgons slither past and whisper to their friends around them.

"Don't mind them. Just keep your eyes on me."

His face remains neutral for a moment.

"Pretend you are having a good time and listen carefully. Laugh if you understand."

I laugh the most horrible laugh I can cough out. I can see a smile on Bellamy's face. I may have embarrassed myself on my first night as a princess.

"I saw you looking at the other chair."

I continue to smile, but it almost hurts.

"Astrid did not die as a child. She was taken."

Bellamy looks around and lets out a small chuckle.

He spins me around, dips me to the floor, and

 lightly kisses me on the cheek as he brings me back up, and I brace my crown to my head.

"What are you saying? Davina said she died as a baby."

We spin in circles around creatures alike. All of them dance to their heart's content. I can't help but feel happy for them. Who knows how long they've waited to celebrate something like this?

Bellamy pulls me to him. Our chests are touching. Warmth on warmth. Breath on each other's necks, so close he could bite me with fangs, and no one would notice.

"She is the reason you and Sora were sent to the light realm."

He keeps his eyes locked with mine. It's hard to look into his eyes and not feel dread waiting to happen. Like I could be sucked in so deep. I'm losing myself in his eyes.

"Don't tell them I told you."

"So, it is but a rumor. Why would they lie about their child's death?" I smile, trying to blend in with the merriment.

And if someone found out where she came from, she would have been killed by King Alaric.

"There are many things they haven't told you. And they will have my head if I tell you everything. But I can't."

I grab his hand as we twirl around.

"It kills me to keep any secrets from you. It is not of my own free will."

Our movements slow to a shuffling of our feet. Strained by the words and secrets; we hold on to each other closely. Waiting for the right moment to part.

Bellamy and I escape the party and venture to the gardens. The sun is barely on the horizon, so the party should die down soon.

The Sea of Lights is still visible. Its vivid colors are swirling in the night sky and waving at us like it's trying to gain our attention. I'd never tire of seeing its beauty even if I am bound to this kingdom. Something unique as this will forever be etched in my mind.

Bellamy takes me through a maze of rare and unknown flowers to the light realm. Some are dark, and some glow in the night. Some hang, and some are alive and full of color. Each one is different from the last. Each one is a reminder of the secrets this realm holds.

"So, will you ever tell me what your business is here?" I ask, brushing my fingers against a queen of the night tulip.

"Politics. But I'm mostly trying to avoid my insufferable parents." He brings me to a stone bench. "What was it like in the light realm?"

I straighten my dress. I smooth my hair over my shoulder, forgetting the crown on my head. Its presence will take some time getting used to.

"Dreadful to say the least. I wanted to get out so bad. I didn't know my destiny lied here." I laugh.

We laugh.

"I don't get it, though. People fear this place. They think of it as some rancid and savage wasteland for rejects of the court."

Bellamy eyes something in the distance. A figure catches his attention. His eyes narrow in on an object.

"People fear what they do not understand. They are close-minded."

He keeps his eyes in the distance. I look out, trying to see what he does. Unfortunately, my eyes aren't as good as his.

"Bellamy, do you see something?" I ask, looking behind me.

He stands up, facing his ears in the direction that distracts him.

In the blink of an eye, I am surrounded by crow-like wings. They hug me tightly, almost too tight to know what is happening. The thudding of feet tramples closer to us.

"We are under attack," Bellamy shouts.

Guards round the corner with spears in hand. An arrow lands right before my head and takes the crown off my head. Bellamy pulls me up, and I reach for the crown last second, trying to regain my balance.

Bellamy covers me with his wings, and we run to the castle. He hisses in pain. The gargoyles run past us, horns out and stone fists and swords. The swords clash as a mass of centaurs makes their way through the garden, destroying the plants in the path.

Bellamy pushes me through the door.

"I'm sorry, Princess."

He shuts it with him outside. I pound on the door, unable to open it.

"Your majesty, follow me." A gargoyle says.

"What about Bellamy?" I cry.

The stone of the gargoyle's hand takes hold of mine. I can't fight back through his strength.

We weave through the halls. Gargoyles and vampires alike shove their way through to get to the commotion outside.

I'm running so fast I'm sure I hear my dress rip on my feet a few feet back. I keep my eyes on the gargoyle. He's not stopping till he fulfills his order of taking me to safety.

I see Davina, Lazarus, and Sora waiting for me at the end of the hallway. Davina's fierce eyes come to me, her arms open. She embraces me, and I wrap my arms around her, not realizing what I'm doing until she leans away checking my face and body for any signs of distress.

"Are you okay, dear? Did they hurt you?"

"What is going on?" Tears roll down my face. I'm shaking from the sudden terror.

"There's been a breach at the border."

CHAPTER TEN

The next night, a meeting is held with the King and Queen and the private council. The decision to invite Sora and me was made at the last minute. Sora seems rather pleased to participate in such an important task on his first night as a prince. I would much rather look for Bellamy. He never came back after the ambush.

Greer tells me he is alive. He came out with minor injuries besides an arrow to the wing saving me from unknown weapons and enemies. Unfortunately, I never got to thank him properly. He saw what I could not see, and it kills me not to have the same ability.

His wings are so massive, smooth like a crow's wing. They wrapped around me like a blanket. It's almost impossible for someone to move as fast as he did. Yet, I still can't believe it to be true.

I sit next to Sora in the council room. His hands are clasped together as if he's ready for battle. Given that he is a blacksmith, I'm sure he can easily wield a sword.

King Lazarus sits next to Sora. They mumble things to each other, back and forth, leaving me out of the conversation. This is why I don't want to be here. But I'll be damned if I'm ignored. I've been ignored for quite a long time. It's time for my voice to be heard.

Davina rises. Fingers grazing over the map in front of her.

"Thank you all for attending this meeting. I apologize for the last-minute message last minute." Davina straightens the papers before her. "I'm sure you've all heard about the ambush that directly attacked my daughter, Prince Bellamy, and this castle."

My head snaps to Davina when she says, Prince Bellamy. I suspected he held an important title, but Prince did not come to mind. I thought maybe he was part of the private council or even an assassin.

"Our forces killed all but three enemies. However, we believe they were ordered to attack the castle and kill the Princess. This directly violates our treaty with the light realm."

The Treaty was formed hundreds of years before I was born. A malevolent light realm king despised Tenebrisean creatures so much he'd do anything to kill them, sometimes for no reason. He ordered his army to attack even if one night creature were to step out of line. He called them ugly, vicious, and scum of Rhemus. Nothing boils my blood more than a king who thinks he can get away with killing the innocent. Luckily, he didn't commit mass genocide, but perhaps that is what King Alaric is trying to accomplish.

"For this, we have sent out a message to King Alaric, demanding a meeting with him to discuss further action."

No. This will not do. A king that plays his own game will only do as he wishes and only on his time. Trying to reason with him will get us nowhere.

"If I may, Queen Davina." I raise my hand.

All eyes turn to me. Sora and King Lazarus tense their shoulders like I've spoken out of turn. Even the elderly in the council gives me eyes that could kill. Queen Davina smiles as an invitation to speak.

"Of course, Morana."

I straighten my spine. To let it be known, I do deserve to be here. However, I must tell them I intend to uphold my role as the princess and not just stand by wearing pretty dresses and twiddling my thumbs.

"Why are we entering their territory on their terms? King Alaric is no fair king. I've seen that firsthand. He's ruthless beyond measure. Why ask him permission to enter his lands?"

A council member chuckles as he hunches over. Queen Davina's eyes turn red. A displeased look crosses her face. She wants to interject but gives me the pleasure of owning the table.

"He is a King of rule-breaking, and he will continue to be that king. We, as a realm, will always uphold the law. If we attack, then we lessen our chances of —."

"Enough, councilman Hugo." Queen Davina interrupts. The councilman leans back in his seat, sinking into it.

I breathe, daring to speak. "Exactly. He is selfish and full of ill intent. This means, whatever he has planned, won't be for the good of his people. It will be for him. That is why we need to throw his own tactics back at him. He's doing this to cause worry in the kingdom. Who knows how far he will go to kill us all."

The councilmen's eyes linger away from me. I can't read the room very well. They fear Queen Davina, and rightfully so. She still frightens me with her red eyes of fury.

"Send Morana and me." Sora cuts in. He stands with his hands resting on the table. "We know the light Realm. We know every little thing there, down to each blade of grass, every fairy, and every building. We've had our experiences with the guards. So, we know how to protect ourselves."

There is truth in his words. There is no better duo than Sora and I in the light realm. We know the area. We know the people and their weapons. If they are planning a war, we can find out swiftly and undetected.

"You are forgetting one small piece of information, Prince Sora." Councilmen Hugo says. "Your enchantments are still active. You can never step in the light realm again unless you are dead."

King Lazarus clears his throat. "Not necessarily. Their human blood still runs through their veins. Who's to say if they were turned into one of us?"

The room goes silent—a silence that hurts my ears.

I have a long list of possibilities of what they could be. I note the red eyes. Impeccable skin and fast reflexes. Bellamy has crow-like wings. Vampires are at the top of my list. Not just a normal vampire, perhaps a form of mutated vampire. Or a shifter, which I had also expected.

"The choice to become a daemon is purely their choice. I will not coerce them into doing so. As long as they are happy, I see no concern." Queen Davina asserts.

Daemon. No such creature was listed in that history book. Then again, it could have been in the many books she said were in the forbidden section.

Why hide the information from their own blood? Is it, not a gift worth sharing? Could being a demon come with more misery than being a human? If I were to be any creature or to possess any gift, I'd want my offspring to hold the same. To be more connected with them. But these people like to keep secrets. There has to be something they are holding back on.

"How come we weren't born like you?" Sora asks.

Queen Davina sits down, resting her hand on King Lazarus'. She doesn't want to have this conversation in front of so many people, but I must address the subject.

"No one is born a daemon. But all those who are daemons carry brimstone blood. Meaning they have a choice in the matter. The transformation is like becoming a vampire or a werewolf. But the transformation is more brutal and deadly. I could never force it on anyone and keep a clear conscience."

We are at an impasse. Either we stay in Tenebris and stand by and watch a war unfold before our eyes, or we transform into a daemon and partake in a war that involves us in every way.

"I'll do it. I'll go through the transformation." I say.

Sora's eyes meet mine. It's almost as if the light is fading from them. First, it was becoming royalty, then a decision to become a daemon—a rash decision.

"They just said it's deadly. I'm sure there will be some sort of dying in the process." Sora exclaims.

"What good has the light realm done to us, Sora?" I raise my voice. "They left us to rot. They do not have an ounce of compassion for us or any of the night realm. Don't you want to fight?"

Sora's eyes meet the table.

"You are my brother." My lips tremble. "Would you really let me live a life of immortality just to watch you die?"

I never thought those words would come from my mouth. After being an only child for so long, I crave the companionship of a sibling.

My throat burns from rage. Tears swell in my eyes. I wipe them away, ruining the makeup Greer had applied earlier. I don't care how I look to others. I'm feeling too much. So much I want to scream. I'll be damned if I lose more family than I already have.

CHAPTER ELEVEN

Queen Davina kept much to herself the night after the council meeting. She left swiftly after, clinging to King Lazarus without a word to Sora and me. Her demeanor changed once we agreed to make the transformation. I thought it was what she wanted. I thought it was what everyone wanted.

She informed us of what a deadly transformation it would be. I ready myself for the growing possibilities of how the process is. My mind clings to one thing. I'll most likely die and be reborn.

Sora and I await the King and Queen's arrival in the garden. Quietly, we are consumed with our thoughts—conjuring ideas about what this transformation entails. My stomach turns with anxiety as we await our doom.

Bellamy strides through the doors leading to the garden. The iron gates creak. A patch of bandages sticks to his wings. Despite his injuries, he still has a smile on his face.

"Bellamy. You're okay." I stand to face him. "Does it hurt?" I examine his black wings. Blood stains his wings on the punctures covered by the bandages—the parts where he's missing feathers.

"That was a nasty fight. Exhilarating." He turns his body so I can see the backside of his wings.

"I haven't seen you. They told me you were recovering. You *can* recover, right?"

Bellamy laughs. "Us daemons heal faster than most, but when we take a hit on our wings, we suffer more from it. I'll be okay in a week's time. But, enough about me. Are you okay?"

Sora snickers at us. I roll my eyes.

"I'm fine. Untouched. Only a bruise from the fall. Will you be joining us?"

He looks at the carriage, and his smile fades. "Where exactly are you going?"

I hesitate before answering. My throat becomes dry.

"Sora and I have decided to transform," I mumble.

He lowers his head. His wings move in the wind's direction. Pain strains his face.

"The Queen hadn't told me." He rubs his head. "But I'm glad it is of your own free will." He takes his hand behind my shoulder and ushers me to the side. "Did the Queen tell you about Astrid?"

"She hasn't yet. I was waiting for the right time."

Before Bellamy can say another word, the King and Queen enter the garden. Embellished in their black attire, they dress in more leather than the villagers in Rhemus. The Queen wears pants this time, fit with a leather belt with packs of things hanging from her hip. The King wears something identical to his wife. Both appear ready for war.

"Bellamy. Glad to see you've healed. Will you be joining us?"

Bellamy remains facing me. His head lowered. His breathing becomes heavy as if he's angry at something. I look up at him and his dark eyes. They meet mine. Golden flecks spark like fire.

"You said you would tell them everything." Bellamy huffs. "So why keep this one that sent them to Rhemus?"

Queen Davina's eyes turn a vivid red, glowing with rage. The vein in her forehead rises underneath her skin.

"I'm not sure I understand what you're speaking about," she growls. Teeth gritting and jaw tensing.

The tension between the two is unbearable. I look at Sora, and he's standing closer to Bellamy and me, looking like he might lunge.

"The one big secret you've failed to mention upon their arrival. The one you are ashamed of. You have the twins back; don't you see it fit to tell them of the *other* one?"

He's talking about Astrid. He's losing control, and his wings twitch with fury. I don't want to be a part of this. I want to hide in my room or run as far away as possible, so I don't have to witness this horror.

King Lazarus stands before Davina, almost shielding her from Bellamy's words.

"I know about her," I say. "I heard the rumors about her being alive, possibly."

Queen Davina's eyes shoot at me in a fiery rage. Her wings burst from her leather jacket and hits Lazarus out of the way. He stumbles but quickly gains his balance.

"What makes you believe such a thing? She died as a child. And even so, they are only rumors. How did you hear of this?"

"People talk." I lie. I don't want to throw Bellamy under, but something tells me in Davina's eyes that she knows it was Bellamy who spilled the truth.

"See, Morana." Bellamy starts. "This is what they do. Go on, tell them what happened to Astrid. Look them in the eye and tell them how you gave them up to save Astrid."

The air becomes cold. Colder than the ice on the frozen river. My lungs compress tighter and tighter until I force myself to exhale. I'm trying to hold my breath but realize I can't. The ground spins beneath my feet. This can't be real.

"What does he mean, Davina?" I beg. "What did you do that you have so much regret for?"

Davina shakes her head. A tear falls down her face. "I was waiting to tell you. I thought it would be too soon." She looks at Lazarus.

She cries. So much so the gargoyles leave around the corner. Leaving us to our first family quarrel.

"She was seven when we lost her. She roamed too far from the border that separates Tenebris from Rhemus. Before we could find her, Rhemus had taken her. They pointed weapons at us and threatened that we would never see Astrid again if we walked over the border. Then, they threatened to invade all of Tenebris.

"I vowed to do anything to get her back. A year later, I became pregnant with you and your brother. I loved you so much. So much that I had almost healed from the loss of Astrid.

"I was still grieving her loss. Then, I found a human at the border. He was exiled to Tenebris for murder. He begged for his life. But he had information about Astrid. She was still alive. The minute I heard the news, I spared the man's life. No human would do good like that without something in return. So, I made him part of my council. That man is Hugo.

"We planned to send word to King Alaric to request his presence at the border to strike a deal with him. If I sent you two to Rhemus, and you lived there without committing a crime before your twenty-first birthday, I could get Astrid back, and all who live in Tenebris can live free of Rhemus and their threats."

"It was so selfish of me, I know. I live with that regret every day. That's why I almost couldn't believe it when I saw you two so grown up. You were never supposed to come back this soon. I had hoped you'd be the savior to our kingdom.

"And I thought that once we got Astrid back, we could get you two back, and Tenebris would be free from Rhemus. It all sounded like a good plan at the time. I counted the days till I'd see my children again. You both came here too early. And now, Tenebris is threatened, and Astrid's life still remains a mystery."

Bellamy's jaw clenches as I reach for him and cry into his shoulder. Sora comes behind me and rests his hand on my back. I feel pathetic, crying into his shoulder as I only met the man a few days ago. How desperate could I be?

"You used us as a pawn. We did not kill intentionally. It was an accident, and King Alaric saw it fit for us to be sent here. He knew what he was doing. He knew time was almost up. He had this planned from the very start." Sora says. "You fell for his game."

Davina listens carefully to his words.

"I am not angry with you two. I am angry that this has gotten out of hand. We could have lived as a family had you two not been sentenced here. Tenebris would be safe again. King Alaric is to blame. And I am to blame for making such a reckless deal."

Sora and I stand before the King and Queen. I never thought I'd be in this position. I'm still not sure I want to be. So many questions still float in the air. So many things still need to be answered. I can't be certain they will all get answered soon. We are running out of time.

"We can still get her back," I say.

CHAPTER TWELVE

Death has finally come for me. It is not a permanent end. I will not be buried in the ground and left to rot. Instead, I will die and be reborn into something much more powerful than a human has ever dreamt of being. Now that death is finally at my door, I may live my life in peace now, cleanse myself of the past, and embrace the future that awaits me.

Bellamy accompanies us to the cliffside. He asked me countless times if I was sure to make such a big decision after knowing what I know now. I have my regrets. Queen Davina spilling the truth doesn't change a thing. King Alaric needs to be stopped. That's what I am doing this for. To bring an end to this corrupt king's reign.

I have lived most of my life believing id die young. Believing I was worthless. This feeling of hope is unknown to me. But now that I have it, I want to use it to my advantage.

Davina leans on the carriage window. Her eyes never leave the outside. I see the same despair I once had. Still have. Things are coming into play now and starting to make sense, and everything is unraveling.

Occasionally, she sighs. Lazarus comforts her by resting his hand on her hand. He does well to hide his emotions if he has any. Ive yet to see his true intentions.

I've find that Lazarus has much to say when the Queen is quiet. She doesn't hush him or object. I could listen to him talk all day. His knowledge of the armadas of countless kingdoms is endless.

Rhemus's army is carefully built of the strongest and most ruthless warriors in the land. The centaurs are of the highest rank. Their muscles top that of a human just by nature. I've seen that firsthand when the castle was under attack. If given a chance, one could easily have forced open the castle doors made of stone, even with the gargoyles standing guard.

Next in rank are what we call elementals. Those who wield the elements at their will. They can start forest fires with a snap of their fingers or spin a hurricane with the tap of their foot. If they have enough energy, they could start an apocalypse.

A water-wielding elemental was a friend of mine once. Kuae was her name. I watched her manipulate the village courtyard's water fountains as a kid. She'd form beautiful mermaids and fairies. Ones that told stories of sea monsters and far-off lands too far for us to travel. She would end the stories by spraying us with a mist of water on a hot summer's day.

There were conspiracies that King Alaric would order such beings to be sent to the Hesai Islands off the coast of the West Village. It is a training camp for those who wished to join the army and those who were forced as their gifts were too powerful not to protect the land. Or better yet, the King and his riches.

I never understood what made King Alaric so vindictive. He followed the ways of the Old King. He died many years ago. So, the question arises, why does he hate the entire population of Tenebris? One would think that after years of war, a King would finally see the wrong in the world and correct it. King Alaric is not that king.

With this transformation, I would be able to choose how I die. Upon looking at the map, Siren's Cove seemed like a good place to die on a full moon. They ask me why I choose such a place, but I never explain that I wanted to die off the cliffs near the east village. I will keep that secret until the end if there is ever an end.

The shoreline comes into view as we round the steep snow-covered mountains. The Sea of Lights showers over the crystal waters. As we edge closer, tapering rocks form at the bottom of the cliff. Similar to the one I so wanted to throw myself off of.

"Are you sure you want to do this?" Sora whispers to me.

I keep my eyes locked on the violent waves ahead. The gray waves turn to white foam as they hit the rocks.

"I've been ready to die for a long time now."

Sora leans back, unsure of my response.

The horses stop at the bottom of the cliffside. The full moon is in view. Igniting every dark shadow and face about to witness my death. The death that I had been longing for.

"This isn't the first place I'd imagine someone would want to transform." Davina sighs. "Most people just take a dagger to the heart."

"Where did Astrid make hers?" I ask.

Lazarus, Davina, and Bellamy all glance at each other. Short of words, their mouths tense.

"She never made the transformation," Davina mumbles, gripping the hem of her sleeve.

I stop before walking further up the cliff. Turning to them, I feel a chill down my spine.

"Once you make that transformation, you are stuck in that body. Forever. Aging will cease. You will not grow old physically."

They should have mentioned this as well. If I was any younger, I might change my mind. But seeing as I am almost twenty-one, I could be happy living in this body even when I'm eighty years old. It's not like I have family waiting for me back home, so it wouldn't make a difference. Raisel, maybe, but even fairies live for a long time, but they are not immortal.

"That's why we had to ensure you were ready for an eternity in your physical body."

Looking at Sora, the lights in his eyes fade. Then, horror-stricken, he freezes.

"I won't do it if you won't. Tell me now."

"It isn't that." He starts. "I've always had a vision of when I am older. I would marry someone and live a long life with them. Have kids and be a grandparent. And die in the flower fields of the north village. It's strange to think my death is only minutes away, and I will remain in this body."

"If it makes you feel any better, Sora, my mother looks like she could be my sister. They are youthful like Davina and Lazarus."

Bellamy rests his hand on Sora's shoulder.

"Well, ladies first," Bellamy says.

I gaze up the cliff. A voice in my head is saying, *No. Don't do this. Turn back now. This is not worth your mortal life.*

I push the thoughts from my mind and start up the hill. Bellamy by my side. He's silent as we climb the barren cliffside. My heart races with each step. I'm running out of breath. The wind soars past us, almost making me lose my balance. Bellamy catches me many times without a sound.

The top.

I am finally here.

My tomb.

I stand so close to the edge I might fall off without a second thought. I want to be ready for this. Ready to plunge into the needle-like rocks so that my body may be impaled on impact.

The ocean mist sprays my face.

"I'll fly with you the whole way down."

"Why do such a thing?" I ask.

"No one deserves to die alone, Morana." He says. "I was alone when I made mine. If I could go back and change that, I would."

My cheeks burn with anticipation, and my heart races and pounds inside my chest. The pulsing in my head makes it hard to hear the crashing waves.

Flashes of memories go through my mind. My parents, Orna and Kai, are the ones I trust. The ones I will never stop believing to be my parents. Their faces light up my mind. My mother's soft hand is on my cheek as I shed a tear. My dad's warm hug embraces me for one last time.

"On three." I breathe.

One.

"Please don't leave me," I say.

Two

"Never."

Three. I catch my breath.

Our bodies freely fall in the chilly air. My lungs are sprayed with ocean water and the chilly night air. I spread outwards like I am flying. This is the feeling I once craved.

I keep my eyes on Bellamy. His hair was around his face, whipping in the air. His dark eyes stick to mine. I feel the brush of his wings on my hand. I almost cling to it out of fear.

No. This is what I want. This is what I am to become.

The cliff gets further from sight, and I know I'm close. I close my eyes. And right before I hit the bottom, I hear Bellamy's voice call out to me. A fading and comforting voice, meeting me to the very end.

CHAPTER THIRTEEN

There's a circle in the sky, glowing behind blurred eyes. Dots of white light gleam around it. Twinkling as if they are greeting me. Soft sounds of the ocean waves crashing fill my ears with white noise. I am numb. I am not alive.

Water escapes from my lungs as I gasp for air. They burn with every cough. And as I cough, a heaviness weighs me down. A weight on my head that wasn't there before. My neck struggles to keep my head up. The muscles are giving out like a newborn learning to lift its head.

"Morana. Are you alright?" Davina gasps.

They surround me, looking brighter than they did before. The colors are so vivid that it strains my eyes. The gold on Davina's top shines more than in the light of the fire. Her crimson eyes are like a rose in the first bloom of spring.

"Did it work?" I stutter.

I cry into my knees. The pain is still throbbing in my back from the impact. I don't remember it. I am glad I didn't. Surviving something like that would not be a life worth living and the trauma that would come with it.

"Feel your head, Dear."

I lift my fingers to it and caress it. Rough cylinders bulge out of my forehead. It stings to the touch from the saltwater which coats my skin—looking down at my hands. Blood covers it. A single stream of blood travels down my cheek.

Horns.

"Wings." I stutter. "I thought I'd have wings." After seeing Bellamy's massive dark wings, that is one thing I looked forward to having. I want to soar in the sky and travel to places whenever I please. The disappointment creates a pain in my stomach. Like this was all done for nothing. I bring myself back to the real reason I did this.

Davina kneels beside me, wiping the blood from my cheek and onto her handkerchief.

"In due time. You landed directly on your back, where your wings would grow."

"Am I dead?"

Davina reaches for my hand and brings it to my chest.

"Feel."

I listen. *They* listen.

No thump echoes in my chest. The steady pumping of my heart is missing. My heart lay dormant in my chest, never to beat again. I am an alive soul in a dead body. What must I do with this void that now fills my chest?

Davina and Bellamy help me to my feet. I try to catch my balance as my wet clothes weigh me down. Water drips from my dress, and I stand in a puddle of saltwater and blood.

Sora quickly steps toward me and brings me into an embrace. His sudden act of affection paralyzes me. My hands lay on my sides, unsure of where to put them. Everything is still sinking in. I can't even remember the last time I've been hugged.

"You left for the cliff, and I thought that would be the last time I saw you. For a minute, I thought this was all a lie. That they were doing this to keep their hands clean of our death. I didn't believe it to be true. I saw you fall. I saw your body fall onto the rocks. Your body—"

Bellamy steps forward.

"I pulled your body from the Sea before the sirens could get you. Somewhere, they were waiting at the bottom. They smell blood as soon as it drips."

My eyes widen as I realize it was a horrible place to jump from. If Bellamy hadn't been there by my side, they'd have taken my body and ripped me to shreds, and nothing would have been left. Perhaps that ending would have been easier because I can't imagine what life will be like now.

"The full moon is still upon us. We must hurry if Sora is to transform tonight." Lazarus looks to the sky.

Sora's eyes dilate with fear. He swallows.

"Morana, will you do me the honor?"

He brings forth his dagger that he came with to Tenebris. The rusty one I had rejected during his kind gesture at the border. He holds it in his hand, trembling and a somber look on his face.

"You are not asking me —"

"I want you to do it. Right here. Right now. Before I change my mind. I won't have it any other way."

Davina and Lazarus glance at each other. Surely, they never thought one twin would kill the other.

"Will it still work if she kills me?" he asks.

"Yes, but —"

"But what? "

"Are you sure this is what you want? You have already been through so much." Lazarus asks.

Sora slowly nods. Almost undetectable.

I take the dagger from him and hold it before making any moves. Sora never leaves my eyes. I wish he wouldn't look at me. It only makes it more difficult—my first intentional kill.

Should I have told him what I'll do? No. Expecting death is the worst way to go. Knowing how you will die will make it even harder. A plunge through his heart, a stab through his back, even a cut on his throat. It feels wrong to plan my brother's death.

With one swift move, I take the blade across the front of his throat, slicing his skin into two parts. His eyes widen, and blood pours from him, spilling over his clothes and onto the grass. His hands reach for his throat to keep the blood inside. He is sacred. I am scared.

This will work. It has to work.

He gurgles, gasping for air.

Make it stop. Just die already, dammit.

Bellamy senses the fear in my eyes, takes the dagger from me, and throws it into the ocean. I have no time to regret it before the blade plunges into the water. No evidence of his death by my hand.

Bellamy ushers me to the side and hides my face with his wings.

Sora falls to the ground, head hitting the stream of blood. Davina kneels by his side.

"Shh. Hold on, Sora. All is well." She strokes his hair out of his face.

His eyes become dim, and he moves less and less as time passes. For a minute, I think he may have lost too much blood. It pools around him—the blood seeps between the blades of grass, finding its final resting place in the ground.

His movements come to a halt. His arms rest on his sides, paralyzed. Still, his eyes face the stars above, taking them for one last look. He's gone.

We wait.

"He's lost too much blood." I pant.

Davina grabs Sora's bloodied hand. "Come on, Dear. Find us."

Silence.

His sliced throat begins to heal. It stitches itself together perfectly as if I hadn't just cut him. The blood retracts back into his veins.

Sora gasps for air. He flies into Davina's arms as he sits up. Blood covers her, but she pays no mind to it. He cries out in pain. The most gut-wrenching scream I've ever heard from a man before. Chills creep along my spine, but I can't look away.

Wings spring free from his back. He squeezes Davina's arm as the last of the bones in his wings appear deep within his skin. The transformation goes too quickly, and he cries out in pain each second. If I didn't feel pain, then why could he?

The pain dies down, and he takes deep breaths. He loosens his grip around Davina's arms and leans back on his arms. His chest rises and falls more evenly.

"Is the pain gone, son?" Davina asks.

He nods, still unable to mutter a word.

"You have wings, Sora," I mention.

He reaches for his back, gently caressing the silky wings.

He's blessed with wings, and I am cursed with horns. I don't know how I'll be able to look at myself in the mirror anymore. The horns take up half my face. While everyone can retract their wings with a single thought, my horns stay embedded in my head, like a reminder of everything I had endured for a lifetime.

Even with the transformation, I wonder if we could cross the border to Rhemus. I don't know what power I possess or if I am gifted with any. Being a warrior is not something I ever wanted to be, but now, with brimstone blood, I can be the most devastatingly fearsome creature.

CHAPTER FOURTEEN

A message has been sent to King Alaric to request his presence at the border. All we can do now is wait for him to say what I've been thinking this entire time. I want to charge Rhemus at full power. Spare the citizens of Rhemus and storm the castle. Take King Alaric as a prisoner and bring Astrid home.

Sora said my thoughts were not reasonable. I'd be mental to invade Rhemus in such an unrealistic way. Invading Rhemus would only prove further that Tenebris is a place to fear, and everyone who defends it is just as bad. I argued for hours with him on the subject.

When we aren't arguing, Sora takes to the skies. Bellamy and I spend time together in the library, flipping through books for anything information that would be of use to us. He's shown much interest in fighting Rhemus. He'd slice King Alaric's throat and make Queen Inina watch if given a chance.

"Are you almost ready?" Bellamy asks.

I tuck the book into my bag and the last of my food for the road.

We won't be flying since my wings have yet to come in. My wound is healed, but there has been no sign of its arrival. They said to be patient, and I'm trying. It's so hard to be when everyone else has gained their wings, and I'm left with horns that ruin me.

Bellamy is taking me to the City of Drafanel. A more advanced city covered in a dense forest, redwoods, and giant sequoias. Probably to hide it from any enemy eyes that fly over it. Rhemus has yet to learn of its existence.

The city was formed almost a century ago. It is named after a commander of the Tenebrisean army, Drafanel Fallon. His efforts to secure the borders of Tenebris gained much attention during the war. Although he perished in battle, burned to death by a fire-breathing dragon, the Kingdom of Tenebris still wanted to acknowledge him as a war hero. Rightfully so.

"I think I'm ready," I say as I close my bag and swing it around my shoulder.

Bellamy stops me before entering the carriage.

"Let's fix your crown, Princess."

It isn't the same crown that had been used at the coronation. Since sprouting my horns, I find placing the thing on my head difficult. Royal jewelers promptly designed another headpiece similar in style to the crown I had. I keep the crown on display in my bedroom. As a reminder of what I cannot truly be. Normal.

Bellamy looks down at me. His black eyes glimmer in the light of the headpiece.

"Make sure to report back if anything is out of the ordinary. I know the commanders down there take forever to send word." Lazarus says as he pats the horse.

"Got it. Head towards the danger." Bellamy laughs.

Lazarus keeps his face neutral as if he didn't hear a word Bellamy said. I don't blame him, though. Half the things Bellamy says are completely idiotic. I think he does it to pass the time and keep himself entertained.

Sora had rejected our offer to ride with us to the City of Drafanel. He was more interested in flying than venturing through an old city. If I had my wings, I wouldn't be here either. I'd be in the clouds, high on the mountain tops, and swimming in the Sea of Lights. I'd feel the rush of wind through the feathers. Any day now, I'd be able to experience that feeling.

The first hour of our travels is a bore. I am too excited to see something new. Something good. The darkness makes it difficult to enjoy the scenery outside. All I can see in the moonlight is trees beyond trees and occasionally a wandering fox searching for food.

"You know, you don't look bad with the horns," Bellamy says.

I shoot my eyes at him. "But I don't look good?" I tease.

"That's not what I am saying." he situates himself. "I've never seen another daemon with horns. I have nothing to compare it to."

"So, I am lucky?"

"You're making this harder than it needs to be, Morana." He sighs.

"I don't know if you are calling me ugly or decent."

"You are beautiful. That's what you are. So will you stop with the self-hatred? I don't want to catch it."

He smiles as his eyes turn to the window.

I can never tell if Bellamy is being sarcastic or truthful. He jokes half of the time, and the other times he keeps to himself, wallowing in his mind. He puts on that act for those around him but never hesitates when I enter the room.

We share so much in common. Our taste in literature is nearly the same. Once, I caught him reading a romance novel written years before I was born. His cheeks reddened once I saw what he was reading right over his shoulder. Let's say his interests are not what I thought they'd be. Now, he makes sure to read in the privacy of his quarters, where I can't tease him for it.

"Will you ever tell me about Kiveha?" I ask.

He breaks from his trance and runs his hand through his hair.

"What would you like to know?"

"Everything."

"It is a place where light and night creatures roam together as a population. There is little to no crime. And if there is a crime, then it's only small quarrels within separate homes. Fairies and goblins, gorgons, and centaurs live peacefully within the land. Their union is frowned upon by Rhemus. Once King Alaric realized he couldn't invade the land so easily. He gave up on trying to conquer it. He is a cowardly King with big ambitions."

"So why do you live here in Tenebris? It sounds like Kiveha is a dream world." I say.

He shifts in his seat and rubs his knuckles white. He becomes visibly uncomfortable at my question.

"You don't have to answer that. I'm sorry."

He stays quiet for a moment.

"It's not that. It's just complicated. Kiveha and Tenebris allied long ago. I come here to relax once in a while. Think of it as part of the alliance."

"Is that where your family is?" I ask.

He nods slowly as if not quite hearing my words or not wanting to listen to them.

"I see." I swallow. "Do they rule over Kiveha?"

He nods again. I leave it at that.

I want to know more. I want to know what life is like for all creatures of all backgrounds. It sounds like a haven for those who aren't so fortunate. Why can't the other kingdoms follow Kiveha? Those other kingdoms should want to have peace within their territory.

I imagine the King and Queen of Kiveha being very busy rulers and ruling a kingdom of creatures and humans alike. To keep everything in order. To keep Kiveha the perfect country that it is. Perhaps they have no time for Bellamy. So, he sought out peace here in Tenebris.

Through the trees, I see the stone wall. It's protected from those who have ill intentions. Its walls are enchanted to detect any evil thought of burning the place to the ground or harming anyone in it.

It is a magnificent type of magic, yet a powerful one. A magic so powerful King Alaric's army may not get through. It would have taken a very special kind of witch to create a powerful protection spell that could protect all citizens and the wall. One day, I hope to meet this witch.

The carriage comes to a halt as we pass the stone wall. Gargoyles stand guard at the gates: spears, swords, and arrows at the ready.

"Good morning, Princess Morana. Good Morning Prince, Bellamy."

"Morning, Captain Marcel. Lovely night it is. I've brought the Princess to show her the city."

"Yes, sir. Everything is as planned."

Bellamy raises his finger to his lips to hush the gargoyle.

"Thank you, Captain Marcel."

The captain leads us to a boarding station for carriages. The door opens, and Bellamy exists first. He holds out his hand for me to step down. I notice he's shaking, but I do not say anything about it.

Eyes are on me as I step foot outside the carriage. Vampires, werewolves, and goblins all bow in unison. I look at Bellamy, who acknowledges their honor. His chin is high, and his regal appearance amazes me. He knows this life so well. He's lived it for years. When will I be able to hold myself as he does? Unafraid and confident.

"This is all for you," he whispers.

I'm at a loss for what to do. I stand awkwardly in their presence, waiting for them to rise. I don't want this kind of attention. I want to enjoy this night and have fun without the title of princess or any royal title to my name.

"It's time to meet your people," Bellamy says.

"I don't know what to do. Or say. I am not royalty."

"You are royal by blood. It runs in your veins. You know what to do, just don't make a fool out of me." He laughs. I elbow him in the ribs. "Or yourself, your majesty."

The gargoyles stand guard around us, spears and swords in hand, ready to strike if this situation demands it. I know this place is well protected but can't trust it entirely. Every kingdom has its group of people who want to overthrow it. And those people could find a way around that magic to tear it down from the inside out.

"Meet, Nesrin," Bellamy says. She curtsies to me.

Her tawny hair falls over her shoulder in loose curls. Her face is pale, and her lips are red as a rose. Her eyes are golden and alluring. She is stunning in the way she presents herself. I can't take my eyes off her.

"Hello, Princess Morana." She bows.

I return the gesture. "Nice to meet you, Nesrin."

I look at Bellamy. I'm not the greatest at starting conversations. Sometimes I stumble on my words and sweat like a sinner.

"Nesrin owns the bookshop in the center courtyard. I'm sure you two will get along just fine."

"Yes, your grace. I have all types of books. Prince Bellamy loves poetry, adventure, mystery, and even romance books."

Bellamy's face turns red, and he lowers his chin.

"Oh, I know much about his love for romance novels. I'll stop by sometime and have a look around."

"Thank you, Princess." She curtsies. "It was a pleasure meeting you."

We watch Nesrin as she skips down the road. We turn to each other.

"She always finds a way to embarrass me," he laughs.

"What is she? She looks human, but I've never seen a human with her eyes. I could look at them for days."

Bellamy leans to my ear. "She's a succubus. One of the few in town. Get on her bad side, and you'll find yourself in bed with the devil."

"Did you find out the hard way?"

Bellamy rubs the back of his head. He always does when he's nervous or embarrassed. That's what I know about him, at least.

"Once. I thought I'd be brave enough not to succumb to her evil mind."

I hit him on the chest. "I don't want to hear about your naughty fantasies Bellamy."

I turn and walk in the opposite direction. He really knows how to get underneath my skin.

Bellamy catches up to me without a word. Drafanel citizens bow as I walk past them. I lightly bow my head as we continue walking.

This city is bigger than the village near the border. Better even. The fresh scent of bread travels through the air, and my nose turns upwards to find the smell. No scent is better than freshly baked bread straight out of the oven.

Lanterns light the street in fires of blue and orange. The mixing of colors makes for the most beautiful scenery. Even the roads of Rhemus could never compare to the sheer beauty of this place.

It makes me feel bad for the citizens of Rhemus who don't have this kind of luxury. They've been lied to for hundreds of years. They were told that Tenebris wasn't a place to live and thrive. Told by their king that all creatures who lived here would tear them to shreds. I don't think these creatures have any ill will toward humans. I guess they feel pity for them.

We pass a jewelry shop. The jeweler is a goblin, a small wrinkly, old thing. He smiles with his elongated nose and pointed ears as we admire the gold and silver necklaces in the window. Raw and smooth Crystals sit on a table of a red tablecloth. I see myself spending too much here.

"Do you like it?" Bellamy asks.

"Everything I had known back in Rhemus made Tenebris seem like a torturous place. This is nothing as I had imagined."

His face lights up.

"There is more to see. More people to meet. You won't be disappointed."

The buildings tower with vibrancy like none other. The buildings are made of stone, brick, wood, and other materials. Each is designed to fit the heavenly aesthetic of the City of Drafanel. Lanterns line the entire city, igniting it like an enormous parade. Creatures and those disguised as humans walk the streets with bags of food and other objects. There is so much to look at. I fear that if I blink, I might miss something along the way.

I'll never get tired of this. I hate myself for not finding this place sooner. I wish Sora were here to take this all in with me.

We pass an iron shop full of swords, spears, and other interesting weapons. The ogre who runs it does an excellent job carving the blade into a precise figure—one fit for battle. People here really pride themselves on their work.

"How does this place thrive?" I ask.

Bellamy focuses on the weaponry, admiring the ogre's careful handwork. The ogre nods to us as we pass by.

"Davina and Lazarus make sure their people are well taken care of. Low taxes, but all that money goes to rebuilding and making things more efficient. This is what a kingdom should be."

He strokes the blade of an iron sword.

Rhemus can never compare. King Alaric is greedy, no doubt. That's why most of the villages in Rhemus suffer from disease, uncleanliness, and a lack of nourishing food. He puts all that money into his castle and other extravagant treasures. The taxes are so high that the citizens of Rhemus often go hungry because they cannot afford food. Most have now made a system of trade, but even then, sometimes, that doesn't work.

People are suffering under the hands of King Alaric, and they feed into his lies. He takes what he wants only for his benefit. He wants control of the people and the entire population of the continent.

"Come on." Bellamy takes my hand. "I want to show you something."

We weave through the crowd of people. I smile and nod when they bow to me. We pass many shops that catch my eye. I want to stop, but Bellamy has other plans.

We come to a courtyard with a grand marble fountain in the middle. The fire reflects off the crystal waters into the air, forming a light show. Orange, blues, and greens shoot into the air like a magnificent light spectacle.

I look over to Bellamy, his eyes set on the lights in the sky. For a minute, I see a fleck of color in his black eyes. His eyes are void of nothing, only filled with light and beauty.

"Where is everyone?" I ask. "How could they miss this?"

Bellamy grips my hand tighter to gain my attention. I look into the sky. The stars are dancing, twinkling down, and clashing with the water. The Sea of Lights is right above us. This view does not compare to that from my bedroom window.

"How is this possible?"

"I had a few arrangements made with the witches of the Gerofeld Forest. Their magic can manipulate any element to appear like anything they want."

"You had this arranged?"

"Are you surprised?" He chuckles.

"A little. This isn't like you to do something nice if it doesn't benefit you. What do you get out of this?"

"Behind this rough exterior of mine, you may be surprised to find that I love seeing you happy, Morana."

CHAPTER FIFTEEN

The wound on my back has stopped hurting. Occasionally, a sharp pain will strike through it, making me pause whatever I'm doing and breathe through the pain. All that's left is a gnarly scar on my back right where my wings are supposed to be, but they still haven't shown up. At this rate, I don't think they ever will.

Sora has been flying. After getting used to their weight, he asked Lazarus to show him how to fly, much like the bats surrounding the castle. He once flew by my window and scared me half to death when I saw him hanging in the sky. He had been doing it almost all day. And the exhaustion of his back muscles almost caused him to fly straight into a glass window. But that didn't scare him enough to try again.

I am still trying to figure out what I can do with these bothersome horns. So far, I have been able to walk up the stairs and not get winded. The weight of them, though, still strains my neck muscles.

"We've heard news from Rhemus," Sora states. "We have been summoned to the meeting chamber with Davina and Lazarus."

I put down my book. Annoyed because I already know what the news is about.

"Bellamy will be there."

"And? Am I supposed to be swooning?" I tease.

Sora grabs a book off the shelf. "You two have been awfully close lately. I assumed —"

"Doesn't mean I always want to be around him."

He puts the book back neatly on the shelf. He narrows his eyes to the books to ensure each spine is uniform and straight.

Sora is right, though. We have been spending a lot of time together. The night in the City of Drafanel was one. He had gone above and beyond with the spectacle of a light show. After that, he treated me to dinner, which consisted of the most expensive rare meats. It was good, nonetheless. But the light show was enough to impress me.

I don't want to admit it to myself quite yet. I hope my time with Bellamy doesn't end anytime soon.

The King and Queen wait for us in the chamber. Councilman Hugo doesn't look so pleased by how he hardly bows to us as we enter. I take my seat next to Sora. Bellamy is next to me, but I avoid his eyes. His gaze penetrates my soul.

Davina clears her throat, "As I feared, King Alaric has rejected our request to meet at the border."

"No surprise there," I mutter.

"Morana. Enough." Davina says.

"You all act like he was going to say yes. I told you, play by his game. He isn't going to meet us."

Davina shakes her head, annoyed with my outburst. Even I am annoyed with it. If there is one thing I hate doing, it is talking to people who know the outcome but refuse to acknowledge it.

"There is more to the letter, your highness." Councilman Hugo coughs.

"Way to jump to conclusions, don't you think?" Bellamy leans to my ear. I scoot my chair away from him and closer to Sora. He's only a distraction.

"King Alaric will not meet us in person but will send Admiral Caspian and Commander Zion to the border to discuss immediate actions."

I roll my eyes. It's just not good enough. The King is a coward, so he sends his military men to the border. For things to change, King Alaric must be there to discuss further action. We don't need messengers for this type of quarrel.

"Okay, so what exactly are they going to do? They act on the King's orders. Nothing will be solved then. They may listen, but who knows if they will relay such information to him? And what if it's set up? What if his men wait for us at the border with their weapons? They don't want to talk. They want us dead."

King Alaric is someone other than one to speak in a civil conversation. I knew that the moment I had my so-called trial. He would send his highest-ranking troops to the border not to discuss further action but to catch us off guard and attack us head-on. We can't be that naive to fall for his tricks.

"So, we send our highest-ranking officers. Problem solved." Sora suggests.

"With all due respect, your highness. Doing that would put our kingdom at risk. We already have army bases in the northern islands and some near the border. We can't risk taking any troops from those divisions. It would risk the security of Tenebris. We aren't ready to fight."

Sora leans back in his chair. I rest my hand on his shoulder.

"Well, then, be ready. You have known for years now that a war is coming. So why aren't the troops ready at all times?" Sora shouts.

Lazarus lifts his hand to calm Sora. "I think we are getting off track."

Since transforming into full daemons, our enchantments were said to wear off. I didn't know if there was any truth to that. There may be a way for Sora and me to get through the barrier. However, it would be risky and highly doubtful that Davina and Lazarus would allow such a thing.

They have been a little overprotective. I want to understand it, but what was the point of transforming if we can't help bring Astrid back and free Tenebris from Rhemus? It would be crazy not to let us go.

"Perhaps we could send a few low-ranking troops to the border to discuss matters. Then, we could hold interviews for the best candidate." Councilman Hugo says.

"And risk their lives?" Davina cuts in.

I slam my hands on the table. They jump.

"Everything we do is a risk. We have troops for a reason. Why not use them? The minute they joined the military is the minute they knew they'd be risking their lives for Tenebris and you. There is no easy way to do this. So find a way, and stick with it."

Their eyes go wide. I leave an echo of silence in the room. My hands turn to fists on the table. My hands burn. So hot that they may explode.

"Morana, your hands," Bellamy says.

"What about my hands? Do you have a plan they will like?"

"Look at your hands, woman." Bellamy raises his voice.

My hands encompass in a flame of fire. Burning with passion and rage altogether. I bring them to my face. My hands are on fire, but not burning me to the point of scorching them. I play with it in my hands. Tossing the flame back and forth between the two. Amazing and frightening.

"So instead of wings, she wields fire," Bellamy adds.

Davina and Lazarus's faces light up. Surprised but happy that I'd discovered a gift. I wasn't expecting such a gift or any at all. I was preparing myself for a life full of normalcy from my horns from here on out. I expected just to be known as the princess with horns. Now, I am much more than that.

CHAPTER SIXTEEN

Rhemus.

The one place I despise. Rolling grasslands and dreary farmlands will never cease to haunt me. Even in my dreams, I'm still haunted by its presence and the wicked king with no right to claim the throne.

I'll never forget the day Rhemus's troops barged into my home, destroying it. They searched for anyone who was sixteen or just over the age. They ransacked the place, looking in every corner and crevice possible. Luckily, I was the only sixteen-year-old girl in the home. They only took boys. Boys are their treasure.

My friend, Enver, who had just turned sixteen three days prior, was taken from his home by the military. I can never forget his scream. His mother cried for him. I never saw him after that. His mother became depressed and eventually passed not long after his kidnapping because that's what it is—taking children from their homes to fight for a country that doesn't care about their well-being.

I had told myself I would never have kids in Rhemus. Why would I bring a child into the world if they were taken at a young age? Most don't come out alive from the military base. Harsh weather and brutal training kill most.

Even now, living in Tenebris, I still don't see myself bearing children in the future. As long as Rhemus controls Tenebris, I can't bring a child into this world with a clear conscience. I can't lose a child as Davina did at such a young age.

Losing Astrid must have been torturous for her. She lost all hope. Thought she was dead. But it was stupid of her to bring more children into this world only to use them as pawns to get back her firstborn. I could never do such a thing, not even if it were to save the kingdom. My kids will always come first.

Now that I am Princess of Tenebris, much is expected of me. I've spoken out of turn more times than I can count. But, unfortunately, I'm not the most well-spoken and talented princess that people would expect. Now, I feel Davina and Lazarus regret crowning me. I feel like all I have done is disappoint them.

A knock on the door startles me. I hurry to the door, straightening my dress.

"What are you two doing here?"

Bellamy and Sora look at each other with concerned looks. Both of them avoiding my eyes.

"Can we come in?" Bellamy points.

I open the door for them, and they hurry in like something is urgent. They speak to each other through eye contact.

"What is it? I was reading?"

"The book can wait. We have an idea, but I don't know if you will like it." Sora says.

I cross my arms, waiting for them to give me more information. I become impatient with their hesitation. I contemplate ordering them out.

"Bellamy and I were talking after the council meeting. Tenebris will stand no chance against Rhemus if we send any rank of troops to the border."

"And? You're telling me this, why?" I sit on the vanity, straightening the brushes and hair accessories Greer has laid out.

"It's risky, but we have a plan. It will only be between us three. Davina and Lazarus cannot know. We will go into Rhemus, find Astrid, and bring her back."

I close my eyes and sigh. Pinching the bridge of my nose.

"That doesn't seem like a solid plan. We can't just walk into his castle and expect to walk out alive. They have protection, too, you know."

"We've got an inside man. A satyr by the name of Echo. He knows the castle inside and out. He can lead us to Astrid, and we can safely get her back here."

I shake my head. This plan is a death wish for everyone. Not only that, but the plan has no base to it. They have an outcome of what they want to happen but no real idea of how to avoid getting caught. Sora and I know what the castle holds. Bellamy has no knowledge of its secrets and weaponry.

"How would we even get there? Horses could take days. And not to mention, I have no wings, so flying is off the list."

"I'll carry you." Bellamy teases.

"As displeasing as that sounds, I must decline. How do we even know we can trust this Satyr? If he works for King Alaric, there's no telling what traps lay ahead for us. And what if she isn't even alive?"

Sora and Bellamy fall silent. There are so many holes in the plan and nothing to go on. There are so many ways this could turn out. We could find Astrid dead, find ourselves in a trap, and die ourselves. Or, find Astrid alive and still fail. We need a whole division of troops by our side to even have a chance at survival.

"She's alive," Bellamy states. "She *has* to be."

"King Alaric, no doubt, has been torturing her all these years. But, even if she is alive, there's no telling if she can understand what's going on. Magic and torture can do a lot to the soul and mind."

Bellamy straightens the cuff on his shirt. Sora lays back on my bed. Crumpling the neatly ironed sheets Greer worked so hard on.

"Just admit it. You two don't have a clue of what you are doing." I glance at both of them, their eyes on the floor.

"Come back to me when you have an actual plan that won't get us killed."

They throw their hands in the air from defeat. I usher them out the door without a word more. I cannot hear anymore from their mouths. If I do, I'll punch a fiery hole in the wall from anger. And as much as I want to test my magic, Bellamy said not to let it consume me.

I avoid dinner. Bellamy came by my bedroom before to invite me. I said no through the door, and he had not a word to say. I listen for his footsteps, walking away from the door and down the hallway.

I let Greer enter the room to replace towels and other garments in my drawers. She never asked questions and never said anything that may upset me. Instead, she always comes in with a smile on her face.

I feel more anger than usual since Bellamy and I discussed daemon magic. The minor things upset me—even the tiniest fleck of dust on the mirror to a fraying thread on a dress. I feel the fire build up when my slipper doesn't fit right or when my bed sheets won't pull up any further.

I try to rip out my horns. It doesn't budge. They are embedded into my skull, and If I pull them out, my skull will come with it. I hate what these horns have done to me. I wonder if Sora feels the same way. Does he feel the same rage as I, even with his wings?

There has to be more to this life of a daemon than rage. Davina and Lazarus show no signs of anger, only when we discover their secrets, but anyone would do that. Bellamy is an ass sometimes, but even then, he controls his emotions so well. I've never seen him in a fit of rage.

If Sora is feeling a certain way, he hasn't told me. Maybe he's ashamed or scared. Or perhaps he's completely fine. He does have the wings of a crow. I'd be happy about that too. He gets to fly with the birds and the bats and live a free life. While I'm confined to the earth.

I take my shoes off before exiting the bedroom. I don't want anyone to hear me walk the halls. This place echoes too much. Even the slightest breath can be heard from feet down the hallway.

The library is luckily on the opposite end of the dining hall. So, I have no trouble avoiding the others. They can't know what I'm about to do.

I'm careful to hold the library keys tightly so the ring doesn't echo through the castle. The towering doors creak ever so slightly. I hold my breath as I open them, letting out my breath once I can fit through the door.

It's dark, and the only light inside comes from the moon outside. I carefully light the lanterns.

The restricted books lay just beyond a small door in the corner of the library. Unfortunately, she had never given me the key to it, so I find it necessary to break in.

I am no expert lock picker, let alone a thief. But, if I'm going to get the answers I need, I'll do anything to get that information, even if it means going behind their backs to do so. My back feels cold, as if someone is watching me. Someone probably is. I don't put it past Davina to have this place guarded.

The lock is more intricate than I figured. I have yet to see a key that looks like it would fit. Knowing Davina, she probably has it in her bedroom or inside her dress. I don't have it in me to rummage through her room.

The lock is a type of dark metal—iron, almost from the looks of it. Iron takes a lot of heat to melt.

So, if I can conjure up enough heat, maybe I can melt it and suffer its consequences later.

I grab hold of the iron lock.

This has to work.

I think of everything that has ever brought me pain. All the grief I've suffered through the years from those around me: King Alaric and his nasty way of ruling a kingdom. Davina and Lazarus come to mind. Their reckless parenting is what got us here. It's what got me to transform into a daemon. Now, I live forever in this same body, cursed with these horns, and cursed to live in this body forever.

I can never forgive them for giving away Sora and me. They didn't try hard enough to get Astrid back. All the secrets they kept from Sora and me. All of them came crashing down all at once.

The death of my parents. They were the only people I cared about besides Raisel and Sora. Dead because of King Alaric. That wicked king.

As tears stream down my cheeks, I notice my hands are on fire. Orange flames ignite my hands. The heat doesn't bother me, only a slightly warm, tingly feeling. My finger twitches.

The iron is glowing red. I close my eyes and continue to think of all the terrible things in my life. The anger and the dishonesty.

Bellamy, that stupid, charming boy. Thinking the three of us can storm King Alaric's castle—reckless thinking and always looking for a fight. He, too, is filled with anger, but what about? He's filled with secrets, just as Davina and Lazarus are. Why does everyone lie? Why keep secrets from those who are blood? I hate that man. And I hate myself for falling for him.

Iron is dripping on my hands. I stand unfazed by the heat. It's melted enough to get through. I release my hold on the lock—strings of glowing, red, melted iron streak from my hand. I didn't expect it to stick so much. I pick off as much of it as possible. Melted iron sits in a puddle beneath me.

I push the door open, and a wave of heat hits my face like no one has been here for years. A heavy layer of dust sits on the tables and books. The lantern barely gives off enough light as I light it. The musty smell of old books fills the air. I watch where I step, careful not to sweep dust into the air.

Davina was right. This room is filled with the books she mentioned. All forbidden and hidden from prying eyes. More secrets to uncover. I feel it, though. I can feel what I am looking for. It's in this room. I have to search well enough.

More history on Tenebris, mythological creatures, and more. Spellbooks, magic books. It's all here. I've set my eyes on all the forbidden knowledge anyone could ever know.

The Book of Daemons. That's the one I need with the black leather and gold trim. This is the one.

The pages are crisp from lack of use. I carefully flip through the pages. Many of them are hard to read, written in a language I have never seen before. Symbols and glyphs go on for pages.

I stumble on a page about daemon magic and where it comes from. I delve further into it. Daemons with no horns or wings have magic, but not at the total capacity of those with horns and wings. Their magic still lies within the brimstone of The Inferno. Some may wield fire, others may wield ice, but all of them may have the strength of a basilisk.

I pause.

The doors to the library creek. I freeze.

I hurriedly close the dusty book and slide it back into its place. They will know I'm here the minute they see the hardened iron. I am done for. Davina will take back the keys and never allow me into the library again.

Footsteps. They get closer. Heavy boots echo closer. There's where to hide. If I leave this room, they will see me. I back up to the shelves, keeping myself hidden in the shadows.

"Hello?"

It's Sora. Maybe I can trust him. He's my brother. I had given him no reason to distrust me once. Surely, he could refrain from ratting me out.

I creep around the door, my face in the light of the lanterns.

"Morana? What are you doing here/" He looks to the ground of hardened iron. "Did you do this? Davina —"

"Davina won't find out unless you tell her."

"You didn't come to dinner. So, Bellamy went to look for you in your room."

I close the door behind me, holding onto almost nothing by the melted doorknob.

"You aren't supposed to be in there," he whispers. "You melted the damn thing."

"If anything, Sora, I'm claiming what is rightfully mine. We have every right to know what's in here. We are family, remember?"

"Yeah, well, even families have secrets. If she didn't give you the key, there's a reason for it."

He crosses his arms, anxious to get out of the room. Even he's scared of Davina's wrath.

"This directly involves all of us." I place my hands on my hips. "If we are going to rescue Astrid, we need to know what we are against. And by doing that, we are powerless without knowing what we are capable of."

Sora looks around. He shuts us inside the forbidden room.

"Why do you care so much about Astrid? Why do you care so much about someone you don't know?"

I take a breath in to calm myself. He's doing this on purpose. He's trying to set me over the edge.

"This is just about Astrid. This is about Tenebris. She's being used as a pawn. As long as King Alaric has Astrid, Tenebris will never be free from Rhemus. Why can't you see that? This war concerns us too. King Alaric had our families killed. Don't you want revenge?"

Sora pinches the bridge of his nose and lets out a breath.

"Fuck, Morana, slow down." He shouts. "Look at yourself. Your hands."

I look at my hands. Fire surrounds them in a blue hue this time. Hotter than the first time, but still not enough to hurt me.

"This is why Bellamy said not to let it consume you. Instead, you are letting this rage become you. What makes you think you can do a damn thing about Rhemus if you can't even control your emotions?"

Tears flood my eyes. I fall to the floor and bring my knees to my chest. The fire slowly withers away. Sora stands above me momentarily, kneeling beside me and placing his hand on my back.

Everything comes crashing down on me. My sobbing is uncontrollable now. My eyes and throat hurt—even the horns on my head throb.

The door bursts open. I grasp my knees, and Sora loses his balance and topples to the floor.

"Morana? Is everything okay?" Bellamy looks at Sora. "What did you do to her? You can't be in here."

"I — I just wanted to—to." I curl my face into my knees. My tears spill, and I can no longer keep my emotions at bay.

"We have to get her out of here. She's going to set this whole place on fire." Bellamy takes me under my arms with the help of Sora.

"I can't believe you melted the damn lock. Are you insane?"

They guide me out of the forbidden section on each arm. The fire is still blazing in my hands. Hot and full of rage. I can't seem to get a grip on myself and my mind. I'm stuck in this loop of anger and hurt.

"Davina will no doubt find out about this," Bellamy says.

"Not if you don't tell her."

"I'm not going to tell her. But they will find out regardless," Bellamy replies.

The fire dies down as I catch my breath. Tears stain my face with red lines. My eyes are puffy, and my face is stiff with dried tears. I rub the palm of my hands, waiting for everything just to be quiet.

"I'll take her to her room," Bellamy says.

"Do you think that's the best idea?" Sora crosses his arms, shielding me from Bellamy.

Sora looks at me, concern plastered all over it.

"Will you be okay?" Sora asks.

I nod. "I'll be fine. I think I want to go to sleep."

Sora leaves the library and shuts the door behind him. We listen as his footsteps ring down the hallway until complete silence.

Bellamy looks at me, eyebrows furrowed. I take a breath to stop myself from crying again.

"Morana." He caresses my cheek. Everything in me halts and focuses on his touch. His fingers ignite my nerves. "You are not broken. Fix your crown, and let's figure this out together."

He leans inches away from my face. "Princesses don't cry. Especially one as vicious and beautiful as you."

CHAPTER SEVENTEEN

"Good afternoon, your majesty."

Nesrin scoots around the corner of the counter and curtsies before me.

"Please, call me Morana. No curtseying."

Nesrin bows her head. The formalities sicken me. I'm still trying to accept who and what I am. Aside from the suicidal tendencies I once had, I want to feel like my old self— unnoticed and unimportant.

Sora and Bellamy had begged me to accompany me to the city. Sora insisted I needed someone to be beside me at all times. I politely declined the many times he asked. Besides, he knew I'd be well-guarded if anything were to happen. After the ambush, nothing has been the same.

"I am here not as a princess but as a mere citizen of Drafanel." I stroke the spine of the books on the shelf.

"Anything for you. What are you looking for?" Nesrin asks.

"I want to have fun, Nesrin. I am bored of the castle. What is there to do here that might excite me?"

She flips through a book on the shelf, ensuring it's clear of rips and creases. She keeps her books in pristine shape, given the number of hands that have been on them over the years. I am curious how she does it, keeping every book in place and ensuring the books are returned in the same condition as they left. I don't doubt that shed hunt anyone down if they were to ruin her books.

"I have one thing in mind." She smiles. "How much fun are you willing to have?"

A devilish look flashes across her face. Her gold eyes glow.

"Have you ever mounted a bat?"

My jaw drops open. "Excuse me?"

"Bat riding," she repeats. "We do it for fun here in Drafanel."

I cross my arms tightly across my body. "You're joking, right? The bats that circle the castle? Those abnormally huge bats with gnarly snouts? You ride those things?"

"I mean, not daily. Once one familiarizes itself with your scent, they are usually easy to tame. It's a good way to get around for some."

"Yeah, I'll take a horse, thanks."

I scratch around the edge of where my horns jut out of my head. The itch never stops, like it hasn't healed all the way. An annoying itch that is a constant reminder of what I have become and will always be.

"You asked me what people do for fun here, and I told you. Unless you'd rather be sitting here reading books all day, daydreaming about Bellamy."

She covers her mouth, regretting the words that came from her mouth. Her cheeks redden.

"I apologize, your majesty— Morana, I mean." She curtsies and almost trips on her dress. "Forgive me, please."

Her embarrassment amuses me, but I feel slightly ashamed for laughing at her.

"What makes you say such things, Nesrin?"

She flattens her dress and sits on the wooden chair beside her. It creaks at the weight of her.

"I just thought you two had something going on." She breathes. "When he brought you to the fountain a few days ago. I saw the way you looked at him, the way he looked at you —"

"You watched us?" My hands start to burn, but I take a breath before they ignite.

"I had to see if what you two have is real. I was only curious. As is the entire City of Drafanel."

For a moment, I thought she had followed us to spy on Bellamy. They have history together, so I could see her doing just that. Bellamy had said it was forever ago. He had no emotion when he spoke about her. I find myself wondering why I care so much about it and why I care so much about him.

"He never started reading romance novels before you arrived." She mutters, carefully not to invoke my emotions.

"Really?"

"Yes. He has never been the romantic type. Simple one-night stands, drunken nights. He was a mess sometimes. I even doubted his ability to wield a sword."

I sit in the chair next to her, processing past events since I entered Tenebris. All from the moment I met Bellamy up until now. He's always been there. Maybe not every waking moment, but he's been there through hard conversations, even my own death. I was blind to it at first and unknowingly pushed it away because of more pressing matters.

I may feel something for him. Not just a friendship, but perhaps more, now that I think about it. I can't bring myself to admit it out loud. I don't think I'm ready for it. But I know wholeheartedly that my heart ignites when he's around.

I shake my head to dismiss the thought. I don't want to have this conversation with her. Not now, at least, until I'm ready to even admit to Bellamy.

"So, these bats. Where do we find them?"

The guards follow us on a short walk to a valley outside the city. I asked them to follow behind us, so we'd have privacy. It isn't needed much, though. Most of the time, we never say a word to each other.

In the distance, wailing echoes through the sky. It shakes the trees and rustles the leaves and forms a hissing noise through the forest. With each step closer, my stomach flutters. I'm beginning to think this was a bad idea.

"Now, don't make any sudden moves. Walk slowly, and don't look them directly in the eye." Nesrin warns as we round the corner.

The open valley, dead from the winter's storm. Gray clouds swirl in the sky, conjuring a storm of sorts. The open sky is filled with enormous bats like the castle's. This is their spot. Just to the left of us is a big cave, their home for when the sun is bright.

"I didn't think there would be this many here. How many are actually in Tenebris?" I ask.

Nesrin climbs on a rock, making her much taller than I am. The guards stop way behind us. For all they know, we've come to admire the bat's beauty and not ride them. We have to make haste.

"There's many in the land. I think of them like the dragons in Rhemus. They protect their territory."

They are beautiful and free. Their wingspan is bigger than I'd ever seen and probably much bigger standing next to one. I am seconds away from diving into this one.

"Okay, since you've done this before. Why don't you stay here and observe?"

I nod. My muscles tense at the sight of their massive wings.

She treads through the barren land, ruined by the winter storms. Weaving her way around the boulders that surround this place. Her steps are timid but confident. I can tell she has done this before.

She approaches a bat that is resting its wings. It crawls on the ground. She's so small compared to its massive size. She stops before it. Waiting for it to notice her presence. She will have to let it smell her scent before even touching it.

She waits. The bat notices her and takes a step back. She doesn't move. It sniffs the air around her and huffs in her face, strong enough to blow her hair off her shoulder.

She lifts her arm in front of her, the bat noticing her arm. It smells like her. It begins to crawl around her, getting a feel of her to see if she's a threat. My knuckles clench as each minute passes.

With her hand outstretched, the bat nuzzles its snout into her hand. That is her cue that it is safe to pet it. She talks to it, scratching it behind its ears. It looks relaxed with her.

She looks to me and ushers me to come her way, to do the same thing as she does. I look back to the guards, their hands on their swords. I'm hoping they won't have to wrestle with an enormous bat if things take a turn for the worst.

I walk Nesrin's path, avoiding the boulders. Each step sends chills down my spine. I breathe in and out. Relaxing before approaching the creatures. They can sense fear.

Nesrin is still petting the one she became friends with. The other bats pay no mind to us being there. They must be used to people being around them. They are soft but vicious creatures when provoked.

"Let it come to you first. Keep your breath calm." Nesrin says quietly.

I stop before the creature. It sees me. And for a moment, I fear it may want nothing to do with me as it turns its head opposite my direction. Until I shift my weight on the ground, it turns to me slowly and comes to me. Its claws dig into the dirt.

I keep my eyes down, as Nesrin had said. I breathe steadily. Keeping good thoughts and shoving away any thoughts that may provoke my fire. I wouldn't know what to do if I lost myself here. Completely unprepared and helpless. I am still determining the extent of my powers.

Its whiskers brush against my arm. It's tickling me through my cloak. I stay still as ever. My chest rising and falling is the only thing that moves. I focus hard to keep it at a slow pace.

It circles me. I look over to Nesrin, who's scratching the bat's ears. Little babies they are.

I lift my arm before me and wait for it to smell me. It licks the tip of my horns, curious about what they are. I close my eyes for a moment and hold my breath. Its hot breath washes over me.

For a moment, it looks like it has no interest in forming a bond. It comes closer to my hand and pushes it slightly, but rough enough to make me fall to the ground. I'm stunned and freeze on the ground. The bat towers over me. It leans its head down and nuzzles its head into my chest. I hesitantly raise my hand to its ears. It doesn't flinch.

I come to my feet, and the bat nudges me more, but I keep my stance sturdier now.

I smile.

"So, what's the trick to mounting it?" I ask Nesrin.

She's already mounted the thing.

"Bow to it; if it trusts you, it will bow back, then climb onto its neck and find your place."

I keep my arm resting on its ears. It growls, but not in a vicious way. A growl like he's relaxed. A purr almost.

I take a step back and take a low bow to it. I bend, waiting for it to do the same.

It's talons scrape against the ground as it steps back. I peek from behind my eyelashes. It's bowing before me.

I look at Nesrin, who is smiling.

While the bat's head is down, I put it once more before climbing over its head and onto the furry part of its neck. Its smooth fur feels like a cloud. I shift my body to a comfortable position.

I look down from the bat. Its height is massive, like a dragon's. There isn't much to hold onto, but I tighten my body around it, hoping I don't fall off.

"What the hell do I hold onto?"

Nesrin smiles. "Just whatever you can hold onto." She laughs and squeezes her legs against the neck of the bat. It flaps its wings, and cold air swirls around us, making my hair wisp in my face.

The bat takes off, and I grab its fur as tightly as possible without hurting the creature. Although, with its size, not much could hurt it.

We lift from the ground, and the other bats surround us. Flapping their wings in the air, creating a tornado of snow and air, makes my eyes water.

"This is amazing," I yell to Nesrin.

"You wanna race?" She points. "To the castle.

Off in the distance, the castle lights flicker on the mountain in the moonlight. The Lights of Serderis reflects off it, making it glow in various colors. It's breathtaking, and if this bat could fly forever, I'd stay here, admiring the castle's beauty.

"What's the prize?" I flip my hair off of my face.

"If I win, you have to tell Bellamy how you feel about him."

I flinch.

"And if you win, I'll tell him for you." She laughs. 'Ready, set go."

She takes off before I can say a word. I do the same and am only a few feet behind her.

I look below us, and I can no longer see the guards. They're probably following us from the ground and sending word that we've run off. That *I've* run off. Once Queen Davina gets word, she will have a fit when I return to the castle.

The chilly wind pulls back my hair as we glide in the night sky of Tenebris. I'm starting to get used to being in the air. I could be up here all day. Forget the carriage. This is how I want to get around. It's faster and more fun.

The bats are gentler than I had thought them to be. Perhaps I could name this one and claim it as my pet, a personal bat for transportation. Then, I could fly with Bellamy and Sora.

The bat's fur wisps in the wind. I loosen my grip on the fur, testing my limits. Nesrin is beside me with her hands outward, embracing the cold air. I do as she does. We look at each other and smile.

The castle is close. Its crystal tower gleams in the moonlight. We soar over the snowy top mountains, coming so close to them that I feel as if I can feel the snow that covers them.

Nesrin swerves before me, and my bat turns to avoid it. I grip its fur, catching my breath, hoping I wouldn't topple to the ground, and I have no wings, so I'd be dead for sure this time.

We circle the castle. The gargoyles stand guard at the front gates. They notice us in the air, and they point to us. We wave, but they look more worried for us than happy. Two of them return to human form and storm into the castle.

Nesrin makes a free fall to the ground and lands her bat on the walkway leading to the castle. The gargoyles run to us with spears in their hands, horns, and red eyes gleaming at us.

I jump off the bat with my hands in the air.

"Do not fire. I am Princess Morana."

Their spears lower, and they back away. All but one. The gargoyle turns to his human form—red hair and brown-eyed man no older than Bellamy.

"Your majesty." he bows. "There has been word from King Alaric. Please, allow me to escort you to the others."

He catches his breath as if something is urgent. Can gargoyles even sweat. His forehead is glistening.

Nesrin comes behind me. "Looks like I won. You know what you have to do. And what's with the weapons?"

I turn to Nesrin and grab her hand. "Care to see the castle? There's something I need to attend to."

We follow the guard into the castle. He leads us into the throne room and not the council chamber. It must be urgent of they aren't calling us to the official chambers.

The group of people turns to Nesrin and me. Bellamy, Sora, Davina, Lazarus, and the other council members all turn without emotion—all except Sora, who has tears running down his face. I release Nesrin from me.

Greer stands near the doorway.

"Will you please take her to freshen up? She is invited to dinner. Find her a change of clothes too."

Nesrin looks back at me with fear. As much as I want her by my side, this is not the time for it. I cannot expose her to the troubles of the kingdom.

"What's going on?" I walk up to the group. They huddle around a wooden table. "Sora, what's —"

CHAPTER EIGHTEEN

I look down at the table, covered in blood and mangled bodies. A faun with dark fur, broken horns, and a gaping hole in his chest lay sprawled on the table. Sora kneels next to him, gripping his bloody hands, unaware of the bloody mess he's covered himself in.

Next to the faun is something from my worst nightmares. Raisel's tiny body, dead on the table, bloody from the neck down, wings broken and fragmented into pieces. Not much is left of her.

I catch my breath and choke on the air.

No. She can't be dead.

I fall to the ground. I don't remember starting to cry, but it's unstoppable now. The tears blur my vision. I shake with anger and demise. A lump in my throat forms, and I am unable to swallow it. My chest tightens with every breath. My lungs burn so much that it feels like I'm breathing fire.

I let out a wail so loud that Bellamy flinches. Sora comes to my side, crying and holding me to him. I reach around his back to keep myself from falling over. The others stand over us, at a loss for words, unable to speak in our presence.

"Why?" I cry. "She didn't do anything."

Davina reaches down to rest her hand on my shoulder. I pull away. Even Bellamy stands back. Although, I slightly wished he would come to me and comfort me too.

"It wasn't supposed to happen." Sora cries.

Bellamy kneels to my level, careful to give me my space. He looks into my eyes. His black eyes are an ocean of mystery, pain, and never-ending sorrow.

"They were left at the border, unharmed by our people. A werewolf roaming the border brought it to our attention." Bellamy sighs and reaches to the table, a crumpled piece of paper.

"It reads." Bellamy clears his throat. "To keep Tenebris from any invasion attempt, I bring you the loyalists to Sora and Morana, Raisel of the east, and Stornyn of the north. Both were found guilty of aiding the criminals. Both were sentenced to death without trial. If anyone of Tenebrisean blood steps foot over the border, the princess will lose her life."

He folds the paper and sits back on the table, never losing eye contact and staring deep into me, trying to read me.

"I assume these people were friends of yours?"

I nod my head, unable to speak. Bellamy wipes a little tear from my cheek.

"Stornyn became my guardian after my parents died," Sora mutters. He leans away from me.

"Raisel was my best friend." I breathe. "She's all I had after…after."

I lower my head. I can't force the words out. This is too much. This never-ending pain. It strings like a rope connected to my soul, continuously tugging my heart till it's almost out of my chest. The pain pulls and pulls till I lose my breath. I open my mouth, but no sound emerges from it.

Bellamy shakes his head and rises to Davina and Lazarus. Sora brings me to my feet. I turn my body from the corpse on the table. If I get one more look at them…

"This is getting out of hand." Bellamy starts. "They are provoking us into a war. We must do something. You have waited long enough for war. Now is the time."

Davina crosses her arms. "Do you think it wise to do that? The minute their people send word to the King that we are on their territory, they will kill Astrid."

"That's if she is still alive." Bellamy shouts. "You are running out of options, your majesty." He says mockingly. "You have lost your daughter either way. I'm sure you do not want to lose another one."

After taking a rather long hot bath, I finally muster up the strength to get out of my towel and dress myself. I lose track of time just laying on my bed, towel wrapped around me, thinking of everything up until now. I try to force the picture of Raisel's mangled body from my mind, but it keeps coming back with a sting like venom.

Greer has yet to come to the room. She's giving me space. Part of me wants her here, but I don't want her to see me like this. Torn. And if I get angry enough, I don't want to hurt her. I don't want her to see me as a monster. *I am not a monster.*

I stand behind the double doors that lead to the dining hall. I take deep breaths. I have to keep myself together, not just for myself, but for everyone. I don't know what I am capable of yet, and I don't want to find that out during a perfectly made meal with my new friend.

The doors creak as I push them open. How am I the one to always get to dinner last? Everyone is already here. Even Nesrin, who had a change of clothes. She looks stunning in a simple black dress with red crystals. Her hair is up and away from her face, making her golden eyes pop. They match so well with the castle. She looks like she belongs here.

"Morana. Glad to see you." Lazarus says as he tips a wine glass to his lips.

I nod, taking my spot next to Nesrin.

"You look lovely," I say.

"You as well, Princess." She pushes her potatoes around on her plate. "I must say this castle is exquisite. And the dress. I've never worn such an expensive dress. We have seamstresses in the city, but their needlework is nothing like this."

Davina smiles as she listens to our conversation. I avoid making eye contact with her, in fear she may bring up Raisel and Stornyn's deaths. I'm not ready to talk about it. I don't know if I ever will be.

"Nesrin, you are welcome here anytime. We love having guests."

"Thank you, your majesty."

I fill my plate with potatoes and vegetables, and bread. Just looking at the meat makes my stomach turn.

Sora's head is down, poking at the food on his plate. I don't know what to say to him or If I should say anything. What do you say to someone after such a loss? I can try to comfort him, but doing so may only make it worse.

Then, silence.

"I saw Morana riding a bat earlier," Bellamy states.

Davina's fork and knife falls onto her plate, causing a loud ring to echo through the dining hall.

"She did what?" Davina says.

"Right before they came into the castle, both were in the sky on the back of those huge bats that circle the castle."

Davina turns to me.

"That is reckless, Morana. How did you do such a thing?"

I look to Nesrin to urge her to answer the question. I don't want to speak to her. Nesrin gawks at me in resentment.

"It's a sport, your majesty. In the City of Drafanel, we have races with bats. Some are tamed, and some are wild. We do it for…fun." Nesrin trails off.

Lazarus has a slight smile on his face. Something tells me he is all too familiar with bat racing in his younger years. Or he's gambled away plenty of money on the races.

"Were these bats tamed?" Davina asks.

"No." I cut in. "We found them in the valley."

Davina looks like she may lose her mind. I get she's just being a mother, but I am almost twenty-one. Just because she lost out on twenty years of my life doesn't mean she should be controlling my life now. I survived long enough without her.

"Was it terrifying?" Lazarus asks.

"More than anything."

"I bet there's never been a princess to walk these halls who tamed a bat and rode it for fun." Bellamy laughs.

Davina shakes her head. We all laugh except Sora, who has yet to say a single word to us. I feel for him, I really do. I am saddened by Raisel's death, but it also fuels me with an anger I can use to fight against Rhemus.

CHAPTER NINETEEN

I convinced the stable master to find a place for Nox on the castle grounds. I won't dare keep him in a small stable but keep him nearby with his other companions. After much thought after dinner last night, I found that I'll need Nox in the future, whether it be for transportation or a war.

Sora still hasn't come out of his room. Greer had talked to Lachin earlier. He wanted to avoid being seen. He won't let anyone in his room. His thoughts are still tainted by Stornyn's bloodied body in the throne room. I don't know how to approach him. He has to come out sooner or later. Not for anyone but himself.

I'm trying to shove every thought of Raisel from my mind. My best friend died because I spoke out. Dead because I defended a harmless creature. Dead because I defended myself. How can the people of Rhemus turn an eye to this madness? This madness that they call home.

I had a plan to one day bring Raisel to Tenebris with me. I don't know if she would have done it. But I know, I'm confident I could have convinced her. If she had only seen the beauty of Tenebris, she might be alive right now.

Others may see Raisel and Stornyn's death as a minor inconvenience, but I see it as a huge opportunity to avenge Tenebris. Their death wasn't unnecessary, but the meaning behind it for King Alaric leaves an opportunity for Tenebris to break their walls. Show them who we really are. We are fearsome creatures and vengeful daemons. I want to see Rhemus crumble for the deaths of the innocent.

"Good evening, Morana. How are you feeling?" Lazarus asks.

Davina's back straightens in her throne as I approach them. Lazarus remains unfazed by my presence.

"I need to speak to both of you." I fidget with my fingers.

"Go on, dear."

I push myself to speak, but it strains my throat. "I cannot sit idly by and watch more people of Rhemus die. Not all citizens there are cruel. Most of them are brainwashed by the tyrant king. I want to lead a legion of Tenebrisean fighters."

Davina grips the arms of her throne, digging her nails into the gold frame.

"What brought this about?" Davina says behind her teeth.

"You're doing nothing for the people of Tenebris. A war is coming, and you have made no such plan for your country. I want to help fight."

"I hope you are not doing this because of the death of your friend." Lazarus starts. "I'm sorry for your loss. To you and Sora both, but their deaths do not warrant a war started by us."

I ball my hands into fists. I try to breathe and calm myself. I can't show them how out of control I am with my powers. That would only give them more reasons not to let us invade Rhemus.

"I think you're forgetting a small detail." Lazarus breathes. "If we invade, they kill Astrid. After that, who knows what else they will do to our people."

"Cowards."

Their eyes flutter.

"You are all cowards. You refuse to do anything because you are comfortable. Astrid may be alive, but what's the point if she's in enemy territory? Don't you want to get her back and protect the people of Tenebris?"

My fists are burning now, but I don't dare look down. They might be glowing with rage by the way Davina and Lazarus eye my hands.

"Are you accusing us of something, Morana?" Davina asks. "If it wasn't for us —"

"What can you possibly say to make this better? Would you have liked it better if Sora and I stayed in Rhemus just a little longer, so you'd get your daughter back? The only one you seem to love."

"I love all my children." She stands, fuming, as her voice roars through the room.

"You love them enough to use them as pawns. You could have found other ways to get Astrid back. You could have had us. And now, your children are trying to clean up your mess."

Davina stands from her throne. King Lazarus eyes her from below. By the look in his eyes, anger arises. I may have gone too far.

"Morana, there is much you do not know, but one thing you *will* understand is that I am keeping Astrid alive by not starting a war. King Alaric will not hesitate to kill Astrid when he gets word of our intrusion. That is why I will not allow you or Sora, let alone anyone, to go across the border and risk her life."

I stand, chin high, shoulder back. I will not back down.

"Your majesty, you would be doing Astrid a favor by killing her. Your daughter is suffering, and you are the cause of it."

I spin on my heel and storm out of the throne room. My voice bounces off the high ceilings. Neither of them chases after me. And if they do, I will only run faster.

My hands simmer down as I walk further away from the room. With each step I take, the burning dies down.

I turn the corner and slam into a tall body, my nose scraping against the buckles of a black leather halter. I hold my nose and wait for the pain to subside. My eyes water.

"Whoa," Bellamy says, checking if I'm all right. "What's the rush? I heard all the commotion."

"We need to get Sora now." I pant. "Summon Nesrin. She is to be here immediately."

I've let many things slide since arriving here. The secrets and nonstop lies. I let them all go without perfect judgment. I hate myself for it. I regret agreeing to stay here. I regret going to the blood reader. I could have lived the entirety of my life without knowing who my birth parents are. I could have rejected the crown. Yet here I am, falling prey to everyone's lies.

Nesrin is the last to arrive. I had the guards work fast to get her here in good time. She frantically enters the room without a word.

Sora sits in the chair of my vanity with his head lowered. I know he has been crying again.

"What's going on?" Nesrin asks.

"I blew up on them," I say quickly. "I exploded, and I can't handle this any longer. We have to do something. Break the rules. I don't care what it takes."

Sora shoots up his head. Eyes red from the tears and hours of crying. I know I should have let him grieve, but this can wait no longer. Later, he will know that my intentions were for the good of all of us.

"Slow down. What are you talking about?"

"I'm saying we need to do something. The four of us."

"Are you proposing the plan Bellamy and I had come to you about? The one you rejected?" Sora stands, arms crossed. His gold-lined jacket glimmering in the firelight.

"Yes." I sigh. "We need to go to Rhemus. Get Astrid and bring her back. At least we can do that."

They look at me with worried eyes, scared that I've become someone else. I've gone mad. Perhaps the brimstone blood is taking over my mind. The horns. They have altered my mind ever since they sprouted from my head. They ache, and I want to rip them out for causing so much grief.

"That's if she is even still alive." Bellamy states. "King Alaric could by lying. And with him, it's hard to tell."

And that is a risk I am willing to take.

"We can ride the bats—Nesrin and I. You two can fly since you have wings. We will go to the Hesai Islands first. We can see their army, see what they are capable of."

Bellamy paces back and forth, finger to lip, as he chews on the skin around it. His hair flowing behind him with each step.

"I think you're out of your damn mind," Sora says.

Nesrin cuts in. "I am no warrior, your majesty — I mean, Morana. And if we were to get caught, my punishment could be catastrophic. I could be tried for treason."

I rest my hand on Nesrin's shoulder. "We will protect you. Nothing will happen to you. I will see to that."

Her shoulder relaxes, but my words still don't help her anxiety.

"If we took a legion, or even smaller, Davina and Lazarus would know. They'd be notified the minute we asked. So, the four of us are all Tenebris has." My voice shakes.

They fall silent. Lost in their own minds. They are contemplating the worst of it all. And I expect them to. This isn't an easy decision. They'd be putting their lives on the line and the future of Tenebris.

"I know one person that could help us," Bellamy says.

We turn to him.

"His name is Xanthe. He's a gargoyle. He's one of the guards here for the castle."

I cross my arms. "What makes you think he would help us? He works for Davina and Lazarus."

"Contrary. He works for me. He and I are both from Kiveha. He will do as I order him. He's been loyal to my family for years now."

It's risky. Xanthe is still a guard for the night realm. I'm trying to limit the number of people involved in the plan. The more people who know, the bigger chance we will get caught. Bellamy seems so sure of it too. The last thing I want is for this plan to fail.

"Fine. But if he gives me any reason he might reveal our plan to Davina and Lazarus, I will crumble him."

Bellamy throws his hands as if to keep off my bad side. The corners of his mouth twitch into a smile.

"What's so funny? Prince of Kiveha?" I ask.

Bellamy brushes his foot against the rug. "I just find it funny that Sora and I come to you with the same plan you had rejected, then propose it yourself."

"Listen, I don't need your snide comments. I'll go to Rhemus by myself if I have to."

Sora's eyes shoot at me, eyes fuming.

"You will do no such thing. We are going to help. If one person goes, all of us do."

CHAPTER TWENTY

The sun and it's orange light shines on the mountaintops, making them glisten with the melting snow. The weather is still cool, but the temperature rises each day with the coming of spring. I'm anxious to see the true beauty of the blooming season in Tenebris. And even though it comes alive at night, I'd spend my days just watching the sunrise.

My eyes have gotten so used to the moonlight. They begin to ache in the light of the sun. I admire the night's beauty, but nothing compares to the bright days when no one is around. When everyone is sleeping soundly, and the birds chirp the day away.

We sneak out of the castle one at a time. Each of us carries weapons of every kind. Most of them come from the armory. Nesrin had found a way to distract the guards long enough to give us time to grab what we needed.

I was never fully trained for battle, but what's a better way to prepare than head-on? I'm only skilled with the use of a dagger. Swords and spears, bows and arrows are foreign to me. I have my fists of fire, but even that has many unknown abilities to it.

"Bellamy is right behind me," Sora says, panting.

He rests against a tree, the sword from his back scraping against the bark. I'd never seen him so formal, so warrior-like. When I first met him, he wore nothing but a simple white tunic and a black cloak with pants that might have been too big for him. Now, he's a prince who is about to fight for his kingdom.

Bellamy jogs down the path, holster dangling from his hips and obsidian swords crossing his back. His hair is tied up and away from his face, revealing years' worth of scars.

Bellamy's guard, Xanthe, runs behind him in human form. The same guard that came to me when news of Raisel and Stornyn's death came. I am still weary of his part in this.

Nesrin leans over to me. "Did you ever tell Bellamy?"

I keep my gaze on Bellamy. "I was preoccupied."

Nesrin smirks.

Thoughts of Bellamy's lips on mine consume me. I blush. I turn to try and hide it. I feel like such a little girl swooning over a handsome prince.

"We need to leave now. Xanthe will have to ride with one of you."

Nesrin and I look at each other, waiting for the other to object.

"He can ride with me. Hope he's all right with heights." Nesrin laughs.

"I will be fine." Xanthe replies.

We walk to the bats that are hidden in the trees. They're jittery this morning due to the sunlight. We will have to find a cave for them sooner or later. I can't risk losing Nox. Otherwise, we would all be stuck, and I'm not about to have Bellamy or Sora fly us home.

Xanthe mounts the bat and sits behind Nesrin. "Keep your hands above the waist now." She says.

Xanthe gently rests his hands on her shoulder, still unsure how safe and secure it is.

Bellamy and Sora's wings rip through their backs. Sora is still in pain from them being so new to him. Bellamy's much bigger than Soras. But in due time, Sora's would be just as big as Bellamy's with more training and practice.

"Keep close to the shore, and don't fly too high," Bellamy says, tightening the buckle on his chest. "Any hint of danger, we all turn around. We will meet at the island right outside Hesai. There aren't many guards there. We can assess further once we all land safely."

We nod our heads. I look at Sora. He's in a stance, ready to jump into the air and take off. He fastens his buckle tighter across his chest, waiting for the go.

"Are you sure about this, Morana?" Sora asks.

"As sure as it is daytime."

The further we reach Rhemus, the more my stomach burns with anticipation. The enchantment has been broken, but some part of me thinks it hasn't, and once we reach the border, Sora and I will burn or die, or any gruesome death. Perhaps sound an alarm to the King. Davina and Lazarus were positive that once we became daemons, we could travel to and from Rhemus as we pleased. After all the lies, I still hate myself for believing them so easily.

Nesrin hoovers beside me, Xanthe looking like he may vomit at any moment. I smile and hide my face to save him from embarrassment from Nesrin. She'd never let him forget it.

Sora and Bellamy fly higher than us by a couple of feet. Once in a while, they exchange looks, probably talking about the island or me. If it is about me, I'd never want to hear what they have to say.

The tree line comes into view. That's where the enchantment lies. Sora comes to my side.

"Are you absolutely sure of this, Morana?"

I never thought of entering Rhemus again. Not just because of the enchantment but because of everything I didn't have in Rhemus. Even at the time when Raisel was still alive, I never once thought of seeing her again. I was prepared to die that night. I walked over the border. Now I am here, trying to save Tenebris. Save Astrid. And for what? Raisel is dead. Hatred only consumes me and fills my veins. That is the only reason I seek to destroy the King.

Bellamy comes beside me. "Once we get further to the shore, there's a cave there. The bats can't go much longer in the daylight. We can rest there and make a plan."

Nox hasn't gone this long without resting, and I'm surprised. It probably was a bad idea to bring them, but there would have been no other way to escape if we had to.

The water deepens in color as we near the shore. Rocks bulge out of the water, pointing upward, to act as a shield from enemy ships and armadas—the same rocks, much like the ones that impaled me that night at the cliffs.

Flashes of blood mixing in water disturb me for a moment.

The roaring waters crash against the sides of the cave, causing a rumbling, thunder-like sound throughout the cave. Too loud to hear anyone from the inside and loud enough to keep us hidden from the outside world.

The bat's wings send a gush of air through the cave as we land. Xanthe helps Nesrin off her bat. Catching her by the waist. Her face goes red. They turn from each other swiftly.

It's hard to see into the blackness of the cave. Unknown to how deep it goes, unknown to what lurks inside it. It's safe to say that I'll be camping as close to the entrance as possible to avoid certain death.

"We can rest here for a while till the sun goes down. That's when everyone will be asleep. Then, maybe we will have a better chance of getting to Rhemus unseen."

We'd risk being seen if we started a fire. The smoke could alarm the army, or the smoke could become so dense we could be seen for miles. Keeping warm will be difficult for all of us.

I bring out a container of blood. Too small for Nox to be fully satisfied, but just enough to hold him over till we can leave the cave. I'd let him rip the soldiers to shreds at any chance we get. He'd be feasting, and I won't stop him.

Nesrin stands by the edge of the cave, watching the waves crash against the jagged rocks. The mist of the ocean sprays on our feet. The smell of salt lingers in the air. It is a familiar scent. One that brings memories of plunging to the depths of the sea.

I'm reluctant to tell anyone of my past. And maybe that time will come in the future. Part of me regrets even making the decision to end my life. But perhaps they may understand. I lived a cruel life before this. Could my actions be justified?

"I've never stepped foot outside Tenebris," Nesrin says.

"Why would you want to?" I reply. "Rhemus is bleak, nothing but grass and farmlands for miles. No true beauty."

A wave crashes before us; we back up inches to avoid it.

"I don't want to see Rhemus for that reason. It's a new place, you know? I read, so every book is a new adventure. Maybe if I had seen Rhemus just once, I'd want to travel elsewhere. Tenebris is wonderful, but there's always something itching my skin that tells me I shouldn't be there. I should be out seeing the world."

She's got the mind of a reader. Each book pulls her into a different reality. She lives in the stories she reads and falls in love with the characters she grows to know. New people, new places, new life. It's all so intriguing. I'm glad I brought her here with us.

I return to the others. Sora rummages through his things while Bellamy and Xanthe sharpen their weapons.

"Nesrin. Do you know how to use a bow and arrow?" Bellamy asks.

"I thought you would never ask," she says with a devilish grin.

She takes the bow from him and grabs an arrow from the quiver.

"Sora, stand right over there. Hold out that piece of driftwood."

Sora's eyes light up, but not with excitement, but with nervousness.

"Just do it."

He hesitantly stands, holding the piece of driftwood away from his body, many feet away from Nesrin.

"Hold still."

She pulls back the string, aiming the arrow at its destination. She releases it, and the string vibrates. In the blink of an eye, the arrow hits the direct middle of the driftwood. Sora opens his eyes, fearing he would have been impaled.

"I've had years of practice."

Bellamy takes the arrow out of the driftwood. "Can you put those skills into combat if needed?"

"I wasn't properly trained like you, but I can make a quick hit if needed."

Bellamy nods and places the arrow back into the quiver.

Nox and his friend lay curled in the corner of the cave. It's getting entirely too cold just to be standing around. We need to rest before the action happens. I'll be damned if I go into battle with only a few minutes of sleep. Although I know some have yet to have the pleasure of doing that.

I curl next to Nox, who doesn't realize I've laid beside him. His fur is warm, just what I needed to relax a little.

"I'll stand watch for a little while. We can all take turns." Bellamy says.

The sun behind him turns his body into a silhouette. I watch him, slowly fading as my mind wanders to the dream world.

CHAPTER TWENTY- ONE

The ground rumbles, shaking Nox and I awake. There's a moment of silence before it happens again, this time making me jump up and grip my dagger. Even standing throws me off balance.

It's dark out now, and the light from the moon shines into the cave. Creating dark shadows that twist in the night. Nothing seems real. Something seems quite wrong.

"What is that?" Nesrin calls out.

I realize she's standing beside me when she grabs my hand. Her soft hands and long fingernails give it away.

"The sun had just gone down a few minutes ago. Everything was quiet. Then the cave started shaking."

Bellamy stands with his sword, and Sora with his. Xanthe is a full gargoyle, standing still like stone as if he can't be moved.

"What cave is this?" I ask.

Bellamy and Nesrin cock their heads.

"What cave is this?" I ask more firmly this time.

"Cave of the Winds," Bellamy shouts. "What does it matter?"

"We need to go now." My voice shakes. I run to Nox and Nesrin to her bat.

"Care to tell us what's going on?" Bellamy extends his wings behind him. Xanthe returns to his human form, following Nesrin on the bat.

"I should have known." I breathe. "This cave. There are legends of a monster in the depths of it. One that kills everything and everyone. It's only fitting that it just woke up. They are nocturnal creatures."

Sora twists his head to me. "Are you saying that the Calperi is real?"

"There is no such thing," Bellamy shouts. "We wouldn't have come to this cave had I known that."

I secure my pack around my chest. "You wouldn't have known about it."

A loud screech comes from the darkness of the cave. We freeze, waiting for another sound. The ring of it bounces off the walls and our ears.

"Yes, it's real. It's not just a legend."

The Calperi is a legend of Rhemus. Most famously known for its spider-like legs and massive moth wings. Its tail is of a scorpion, deadly and filled with poison. But that's not the deadliest thing. It has sharp teeth like that of a sea creature. Rows and rows of teeth ready to rip an enemy to shreds. Each one is filled with enough venom that can kill a leviathan.

The screech becomes louder. Rocks and debris fall from the top of the cave. We cover our heads, maneuvering away from the pieces of stone.

"Is it safe to go? We need a plan." Sora yells.

"Off the south shore of Rhemus, not far behind the King's castle."

We spring out of the cave, meeting with the crashing waves. The bat's wing extends further than the span of the cave.

Another screech echoes, making the insides of our ears vibrate with each sound. The creature is behind us. I turn to face it. Its body lunges at us. Teeth barred and legs pointed at us, sharp enough to pierce through our bodies in one swift move.

I can't use my magic to defend us. All I feel is fear and terror. I can't conjure enough hatred to spark the flames. All I focus on is getting out of here alive.

Its wings soar past us, and we barely miss it by a few feet. I grab harder onto Nox's fur. He screeches in return. He's running out of energy, and I wonder how far we will go.

"Go south!" Bellamy shouts.

"They will see us." Xanthe shouts. He's got his sword out, ready to take a hit if the time calls for it. Not any of us can beat that terrifying creature alone.

"Take to the skies." Bellamy shoots up into the sky.

We have no choice. I yank on Nox's fur to let him know to go up, and with one swift move, we tilt upward. I squeeze my entire body around his neck, doing everything I can to hold on. I don't dare look behind me to see how close the Calperi is. Its screeching is only a few feet away from us.

Sora and Bellamy put their arms above their head, flying faster than we are, but only because they aren't riding such enormous beasts. They have the upper hand by forming their bodies into spears, making it easier to fly through the sky.

Nesrin and I shoot upwards, hoping the other doesn't fall off. Xanthe has his arms around Nesrin's waist. He's in human form. He would have easily taken Nesrin down with him if he had turned into a gargoyle.

I keep my eyes on Bellamy and Sora, not looking back at the beast behind us. The wind soars past us, and the force of it almost jerks my head backward, brushing against my horns.

We make haste to the clouds. I don't know how much further Nox can go, or even Sora. He's barely had enough flying practice to maneuver like this.

Once we reach the top of the clouds, we pause, hoping the Calperi doesn't break through the clouds. The only sound comes from the flap of the bat's wings and the unsteady breaths that escape us.

Sora pants. "Did we escape it?

I look down from Nox—no sign of the Calperi. Even the wind is still in the moment. Eerie.

"We need to stay above the clouds for a while," Bellamy says. "It's screech probably alerted the camp."

"I guess those legends are true. The Calperi. Why do they camp so close to that awful creature?" Xanthe asks.

I fix my hair and brush my fingers through it.

"King Alaric probably has something to do with it. No doubt, the cave goes deeper and leads to one of their camps. A weapon of war for them."

We slowly soar through the nighttime clouds for a while. In short of words, no one looks at each other. Each of us is in our own head. Most likely regretting this journey. Part of me does. Everyone's lives are at risk. All because I got angry. All because I couldn't keep my anger at bay. I can't help but take the blame for this.

Sora comes to me, resting behind me on Nox. He's exhausted from flying for more than he's used to.

"Bellamy thinks Astrid is dead."

I keep my head forward. Wanting to ignore his words.

"What if she is dead?" He asks. "What if this is all for nothing?"

I loosen my grip on Nox's fur.

"She has to be. And if she is, then we still have Tenebris to fight for." I tighten my grip on Nox. "All the more reason to kill the King."

We hit a gust of wind, and he grabs my shoulders to brace himself.

"The five of us cannot take on an entire army. Please promise me that if things get to be too much, we retreat. No hesitation."

I continue forward. Taking his words into consideration but remaining quiet.

I can't be wrong about this. I just can't.

CHAPTER TWENTY- TWO

Rhemus. We met again. Now dead from the harsh winters, the grass goes on for miles, so much so that I cannot see the borderline. Nothing exciting to see. Nothing pleasurable to the eye. It hurts my head to look at it. Or perhaps it's the horns that have been throbbing all night.

The castle remains just as I had last seen it. Tall, gray, and nothing but a fortress of death and wickedness. Surrounded by a patch of trees, more is needed to protect it from enemy fire.

No posts along the shoreline wait for us. No guards, no squads ready for battle. It's completely quiet and vacant. But I cannot be fooled by the silence. They will be lurking in every corner. Infiltrating the castle is going to be more difficult than entering their territory.

We find a small cove off the south shoreline. I jump down from Nox, and Bellamy helps me down, grabbing me by my waist. Nesrin looks at me with a smile. I brush it off and try to hide the redness on my face.

"You and Sora know these lands better than all of us." Bellamy brings out the map. "What are we up against?"

I smooth out the map on a rock. Squinting at it because the only light comes from the moon.

"Centaurs, with spears. That is from personal experience. Elementals are the ones we need to watch for. Their elemental magic can be deadly if facing the wrong wielder. However, I'm not completely sure if they protect the castle. But let's just go in believing they are."

Nesrin twists her hair around her fingers. "I should stay back. I will be of no help with hand-to-hand combat."

Bellamy reaches behind him and hands her the bow and quiver of arrows. "Use sparingly. You can shoot from afar if possible. Take to the skies if all else fails."

Nesrin nods. "I have other abilities that don't require me to be so close."

We look at her.

"I'm a succubus. I can travel through dreams. If the King or Queen is asleep, I can distract them."

Bellamy smiles a wicked grin, almost laughing.

Nesrin shrugs her shoulders.

"Can you do your…thing?" he asks.

"Her what?" I cut in.

"You want me to dream fuck the King?"

Sora turns his head to keep from laughing out loud. Xanthe wanders in the other direction, hoping to avoid this silliness. The grin on Bellamy's face does not go unnoticed.

"Come on. You think we would bring you here not to do that?"

It's funny, but to hear Bellamy even suggest she do such a thing angers me. For him to even know about it makes me question what else they have done together. I can't be angry, though, considering I haven't even told him how I feel about him. I hate myself for even thinking like that at a time like this.

"So, you can stay back and do your thing," I say. "Back to other important things."

Bellamy nudges Sora. I pretend it doesn't happen.

"There is a tunnel that leads directly to the dungeon of the castle. That is where she most likely is." I point to a spot not far from the castle ground and slide my finger in the direction of our route.

I look up to make sure they are all paying attention. All their eyes are on me.

"That route will be our best option. If anything, a few guards may be patrolling the place as a precaution."

Bellamy crosses his arms, listening to my plan. At least he can do that much.

"Everyone understand?" I ask, rolling up the map and handing it back to Bellamy.

"Hold on, we need a signal if one of us gets lost or comes into trouble," Nesrin adds.

Sora rustles through his pack and pulls out a horn. It's small, but it will do. He hands it to Nesrin since she's the only one staying behind.

"Got it."

"Everyone ready? Keep your wits about you. Stay close together. And Nesrin, those bats can get mean and vicious once fired at. Ensure you are mounted to it or able to get on it as quickly as possible. They may be able to give you some time.

We turn away from Nesrin, and she takes the two bats to a patch of trees. If she was to enter the King's dreams, she needed to do it privately, away from the enemies and in the safety of the bats. Those bats know her and will do anything to defend her.

The rest of us take off to the tree line. The shore is close to the tunnel leading to the castle. If we had decided to enter the castle from above, we'd be ambushed by flying arrows and boulders set aflame. With Nesrin occupying the King, that gives us a better chance of distracting him so he can't set off an order to kill Astrid.

Luckily, Bellamy and Xanthe have incredible night vision. I can barely see in the dark, even with the moonlight barely showing itself through the treetops. So many dead branches are skewing my view of the stars.

"Shh." Bellamy stops, putting his hand out to prevent us from going any further.

"There are three centaurs. We need to be quiet."

We turn our view to the tunnel entrance. Muscular centaurs, spear in hand, wearing the emblem of the King's court, stand around, waiting for someone to strike first. I wonder how many people have tried to enter the castle this way. Surely enough for them to place guards here.

Bellamy rounds a tree, each of us following his exact footsteps. I hold my breath, careful not to make unnecessary sounds to alert the guards. I keep my hand on Sora before me, fearing that I'll lose sight of him if all hell breaks loose.

Bellamy takes us to the top of the tunnel. The centaurs are still oblivious to our existence. The boys carefully bring out their swords. Bellamy nudges me back.

Bellamy holds up his hand and counts.

One.

Two.

Three.

They jump into the air and attack the centaurs from behind. Bellamy doesn't hesitate to plunge the sword into the centaur's back, causing the creature to howl in pain. Pulling back the sword, blood splatters on his face. The blood doesn't faze him. He ends its misery by slitting its throat, and its cries become slowly fading gurgles.

Sora beheads one, and its body thumps to the ground. I try to shield my eyes with my own hands but peek between my fingers.

Xanthe does the same with no effort. Each of them unfazed by the bloodshed.

Sora stands bewildered. Looking at the poor creature before him. It was his first intentional kill. His face gives nothing away to how he feels. I can't read him.

"We need to leave now. There could be more patrolling in the area," Bellamy says. "We need to pull their bodies into the tunnel so that no other guards are alerted."

After dragging the bodies into the tunnel, we stare into the entrance. Endless darkness and nothing but hot air come from it. The smell of rotting flesh and food creeps into the air. Covering my nose doesn't help.

"Are you sure this is the way?" Xanthe asks.

"I'm sure of it," I say.

Bellamy leads the way first, his hands igniting like mine but his face neutral. I remember what he said on the balcony. He's always angry, but he doesn't let it consume him. He goes on without a change on his face. Nothing to show he's angry. I've seen him angry once towards Davina and Lazarus. His fist never grew into flames, though. That is the part I have to master.

The water in the tunnel echoes, but I try to walk as near the wall as possible. The tunnel seems to go on forever—a never-ending void. We could be in here for hours.

I hold my breath with each step. I follow close behind Bellamy, his hands of fire leading the way. Sora behind me with his blade out, shining in the light of the fire, and Xanthe beside me doing the same.

"The entrance is right ahead," Bellamy whispers.

My body stiffens. Sora's grip around his sword tightens, and his shoulders become firm.

"Protect the princess," Bellamy whispers to Sora. He ushers Xanthe to his side, standing in front of Sora and me.

The light of the lanterns comes into view. Bellamy's fire dissipates in a haze of smoke. He quickly waves it away. Xanthe stands on the opposite side of Bellamy, both gesturing some hand signal. They must have used them quite often in battle. Sora and I stare at each other with confusion.

Bellamy steps out first, then Xanthe, each with their swords to their chest. I stand behind Sora, who straightens his stance. Swords clash, and bodies fall. I jump at the sudden silence. Sora grabs my wrist in an attempt to silence me.

Xanthe peeks around the corner. "It's clear. Come on."

We follow Xanthe down a hall of empty cells, mostly ridden with rats, bones, and dust. The origin of the bones is unknown, but I'd rather not know. The musty smell thickens in the air.

Bellamy stands at the end of the hall, staring at a cell. His eyes never leave it.

"Bellamy, are you okay?" I say.

His eyes lock onto the cell before him.

I turn in the direction he faces. My breath catches in my throat.

She's alive. Barely, but alive. She crouches in the corner, dressed in rags of filth. Her long hair streams over her face, uncombed for years, and an unbearable stench.

"Is that her?" Sora asks.

Bellamy nods, unable to take his eyes off her. Jealousy builds in me. I have to pinch myself to rid my thoughts of such things.

"How can we get her out without alerting the guards?" I ask.

Bellamy takes the metal bar tightly in his hand. It begins to glow with rising heat. His strength and magic break the bar in one snap. He repeats the process with the others.

"Astrid," I say. I walk to her slowly, careful not to alarm her. I kneel before her.

"I am Morana. Your sister."

She looks up at me. Her face is encompassed with dirt, but her beauty lies beneath—her eyes, dark like mine and Sora's. I reach my hand out to her. She continues to stare at me as if my hand isn't right in front of her.

"We are here to take you home."

"Home," her voice cracks. I wince, fearing it was too loud.

"Yes, home. To Davina and Lazarus. Your parents. Our parents."

She focuses her view on her shackled ankles. Her skin is red, swollen, and possibly infected. They probably give her just enough medicine to fight the infection, just long enough to keep her alive. Claw marks line her skin. Who knows how long she's been shackled to the wall?

"Can you break these off, Bellamy?" I ask.

He comes forward and kneels. Astrid retracts her legs to her body. She's scared. She has every right to be. We are strangers to her.

"It's okay. This is Bellamy. He is our friend. He is a friend of Davina and Lazarus."

"Astrid, don't you remember me?" Bellamy asks. "When we were children, we would play together."

He had never told me of their history. Although they were children, that jealousy steeps in the bottom of my stomach. I wonder when this feeling will ever leave me or if it just comes with being a daemon.

She's hesitant and doesn't make direct eye contact with any of us. The chains rattle as she holds them out for Bellamy. He gently grabs the chains and closes his eyes, focusing on the power within him.

The chains glow. It does nothing to harm Astrid. She sits with a blank stare.

"I can't. If I go any hotter, I may burn her." He drops his hands to his knees. "You could try, you know."

I look at him, eyes wide. "I'll burn her. Just like you were scared to do."

"You melted the lock on the library door. Besides, those who wield horns may have a different magic than those of us with wings. Just try."

He takes my hands and places them on Astrid's chains. Her face remains dark and soulless. It leaves an unsettling feeling in my stomach, like they have stripped her of all her humanity.

"If something goes wrong, I am blaming you." I snarl.

I grip the warm chains. I breathe in and out, grounding myself and reminding myself of who I am and who I will not be. I will not be what weakens me.

I let in that anger that fueled me before, but only slightly, a trickle at a time, like a raindrop. I can't imagine what my magic could do if unleashed full force with no one to stop me. The people I could potentially hurt. I could not live with myself.

The chains glow, and the fire grows hotter. Astrid is still. I keep my breathing controlled. Steadily, I can feel the metal melting in my hands. I hold my focus on the chains, the emotions I'm feeling. The one thing that angers me the most. King Alaric and that one feeling of wrapping my burning hands around his throat.

"Keep going, Morana." Bellamy whispers.

I push that last ounce of anger out of me, slowly controlling how it flows. And once that one drop leaves me, I take my hands away from the melted chain.

"Free." Astrid mumbles.

"Yes, you're free now. But we must get you to safety." I help her up. Her balance is off. Her legs are small, and her body is malnourished from years of neglect. Her bones could snap so easily with one fall. We have to do this right.

"That was entirely too easy," Sora says. "We need to go now." He tightens his grip on the sword.

Rumbling sounds down the tunnel. We stop, listening to the sound.

"Should we alert the King?"

"No, he will have our heads for this. Besides, he is otherwise occupied with his wife. No one disturbs him. We handle this ourselves."

"We are dead either way."

Guards come down the hallway. I don't know how they were alerted to our presence.

"Let's go."

As we head for the tunnel, the guards see us around the corner.

"Stop them. They have the girl." The guard shouts.

The floor rumbles, and the rocks bounce near our feet. The walls begin to cave in. The dust of it swarms our faces. A hand grabs mine, unsure of who pulls me.

Elementals ravage the tunnel, breaking the earth around us, attempting to trap us here. But I refuse to die here. Not in this realm.

I see the end. Moonlight gleams at the end of the tunnel. We are almost there. The light of Bellamy's hands lights the way. The dirt around us blurs everyone's faces. I don't know who has Astrid.

We make it outside in one piece. Nesrin waits for us with the bats ready to take to the skies.

"He only lasted two minutes. Come on," Nesrin shouts.

I mount Nox, and he wails so loud that the entire kingdom of Rhemus hears him.

Sora lifts off the ground, Nesrin and Xanthe on her bat. I skim for Bellamy in the sky. His wings out further than before. He has Astrid in his arms. He struggles to stay in the air with her weight in his arms.

Fiery arrows fly past us.

"Get back to Tenebris," Bellamy yells. "We meet at the castle. Whatever you do, stay alive."

I steer Nox to avoid the fiery arrows. Bombs explode in the sky, steering us off track. I shield my face from the debris. I've lost track of everyone.

More guards have exited the castle now, all of them shooting their arrows and magic at us, all in an attempt to not stop us but kill us. My horns burn, the pain blurring my vision. Smoke swirls in the sky, and my lungs burn because of it.

I hear Nesrin cry out in the distance, but I can't see her. I hope Nox can see through the smoke and escape this mess. An arrow pierces Nox, but not enough to kill him. He's losing his strength quickly. We have to keep going.

"Sora, Bellamy!" I call out. No response. I've lost them completely. I should go back, find them and ensure they are okay, but Bellamy made strict orders to go directly to Tenebris. I'd be walking into a death trap if I turned around.

The smoke is dissipating. We are coming closer to Tenebrisean territory. Still no sign of the others. Hopefully, they made it across. It's better to hide themselves and their wings than an enormous bat in the sky.

I see the trees that divide the two kingdoms. Almost there.

An arrow flies past me, and another one follows, but the second one pierces my shoulder. I cry out in pain. Tears form in my eyes, the pain unbearable. My head spins. I grip Nox's fur tighter to steady myself, the arrow still embedded into my shoulder. I have to get out of here.

My vision blurs. My head becomes heavy, and I can no longer keep myself up. Losing control of my body, I fall off Nox.

A glowing light appears below. Gold. This is it; I am dead. That's the light of the Inferno. I'm done for. Nobody will know what happened. It will only be a memory.

CHAPTER TWENTY- THREE

I never imagined the Inferno would be so furry. Warm, no doubt, but never a comfortable warm. Nothing burns but the horns on my head. My body sways back and forth, side to side, consistently. Maybe a boat in a lake of sulfur. Traveling to my impending doom.

No. My vision becomes more apparent. This is not the Inferno. It's dark, and moonlight glimmers from above. Trees pass in black silhouettes. Nothing much clearer than that other than a very warm body sitting directly behind me.

"Who's there?" I mumble. The body stirs behind me, gently grasping my arm. I'm too weak to fight back. Too scared to look at my kidnapper.

"Don't worry, princess. I'm taking you to the castle."

"Who…Who are you?" I stutter.

I lift my head and notice a horse's head bobbing up and down. Too dark to see its natural color. It walks at a steady pace on a dark trail.

I notice the glimmering jewels on the saddle. Obsidian like the ones at the Castle. He must be a citizen of Tenebris.

"Malik, your majesty. Try not to talk too much. You are badly injured."

I reach for my shoulder. The arrow is gone. Blood stains my shirt and hands.

"I retracted the arrow. Luckily it didn't pierce all the way through."

"Where is Nox?" I ask breathily.

"Nox? I found you alone, princess. No one was with you."

I twist my neck to him, and pain shoots through it and my shoulder. I grasp onto it, trying to breathe through the pain.

"Don't move too much. We will be at the castle shortly."

∞

We meet the guards at the front gates of the castle.

"I found Princess Morana at the border, injured and alone," Malik speaks.

The guards hurry to open the doors, red eyes glowing and alert.

Malik puts my uninjured arm around his back, but even that small movement makes my body ache. I don't realize how badly my legs hurt until I start walking. Each step sends a dull ache through them.

I look at the ground. My dress is dirty and bloody. Pieces of wood stick out from it. Boots covered in dirt and a mystery liquid.

"Morana. Oh, my gods." Davina comes running to me, Lazarus by her side. Each of them holding me up. Malik steps back.

Sora, Bellamy and Nesrin run to me.

"What happened to you?" Davina pushes my hair from my face. She looks at my horns, and her face remains full of worry.

"Malik, how did you find her?" Lazarus asks.

"Your majesties, I was patrolling the border and found her body lying on the ground inside the trees. She was on our land."

Sora runs to me. "I thought you were caught." He hugs me. It hurts, but I don't push him off.

"Where is Nox? Where is Astrid?"

"Let's worry about you." Davina steers me in the opposite direction of the others.

I stop.

"We saw you fall. There's no way you could have survived that fall, even being a daemon." Bellamy looks down at my wounded shoulder. "I'm so sorry I wasn't there for you."

I'm not in the mood for apologies. Everyone came out alive, even if I was on the brink of death.

"Nox is okay." Nesrin cuts in. "I found him at the border. He's back with the others. His wounds are being tended to."

I nod.

"I want to see Astrid." I plead.

I grab onto Davina's hand to steady myself. "Dear, you are in no condition. Neither is she. Astrid is resting. You must too. But dear."

She looks up at my head like before. "There is something you must know."

"What?"

"Your horn, one is broken. Half of it is gone."

I reach up to my head. Rough ivory pokes at my fingers. My stomach drops. I reach for the other one. It is completely untouched.

"It will grow back in time." She says. "Just need to take it easy for a while. "

I step away from Davina and the others.

"This happens, and I don't even get a simple apology? None of us do?"

Davina's eyes widen with fear.

"We risked our lives to save Astrid. And we can't even get a simple thank you. It's almost like you wanted us to do this very thing you kept us from doing." I reach for my horn one last time.

"I break a part of me. Destroy myself and fall to my death, yet you don't say thank you. We did something you were too scared to do."

"I didn't want you to risk your lives," Davina says. Her voice shakes.

"But you did. You just may not have said it. Admit it, Davina. You are glad we went to Rhemus under direct orders not to interfere. We infiltrated the castle and brought back the daughter you have always wanted. I broke a horn to save her. And you can't say thank you."

The room settles in silence.

"Morana, it's not that serious." Sora cuts in.

"So, you just expect to risk your life with no thanks? No appreciation? Pathetic."

My hands begin to burn, and I gladly welcome it. Their eyes linger on my hands.

"I was starting to accept this life, you know? These horns. And then I break it in half, making me look more broken on the outside than the inside."

"Morana, what is it that you want?" Davina asks.

"I want you to admit to your faults. Had you watched Astrid at the border, you might have had the life you are fighting so hard for now. And King Alaric wouldn't be threatening to kingdom."

I storm off before anything else can be said before I light this place on fire. I hate her. I hate how she makes me feel. I loathe her in every way. Mother? No. Tormenter.

CHAPTER TWENTY- FOUR

I am a broken woman. I am no princess. I am a vigilante forced to live a cursed life. I've broken the rules and will continue to do so if it means peace for an innocent kingdom.

Davina and Lazarus offered me the crown without a second thought, unaware of my true intentions. The villain is considered King Alaric, but all signs are pointed at me. Am I the villain for keeping such hidden motives, or those who hid their entire life from me, Sora, and Astrid?

Ever since becoming a daemon, I've felt a lingering burn in my veins—one that isn't painful enough to hurt me but enough to make me notice. At first, it was vexing; now, it is only a comfortable tingle like I've become one with it. Accepting it would mean I've accepted my fate, and I don't think I am ready for that yet.

I look at myself in the mirror. The horn is broken, and the other half is nowhere to be found. Somewhere along the border of the two realms. No way for it to be mended together. A part of me is lost once again. My soul is next. And when it happens, I want no trace of myself on this earth. I want every piece of me buried in the next life and the next, never to be known to another soul.

I travel inconspicuously through the dark hallways in search of Astrid's room. I want to see her and talk to her, if at all possible, in her state. See what other information I can pry from her. From all the years of abuse and neglect by King Alaric and his followers. I prepare myself for the worst.

Her door stands ajar. Either left open for her, or someone visits her as well. At this point, I don't care. I am here for her and no one else.

My suspicions are correct. Bellamy sits by her bed, head down and arms propped on his knees. He slouches over like he's been there for a while.

He snaps his head at me as I enter the room. He stands up and lightly bows his head, acknowledging my presence.

"Morana. Glad to see you out and about."

I keep my eyes on Astrid. She sleeps peacefully. Still, there is no color on her face. She lacks nutrients, but I'm sure she's being cared for now. Her hair, dull brown and purple hues under her eyes from lack of sleep. I can't help but feel bad for her.

"I hope you have rested well. We have all been worried about you."

I come to the other side of the bed, now facing Bellamy.

"Has she woken up at all?" I ask.

Bellamy crosses his arms. "Here and there. Only enough for her to eat, and then she falls back to sleep. She's finally catching up on all the sleep she missed."

Her bony fingers cross over her body like a corpse. She's clean, though. They had to scrub years of grime off her skin and from under her nails.

"How long have you been in here?"

Bellamy shifts from one foot to another. "Not long. I come whenever I can. I try to come often to see how she is. I've only spoken to her once." He shakes his head. "Something is off."

"What do you mean?" I pull up a chair next to her.

"She doesn't talk in full sentences. It's usually one word at a time. Either repeating what someone says or something completely wrong. None of it makes sense."

I caress her bony fingers. "Do you think King Alaric did something to alter her mind?"

He shrugs his shoulders. "It could be anything from years of abandonment, and magic, to pure torture. It's difficult to tell. Davina wants to take her to the Blood Reader to see if any magic was performed on her. It wouldn't be worth it, though. We already know something is wrong. We might as well see what we can do for her."

I stare at her closed eyes. Long eyelashes, pale skin. She isn't much older than I am. Even in this state, she is beautiful—so many secrets hidden in her mind. We have to unravel those secrets if it's even possible.

"How does it feel?" He asks, pointing to the dismembered horn.

"The pain is fading. Just wish it would grow back already."

"It will soon. I'm so sorry, Morana."

Our eyes meet. My stomach drops. I remember my conversation with Nesrin before we rode the bats. She sensed I felt something for him, and she saw something in him as well. I put off telling him. I don't know how much longer I can, though. He makes my stomach flutter each time I look at him now.

"It wasn't your fault. I'm just glad we got her back here safely."

We both stare at her in silence. My lips move as if they want to spill secrets. Not here. Not right now. Not over my comatose sister.

I have so many questions for her. Aside from what they did to her, I'd leave that for last. I want to know about her—things she likes and dislikes. But seeing as she was kept for many years in captivity, she may know none of that. Everything was stripped from her. Her childhood, her teen years. She never had her first kiss. She never got to experience riding the bats as I have. I know she needs to heal. I wish she'd wake up to talk and share things as sisters. Maybe I wouldn't feel so lonely.

Nesrin was hesitant to come back to the castle. She feared Davina and Lazarus wouldn't be so happy with her, given her part in the plan to rescue Astrid. Davina was the first one to mention her name during dinner.

I was ready to hear the motherly scolding. I planned for her too. She never said a word to any of us after I had made it back to the castle.

"So, tell me the details. How does it work?"

Nesrin pours her tea before sitting in the chair adjacent to me. The silver spoon clanks against the teacup before she rests it on the plate.

"You want to hear of the king's two-minute session in the sheets? There's little to no details." She laughs.

I cross my arms and smile at her. Waiting for her to spill it.

"I'm telling you, Morana. There are no steamy details. It was quite disgusting. I could have killed him. But, instead, I left my mark on him. Or in him, to be exact. Inside his subconscious. Anytime he decides to do anything with his wife, he won't be able to stop thinking about me."

I laugh so loud I startle her, but she joins in the laughter.

This is what I needed. Laughter. The anger boiling in me has been trying to surface for so long. It's like a magma pool about to burst from the earth's surface. These days though, I try to keep my days quiet and have little to no conversations with Davina and Lazarus.

"Play on," I say to the string quartet.

They begin playing their ethereal songs. The music rings in my ears like a symphony of faeries. Much like the ones Raisel was. The music makes me miss her more.

Nesrin pulls me upward, I take her by the waist, and we join hands. Our dresses flowing against each other, swishing with each sway and step. The glow of her eyes meets mine, an instant connection.

"I never thought I'd be dancing with a princess." She laughs.

"I never thought I'd be dancing with a succubus."

We smile and continue to dance to the music around us without a care in the world. Not caring who sees. At this moment, it's Nesrin and me together in our own reality.

"I don't mean to intrude on your sad excuse for a party." Bellamy coughs from the corner.

We jump, but our fingers are still locked together.

"We have matters to attend to."

I drop my hands and release Nesrin. "What could possibly be so important that calls you to interrupt us?" I feel it. The burning. It makes me angrier just thinking about it.

Breathe. Just breathe.

"It seems your birthday is in three days' time." Preparations must be made." He halts.

"You didn't tell me it was your birthday soon." Nesrin nudges me.

I pick at my dress, looking for invisible pieces of dust—anything to distract me from the thought of my birthday. I try to steer my mind from the many years of lonely birthdays. Back then, it was just a typical day, full of uncertainty about when I'd eat again or even bathe myself. The thought of my birthday has become a messy topic. A subject I'd rather not celebrate.

"I didn't realize how close it was. I forgot." I mutter.

"You forgot your own birthday?" Nesrin asks.

I take a deep breath in. "No. I wanted to keep it a secret."

Bellamy takes a seat at the table and pours himself a cup of tea using my cup. He winks at me devilishly. I smirk at him in return. He comes in to stir things and then uses my cup. Bastard.

"The entire kingdom is preparing for your birthday. Well, Sora's, too, since you know you both share a birthday. How wonderful. Your first birthday together as brother and sister."

A pit in my stomach opens. I wish I could muster up enough power to throw a fireball at his face.

Clicking echoes behind us. We turn to see Astrid looking much better than she did days before. There is more color to her face, her cheeks rosy, and the light glimmers in her onyx eyes.

My breath catches in my throat. I've barely said a few words to her. Will she be willing to talk to me? Given what she's been through, I'm unsure of what to say to her.

"Glad to see you up, Astrid," I say.

Her dark eyes shift from Bellamy to me, Nesrin, and back to me.

"Sister."

I take a step towards her. "How are you feeling?" I ask.

She looks at Bellamy, and he nods. I find it odd that she would look to him for confirmation. I brush it off.

"Better."

I thought the one-word sentences were the effects of a sort of magic. A spell that can easily manipulate the mind or prevent someone from speaking, or even worse, speaking of the terrible things done to them. This is most likely what we are dealing with. She's unable to tell us what happened to her. She's stuck in her own mind. Like a prisoner confined to only the awful things, she lived through.

Bellamy helps her to the iron chair. She sits with her hands in her lap and back straight. Like a perfect princess. Or Queen.

I turn to Bellamy. "You two have gotten close," I say, keeping my tone neutral.

"Well, I didn't think you would be up to the job of taking care of her. So, I decided to do so."

"No one asked me." I cross my arms. Furious with his words. "She has parents, you know? They wanted her back, so why don't they care for her?"

Bellamy shrugs.

The pit in my stomach opens again, but this time, not from anger but jealousy. I missed the opportunity to tell him how I feel about him. I can't help but think I may have missed it for good. He's becoming awfully close to Astrid.

Why am I like this? It's all my fault. I could have told him. I could have spilled my heart before we left for Rhemus. I can't be sure he feels the same, though. He's been a gentleman from the start. He's said so many things to make my heart melt. I initially rejected him, and now, I feel like I've missed him. He was just within fingertip reach, floating off in the distance to another woman's heart.

I can't jump to conclusions.

"Sora didn't feel comfortable with it. Besides, he's been seeing Xanthe more. Like a lot. Wherever Xanthe is stationed, he's there. They've become close. You were getting close to Nesrin, so I volunteered."

"What Sora and Xanthe have going on is none of my business. Whether it be a simple friendship or more, I don't care."

"Whoa, your majesty," Bellamy chuckles. "I'm sensing some jealousy."

He speaks as if it taunts me. In his eyes, I see it, that glimmer of wickedness. He knows what he's doing to me. I can't let it bother me. He will win if I do. He will taunt me till I impale my ears with a dagger.

CHAPTER TWENTY- FIVE

This day, twenty-one years ago, I came into this world not knowing my own fate. Not knowing I would have no control over it. Events that were out of my control occurred and led me to this very moment. I'm celebrating with new people in a new kingdom. A new life as a daemon of the night realm.

It took days for Greer to choose a dress for me to wear to the celebration. Each seamstress in the City of Drafanel presented their works. All turned down by Greer. Nothing was perfect enough for her, that is, until a lone forest witch came to the castle, uninvited, with a dress in hand like no other had seen.

Greer holds the dress open for me to step into. The corset she laced earlier squeezes a bit too tight, but she says it's all for my birthday. I must be presentable and represent the kingdom of Tenebris.

Finally, something other than black. I grow tired of the dreary colors every day. The halls are dim and dark, the castle decorations are dark, and everything about this kingdom is dark. Hence the very name of it.

She lifts the moss-colored dress over my shoulders. The lace bodice tightens around my body as she weaves the ribbon through.

I observe myself in the mirror as Greer does the finishing touches on me. My horn has almost fully grown back, it doesn't look so hideous anymore, but still, the end of it is jagged enough to impale someone.

Greer lifts the shoes to my feet. She acquired the ones I had asked for. Unfortunately, the heels killed my feet, and they burned at the end of the day. I had to soak them in hot water to soothe them. Now, I wear flat slippers. Much more comfortable.

Greer helps me into the carriage. I requested to be alone on the journey to the City of Drafanel. I want to enjoy the last moments of peace before being bombarded with city folk, music, and many people, including Bellamy.

I arrive at the city gates. Guards stand by with weapons in hand.

I expected Bellamy to be the one to greet me at the gates, but he is nowhere to be found. I shake the thought from my head and continue on.

I set my eyes on Sora and Xanthe standing with Davina and Lazarus. All of them are beautifully dressed in spring colors. Sora and I match our moss green attire. We must dress alike on birthdays to signify our sibling bond.

"You look lovely, Morana." Davina twirls me. Lazarus smiles in the background.

Sora and Xanthe stand shoulder to shoulder, whispering to each other. Their faces are close to touching. I smile, and they return the gesture.

"Where is Bellamy?" I ask.

Davina fixes my hair. "He just arrived. Astrid is with him."

I turn to them behind me. Bellamy holds out his hand to Astrid. She looks around, weary of her surroundings. This place is foreign to her. It's her home, but she will soon find it to be one. She quickly let's go as her feet meet the ground.

I avoid eye contact with Bellamy. "How are you, Astrid? So glad you came."

She looks at me, but not directly. Her eyes linger on my horns. She fixates on them, her eyes moving and observing them like she's never seen them. She's been so deprived of Tenebris' beauty. Everything scares her or fascinates her.

"Horns." She says. "I have those too."

She's never said more than one word. Even Bellamy flinches at her words.

"Astrid, you don't have horns," Bellamy says.

"Yes. I do."

I shrug and continue on. I'm not going to argue with her on what attributes she has and those she doesn't. At least not until I can have a real conversation with her. Her delirium still lurks.

"Happy birthday, Morana. You look lovely." Bellamy pokes my shoulder.

I turned to him. Eyes narrowed on him. "Thanks."

"You've barely said a word to me. Is everything okay?"

I stop at the entrance and spin on my heel. "I am fine."

I continue on before he can say another word to me. I lock arms with Sora and walk through the city's gates. I berate myself for being so cold with him. I didn't even think about it till now.

We are met with the entire city and more, full of fire-lit lanterns of every color, glowing insects buzzing around us, creating a sparkle effect. The music plays in the background. Violins and stringed instruments play upbeat music. People are already dancing and waving to us as we enter the city. Our city.

"Announcing Prince Sora and Princess Morana of Tenebris. Let us toast to the twin siblings."

People raise their goblets in the air. "Long live Prince Sora. Long live Princess Morana."

The announcer hands Sora and me a gold goblet adorned in red jewels- a color of the night realm. Looking at the goblet closer, there are carvings of basilisks and its filled with the delicious aroma of elderberry wine.

We raise the goblets in the air to honor the city's people. Everyone drinks and remains quiet for a moment as they devour the wine. All eyes are on us. I take a sip of the wine and hold back a cough. Definitely strong enough. I'll only need one drink for the entire night.

Davina steps forward. "I would like to say a few words before continuing the festivities."

Sora and I look to each other, worried about what she may say or lie about this time. I had suspicions she would make a speech. I never got the chance to talk to her beforehand. To make sure she didn't.

"Spring is upon us. On this day twenty-one years ago, twins were born on the Day of the Corpse. Our eternal flower is a symbol of our kingdom. We celebrate it's blooming this spring, along with the birthdays of my lovely children."

She takes a sip of the wine and smiles at us. This time. I sense it's a genuine smile. I return the gesture.

"The corpse flower blooms once a year. Living on the top of the mountain, away from harm, we acknowledge the magic it gives our kingdom. No matter how putrid its smell is, we celebrate its eternal bloom. We celebrate Tenebris. We will overcome all that is thrown our way. "

The crowd cheers and returns to dancing and conversing. Kids laugh all around. A wyvern flies over the city, blowing fire into the air joyfully.

Davina turns to us.

"I wasn't going to embarrass you if that's what you thought I would do." She laughs.

"Where's this flower you speak of?" Sora asks. "Is the smell actually that bad? I found information on it in the library once but never looked deeper into it."

"It's terrible." Lazarus interrupts. "Like that of a rotting corpse. Hence its very name."

Sora and Xanthe leave their arms locked like love-struck teenagers. I can tell Sora is happier with Xanthe around. Even though I haven't known Sora for so long, I am glad to see him happy. I want happiness for them both.

"Happy birthday," Nesrin shouts from behind.

We embrace, and she takes me by my hand and pulls me along the path, guiding me through groups of people. With each glance, they quickly bow their heads as I pass.

She twirls me, and we begin to sway with the music. At the moment, nothing matters to me. My worries fly away. I feel lighter, and my spirit is lifted, until I notice how many guards stand by.

After the ambush at the castle, more guards have been ordered at more posts around the city, villages and the castle. It makes everyone stand on edge. As if we are waiting for a war to happen.

There's been no word from King Alaric. We all feared he would retaliate and start a war against Tenebris. It's been days now, and it's been quiet at the border. Something in me fears that something is brewing across the border. Something Tenebris has been preparing for many years now. I know this war is not over.

I quickly dismiss the thought. I can't let the thought of King Alaric bother me on my birthday. Even as his face enters my mind, my stomach burns with anger.

The moonlight peaks at the top of the mountain. I can't see it from here, but the corpse flower blooms tonight.

"Have you seen it before? The flower?" I ask.

Nesrin slows her steps, and we dance, swaying side to side. "Only once. It's true what they say. It smells like a rotting corpse. That's why no one goes up there."

We dance, switching partners every so often to the beat of the music. Laughter surrounds us. and

Nothing can make this moment better than it
already is.

CHAPTER TWENTY- SIX

"May I have a dance with the princess?"

I jump at Bellamy's touch on my shoulder. I can't help but focus on his attire. He stands out amongst the vibrant colors, his black tunic portrays him. I won't admit it to him yet, but he looks stunning. Still, his eyes mesmerize me. The black abyss hypnotizes me and reels me closer to his soul.

"Morana?"

I snap back to reality, and the muffled sounds return to clear.

Without a word, I take him by the hand, and he leads me to an empty space in the crowd. His grip on my hand tightens as we move into position. His hand wraps around my waist. A small gasp escapes me. He smirks as I turn my gaze from him.

One step after the other, I follow his lead, and we dance. One foot after the other. I don't know this dance, but the way he moves me makes me feel like I've done this hundreds of times.

"Are you enjoying your birthday?" Bellamy asks.

"I'd rather spend it with my brother, but he is otherwise occupied."

Bellamy lets out a quiet laugh, and his grip becomes tighter around my waist. My breath catches for a moment. He notices. My cheeks burn.

"He and Xanthe have become rather close. I like it. Maybe once I return to Kiveha, he could accompany me. I think he would enjoy it."

I give him a nasty glare, and I feel my hands burning. The sensation slowly fades after a few breaths.

"You are going back? And you want to take my brother."

I roll my eyes. He takes pleasure in it. He white teeth showing through his lips.

"Of course, you are welcome to see your brother anytime."

He pulls me to him with the sway of the song. People laugh around us, drowning out the conversation at hand.

"One day, I must leave. Kiveha is my home. I am the future king of Kiveha. I cannot disappoint my people."

As much as he is right, I don't want it to be true. The thought of him leaving saddens me. The castle will never be the same without him. I fear the castle and Tenebris itself will lose a spark—a spark that fuels this kingdom.

Just come out and say it already. Dammit, Morana. I will never get another chance.

"Hopefully, you will find a woman worthy enough to have your heart and hold the crown, I hope." I sigh.

I wish I had never said it, and now I can't take it back.

Bellamy chuckles, "And perhaps that may never happen. Being King brings on new responsibilities and burdens. Many things that are out of my grasp."

I turn my head. "How so?"

Bellamy shakes his head. "It's nothing, Morana."

I loosen my grip on his hands, but his stays the same. I shouldn't be prodding at this. I should be enjoying myself. But the curiosity in me sparks.

"It's not nothing," I say. "But if I am to become queen one day, I want to know what to prepare myself for."

His eyes stray away from me. I silently beg for him to come back to me. I crave his gaze.

"Morana, this is your birthday. Why trouble yourself with such things? Let's enjoy the music."

He sways me from side to side. The voice inside me is begging to be let out.

"I am enjoying this. I just want to know more about the duties of being a queen. I need to know what I must do for my people. To protect them from people like King Alaric and those that threaten them."

Bellamy's eyes become serious. He swallows.

"If your kingdom depended on it, would you marry another to unite forces? To unite them as one and make one powerful nation?"

My muscles tense. What kind of question is this?

"I'd do anything for my kingdom. But I'd prefer to marry for love and not for politics. My parents — Orna and Kai, loved each other so much. I can't imagine doing something like that."

His shoulder slumps forward. "It's never so simple, Morana."

We both sigh in unison. Our eyes drifting away from each other. I've never felt so much pull as I do now.

"Can we focus on the music?" He mumbles.

My eyes meet his again. But this time, I know he's looking at me before I notice.

"Bellamy, why would you ask that?"

He pulls me closer to him. Our chests touch. A flame burns through my hands, and I fear he may feel it too.

"My life was set for me by my parents. Being in charge of a kingdom starts when you are born. In this case, you are just learning what your duties are. There will always be things that are out of your control."

I hear it—the snap of realization. Arranged marriages are rarely done anymore, but it serves a purpose to some. Few villages in Rhemus partake in this anymore, but they do it to share wealth and other things. It's something I could never see myself doing. After everything that has happened, how could I let anyone decide who I marry?

No. It can't be.

Davina laughs from the side lines. She's with Astrid and Lazarus. Astrid eyes Bellamy and me.

All the time he's spent with Astrid. He was there to make sure she was alive and well. Stood by her bedside, caring for her. Walking her around the castle.

"Bellamy. Do not lie to me."

There is a shift in the night air. Cooler than spring should be.

"Are you engaged to my sister?"

His throat tightens. "Morana."

As much as I love hearing my name come from his lips, all I want to do is slap him for it.

He looks around, but I keep my eyes on him. Tears are waiting to spill. I want him to say it.

I let go of him, slowly backing away. His arms fall to his sides, realizing that this is the beginning of the end.

"Why didn't you tell me?" my voice cracks.

I peer at the people around me. They are oblivious to this encounter. I want to keep it that way.

I thought I could trust you." I say. "All the time we spent together. It was all a lie."

He holds out his hand to stop me from leaving. "That's not true, Morana. Those were the truest times. Everything I said to you, I meant."

He reaches for my hand. I turn and run out of the crowd. Tears stream down my face. I'm hardly able to navigate with water in my eyes.

I search for Nesrin. She's invisible in the crowd. Davina and Lazarus are otherwise distracted with the city folk and dance their own dance. They haven't a clue what is going on. I see Sora and Xanthe. They, too, are occupied dancing with each other.

I find Nesrin's bookshop down the way. Fewer people crowd this area, but some still linger. They bow their heads as I pass them. I do not return the gesture.

As soon as I open the bookshop doors, I fall to the ground, collapsing on my knees. The pain in my stomach makes no gentle entry. It consumes me and causes my muscles to burn. I let the fire consume every piece of me. Ripping me from the inside.

Bellamy barges in the doors behind me.

"Morana, please let me explain."

"Why didn't you tell me? Why didn't you tell me sooner? If you had told me from the beginning, maybe I wouldn't have fallen in love with you."

He reaches down and touches my shoulder. His touch sends fire through my spine.

"Don't touch me."

He takes a step back.

"The contract is bound by blood. It was made before Astrid wandered over the border." He sighs. I can hear the tremble in his voice.

He comes around to face me. He kneels. Darkness fills his eyes.

"This is what being a royal is. You make sacrifices for your kingdom."

"You were a child," I scream. My throat burns. "An innocent child. Any good parent would never bestow such a curse on their own child. It's wrong. It's dehumanizing."

I turn my face away from him and hide my hands, ashamed of how out of control I'm becoming. My horns burn with rage and sizzle on my skin like my blood is boiling. I wish it would just grow back already.

"I believed Astrid was dead. I wanted her to be dead so badly that I was willing to bribe a witch to cast a spell to kill her. To end the blood contract. But I learned that I cannot cause harm to the other.”

“I wish she was dead too.”

Bellamy's eyes turn cold. “You don't mean that.”

Of course, I don't mean that. But the hatred in me is telling me I do.

“I don't want to marry her. I've *never* wanted to marry her.” He breathes. “You don’t know the pain I’ve endured, knowing I could never have your hand in marriage. Or feel your lips against mine. It was hard to resist it when I found you in the library, crying and begging for things to be different.”

I cry into my knees, leaving no sob unheard. I want him to see the pain he gives me. I want him to feel it. I want him consumed by it. My mind leaves no room for logical thoughts. I want him ruined.

“I will never forgive you.” I cry. “All I wanted was you. I was foolish to let love blind me. Such a stupid thing to do.”

He stiffens. Face turned away from me. Guilty of the pain he's caused. I see a tear fall onto his cheek. And he quickly wipes it away as if it was never there.

“Morana. I do —.”

“Don't say it." I stutter.

Fury consumes me and devours my soul. I hesitate for a moment. I shouldn't do this. The inferno in me speaks as a scream, a ringing in my ears. A constant hum vibrates everything. This is what I have been waiting for. This is what terrifies me the most. Letting go.

Looking down at my feet. They are engulfed in flames. Orange-blue hues swirl together like a fiery storm. The warmth doesn't burn. I feel relief letting my all go into my own power, like I have needed this.

"Morana, don't. "

I let the fire take hold of me. Every inch of me.

I run out of the building with Bellamy trailing me. The citizens gasp and scream in fear. Their horrified faces cling to me. They are scared of what I've become. I am no princess. I am a villain. I am what people should fear.

"Morana, what the inferno is going on?" Sora and Xanthe run to me. Sora's eyes blink at Bellamy. He quickly strides over to Bellamy. "You bastard. What did you do to her?" Sora takes Bellamy by the collar. Bellamy falls to the ground as Sora's fist meets Bellamy's face. Blow after blow, and the crowd gasps in shock.

Davina and Lazarus follow the commotion. "Let's take this away from the city folk. Morana, dear, come with me."

Davina holds out her hand.

I no longer feel like myself. My body is foreign to me. Something else is controlling me. I can't fight it, not with whatever energy I have left in me. The sadness has turned to anger, and I have completely lost myself.

I whistle loudly, calling Nox forth. It takes a short moment before I hear his screeching in the sky. His enormous wings fill the spring sky. He finds me quickly. The crowd runs for cover as Nox lands in the heart of the city.

"Morana, where are you going?" Sora stops me. He pulls on my dress. He's unafraid of the destruction I've caused.

"We live in a kingdom of liars and manipulators. Guard your heart Sora. These people are deceivers."

CHAPTER TWENTY- SEVEN

I have destroyed myself merely from my actions made without thought beforehand. Carelessly, I have opened my mind and heart to people who have no care for mine. No empathy fills their hearts. No conscience occupies their mind.

I should have learned early on not to give in so easily. I should not have believed others' words so easily, so carelessly. I should have questioned everything. I regret what has happened to me. Taking the crown may have been my most reckless decision ever. Draven's death doesn't compare to this. No. It never will.

The fire has gone down, and the only evidence of my grief sits on my cheeks, reddened by the tears that now leave a dry trail. A headache forms where my horns grow out of my body. Everything is throbbing. Everything is maddening.

I left them. I even left my own brother. Who knows what he's done to Bellamy now? If Bellamy is smart, he'll let Sora have it out on him. I hope he does. He will heal quickly, but I hope every punch leaves a bruise on the soul.

Bellamy's face flashes in my mind. His guilt-stricken face. The tears. Oh, the tears. How could those tears be real? If only he had told me sooner. Told me his hand was bound to another of my own blood, but not my blood that flows through me.

It will never work. Tenebris and Kiveha's alliance will never work. I'm surprised it's been steady after all these years. Bellamy has come and gone, hoping Astrid would be back one day to fulfill the arrangement. After some time, though, I believed such a thing would never happen. So why did he bother to return to Tenebris when I show up in the kingdom?

I should have died on this cliff I now stand on. My brimstone blood prevented me from dying a permanent death. I would have been okay in The Inferno. In fact, I still welcome it with open arms. Damn this brimstone blood and this curse that follows me.

The waves crash against the cliffside. Beautiful in the springtime air. The scent of blooming nature fills the atmosphere. I take a breath in, filling my lungs with new air, hoping it will calm this ever-lingering hurt in my chest.

No. The hurt is still there. The anger is still inside me.

Why can't I control myself?

Everyone makes being a daemon seem so easy. Even Sora isn't struggling. At least he doesn't show it. Davina perhaps still has much to work on. Bellamy and Lazarus are calm most of the time. Lazarus more than Bellamy. I'm beginning to think these horns give different emotions than those with wings.

I tug on the horns hoping they will rip from my head. I pull and pull, and nothing changes. The damn Inferno curses me.

Damn it.

"Just come out already!"

I pull as hard as I can, tears streaming down my face. I lose grip, and my hands forcefully slide from the horns. My hands burn. I look down and notice the redness, but on my right hand, small bubbles of blood begin to peak from my skin.

Great. These damned things aren't smooth either.

The blood pools and drips onto the grass. I quickly wipe my hands on the dress that Greer carefully picked out. I will apologize to her later for the mess I made. If I ever return.

Below my feet, a familiar golden light forms. It grows, and just when I think there is no end to its growth, it suddenly stops. It's like the sun is only shining in one spot. Perfectly round. I can feel the energy radiating off of it.

Peculiar. It looks like the blinding light I fell into when we rescued Astrid. Makes no sense as to why It would come up now. I'm certainly in no danger. I'm entirely alone.

I dip my foot into it. A tingling sensation runs up my leg. It tickles almost. The most relaxing feeling I've felt in a while.

I play around with it. Kneeling down to it just to brush my fingertips along the edge. I sink my hand in. A pool of nothingness surrounds my hand. It doesn't feel like water, but it also doesn't feel like air. It is simply nothing.

Deeper and deeper, I push my hand into it. At this point, it's up to my elbow.

I feel the tingling of someone watching me as I glance behind. No one. Besides my hand sticking out of the golden portal, no one else is nearby.

At second glance, I almost think my eyes deceive me. Yes. My hand is sticking out of another golden portal a few feet away from me. I move my fingers. Yes. I'm sure that is my hand. I push further into the void. The hand in the other portal extends.

I pull my hand out completely. Kneeling on the edge of it, I dip one foot into it. That's my foot. I'm sure of it. Further and further, I go into the portal. I'm waist-deep now. And in a moment, I close my eyes and let the portal swallow me.

Grass surrounds me. Darkness. I open my eyes to see I've moved a few feet from where I was standing. No, my eyes are deceiving me. I have just been transported to another location. It wasn't far. But far enough for me to want to test it out more.

I first noticed the golden circle when I pulled the arrow from my shoulder. Blood spilled. My blood. Again, this time, my blood spills, creating the portal. Surely this means it must open by blood, and my blood only.

"Morana!"

I turn swiftly, holding my bloody hand.

Sora runs to me. I search around, waiting for more people to make themselves known. No. It is just him.

"What are you doing here?" he breathes. "We have been looking everywhere for you."

"Don't tell me the others are with you." I sigh.

"No. We split up. Out of all the places to go, you came here?"

I stand by the cliff, holding my bloodied hand. He notices it but doesn't say a word about it. I look down at it. It's starting to clot.

"I had to get away, Sora. This is… entirely too much." When the words come out, I notice the numbness in my voice. Nothing makes sense anymore.

"I know why you left." He steps toward me, resting his hand on my shoulder. "What he did was wrong."

"I don't know what I should be angry about. Him marrying Astrid, or him keeping the truth for me, leading me on?"

Sora turns me by my shoulders. My eyes meet his. The redness in his eyes shows his hurt for me.

"I'm going to tell you this once. You don't need him. I knew something was off about him the moment we met him. Whether he was a young boy or not, when the contract was made, he led you on. And have mercy on whoever breaks my sister's heart. He got what he deserved."

He takes me in an embrace. One that I needed for a long time.

"He may have a black eye in the morning. But he will be fine."

I force a smile at the idea of Sora beating Bellamy to a pulp. I hate it too. I didn't want that for anyone—no matter my feelings for Bellamy.

"Sora, I need to show you something. It might explain a lot. But promise me that this will stay between us two. I don't need Davina or Lazarus, let alone Bellamy saying anything negative about it."

He nods.

I use the tip of my fingernail and draw blood from the cut I made earlier. It stings, but only a little.

"What are you doing?"

I let the blood flow till there's enough to use— the red liquid pools on the tip of my finger. I hold out my hand above the grass. It slowly drips onto the grass.

The grass fades into sparkling gold. Sora's eyes widen at the sudden light. He takes a long step back, almost falling over, but quickly catches his balance.

"Morana, what did you do?" He stutters.

The golden circle grows a few inches more. Big enough for my body to fit through. I walk around it, thinking of where I want to go. Just a few feet from here should do.

I look at him once more without a word and jump through feet first. He lunges after me but misses me just as the portal closes.

"Morana? Where are you?" He fumbles his words.

"I'm over here." I wave.

He turns around. I'm closer to the tree line. He races to me.

"How did you —"

"This is how I returned to Tenebris so fast after rescuing Astrid. An arrow hit me, and once I pulled it from me, blood dripped, making the portal open. Isn't it…wicked?"

A smile creeps along my mouth but quickly disappears as Sora looks at me. His face is full of concern.

"So instead of wings, you can just transport yourself?"

"Seems like it," I observe the cut on my finger. "Just please, don't tell anyone yet. I want to be the one to do it."

"You have my word, Sister."

I have to find out what this means for me. Why have I been chosen to hold such a unique gift? If it even is a gift. I've yet to experience any repercussions in using it.

I walk to the edge of the cliff, Sora beside me. We sit on the edge, feet dangling off of it. Nothing is better than the spring breeze and gentle mist of the ocean. The ocean waves were once an omen of my death, but now I find it peaceful.

"Sora, I don't think I can go back to the castle."

He turns to me, but I keep my eyes on the distant dark horizon.

"What do you mean? The castle is our home now."

I breathe. "I cannot call that place home. Being a princess is not what I wanted. Being a demon is not what I wanted. Being here sometimes feels like a prison."

"And Rhemus feels like Paradise, I suppose?"

I shake my head. "Not at all. I just… want more than this. We are on the brink of war, and I can't help but feel like this may have been our fault. My fault."

His head remains down.

"It's not our fault. And definitely not your fault. If anyone is to blame, it's Davina and Lazarus. They got us into this mess."

I feel the tears watering my eyes. I breathe in to suppress it.

"Sora. I'm leaving. Tonight. I can't continue to stand by and watch Davina tear Tenebris from the inside out. I have to do something. Even if it means going back to Rhemus. Besides you, there is nothing for me here.

Sora snaps his head to me. "If this is about that bastard, Bellamy—"

"This is not about Bellamy. I must do this for the kingdom of Tenebris. I must save this place from any further harm."

I stand up to leave Sora behind. I glance into the dark horizon, gleaming with waves for miles. At this moment, I feel the same feeling I once did when I wanted to end my life. That's what I am doing now. Sacrificing myself to save Tenebris.

Sora trips as he attempts to stand. I bite my finger and let the blood drip onto the grass, and the golden portal opens up beneath my feet.

"Morana, please don't do this." He waits to make any moves. "What about Nesrin? "

The golden portal waits for me, glistening in the moonlight. It begs me to jump through.

"Tell her I love her." I glance at Sora. His eyes beat down at me. The horror in his eyes made me spin with chills. "Tell Xanthe you love him too. I know you do."

I jump through the portal. Sora lunges for me as my head is submerged in the veil of golden light. Its presence takes me where I once had a life.

PART TWO

CHAPTER TWENTY- EIGHT

I open my eyes to see the house I once called my home. Its spirit, once vibrant, is now heavy with demise. Empty of liveliness, full of a dark uneasiness.

The wood still chips around the edges of the door frame from the past storms. It always lets in the harshest of winter breezes. The windows are nothing more than an empty space. The flowers that once grew around the door bloom for this spring, being the only color left in this house of memories.

I step closer to the door. My brain hopes someone will be inside making dinner. Someone with a friendly face. I push the door ever so slightly. My fingertips graze the wood splintering from it. My stomach sinks.

The furniture is just as we left it. Just as I had left it. Dust accumulates around all the crevices and tops. The longer I look, the more chest pain hits me.

"It's empty."

I turn so fast that it seems the air escapes my lungs. I hold it for more seconds than I should.

Enver.

The elemental who I once called my friend. He stands before me not as an enemy but as another lost soul. I never thought I'd see him again. I watched them drag him away to his death. A death that was not set in stone as I had believed.

"I didn't mean to frighten you." He says.

I eye his sword. As if he needed it. The elements bow to his every will. Who knows how powerful he's gotten since training on the Hesai Islands? He could form waves as big as the ocean and then light an entire village on fire in one snap. I'll be sure to watch what comes from my mouth.

"I am not here as your enemy Morana. I'm here as an old friend. But I am warning you. If you get caught, I cannot help you."

I take a step towards him. He glances at my horns, but his face remains neutral. It doesn't seem to bother him. For once, I feel as if I am human again, and I am not defined by these horns that bare so much pain.

"I just wanted to see it one last time," I mutter.

He relaxes his shoulders. He settles his hands into his pockets.

"I'm turning myself into King Alaric." I turn to the disintegrating house.

He leans to the side to get a better look at the house. He smiles. He remembers those same memories that went through my head moments before he arrived.

His face drops as thoughts of him being taken away from his mother flash through his mind. I see the hurt. It's never truly gone away. It never will.

This house catches those memories and keeps them forever.

"I suppose I can't convince you to return to Tenebris?"

I look around for any peering eyes and unusual sounds.

"No."

Enver sighs. "Well, then, there is something you must know. I wasn't sure If I would ever be able to tell you."

I keep my eyes fixed on him.

"Draven's death was planned."

I catch my breath. I repeat the words in my head, ensuring I heard him correctly.

"How can that be? I pushed him over the edge in the act of self-defense."

He takes his eyes away from me and scans the village for any sign of lantern light. If we were to be caught by any townsfolk, this could end up messier than I had anticipated.

"King Alaric agreed to pay Draven to clear his wife of her crime. All so that King Alaric could send you to Tenebris before your twenty-first birthday. It was all a setup."

My stomach drops and begins to stir. I lean against the gate to the house. My head spins.

"That night at the tavern, he had to make you angry. He had to get you by yourself."

"How did he know I'd push him over the balcony?" I ask.

Enver shakes his head. "That's the thing. Draven didn't know. His task was to make sure that you killed him. All for his wife's name to be cleared."

He begged me to kill him. I can still hear his voice in my head. There had to be a reason for him to want to die.

"What did she do?"

Enver's lips press together, unsure if he's said too much already. He's already walking on hot coals here.

"She killed their firstborn."

I had been wondering when I would truly be pushed to the edge. This is it. This is the final moment I look back on my life and regret everything leading up to this moment. Every friend I had made, every smile that I gave. I regret all of it. My life was written in stone before I was born from Davina's womb. Even after being so kind to those who hurt me, they drove me to the top and left me to bear a life of darkness.

"So instead of her being sent to Tenebris, he thought it fitting to send me instead? I killed an innocent man who was just trying to protect his wife?"

I cross my arms.

King Alaric planned this. He saw an opportunity to get rid of me before I was to turn twenty-one, just right before the contract between Davina and him ended. Now I understand why Draven had begged me to kill him. He wanted to save his wife. As much as I hate him for doing what he did, I can't help myself from feeling sorry for him. Knowing that he would die to save his wife, it's heartbreaking.

I begin to walk away from Enver. I simply cannot take any more of this. Lies. And more lies.

I've been lied to again and again. I wonder, though, did Sora go through this same thing when he was younger? Why do I feel like everyone is targeting me? Why do I feel like a pawn in this royal game?

"Why are you here, Enver? Care to watch me turn myself into the King?"

He grabs my arm and pulls me to a stop. He quickly drops his hand as I eye him.

"I make nightly rounds around this part of the village. I always stop at your house to think of where you might be by now. That stunt you pulled by taking Astrid got the entire realm talking. The King is furious."

No one is happy. When does anyone have time for such a complex emotion? I find myself regretting the very thought of loving Sora and loving Bellamy.

"Come, I want to show you something." He ushers me to follow him.

I look at him, unsure if I should even trust him. The memories of our childhood come back to me. Yes, I can trust him. When he first saw me after all those years, he didn't attack. He didn't even question the horns on my head.

I follow him to the woods behind the village. Our feet rustle against the growing grass. I listen for anything that might be threatening in case he decides to take me to my death. I want to be ready.

The trail he follows is unfamiliar. I know this area like the back of my hand. I should have noticed this. Unfamiliar trees and bridges around every corner. Like this place magically appeared.

"Where are you taking me?" I follow behind.

"We are almost there." He glances behind to make sure I'm still following.

We round a grove of trees. Even in this dark light, I can see the trees beginning to regain spring green from the harsh winter before.

"I've never seen this place before," I say.

He opens the iron gates and lets me in.

"You wouldn't have until your eyes were ready to see. Until your heart was ready."

Gravestones. Most of them are tilted from years of nature doing what it does best. Others look new. They all vary in size. Each of them etched with a name, some familiar and some unknown to me.

He stands next to me. "The graveyard doesn't reveal itself until the person is ready to come to peace," he says.

"I don't feel like I'm ready," I whisper.

He nudges my arm to follow him. We stop at two gravestones that tilt side by side. There, Orna and Kai lay in their peaceful slumber underneath the mossy grass. My stomach drops.

Since they died, I never found their bodies, let alone know where they might be buried. I always told myself I didn't need to know. Seeing them dead would not change anything.

"Your heart and mind know better than you do."

He's right. I've denied it so much. I've denied all that I am. All who I was.

"When they took me to the Hesai Islands, I did everything to come back to you. And once the guards discovered my true intentions, they told me everything about you. Orna and Kai are not your parents, and you are a child of Tenebris. It seems everyone knew of your past, all except you."

I continue looking at the gravestones. It seems so unreal to lay eyes on.

"Did they tell you I have a twin brother?" I ask. "He came from the north village. His name is Sora."

Enver smiles. "Family is everything. I'd do anything to have my mother back."

I stop. I almost forgot that his mother passed not long after he was taken.

"I'm so sorry, Enver." I rest my hand on his shoulder. He doesn't wince. "Is she here?"

He nods his head. He points to the gravestone next to Kai's.

"When I was eighteen, I came back to the village. Something called me to walk into the woods. I stumbled upon this. I read every gravestone, thinking I'd never find my mother again. Now, I come here as much as I can."

I needed this. Seeing their names makes me feel a sense of peace that I haven't felt in a long time. I've felt so angry since transforming into a daemon. I thought that was my biggest regret. Maybe this needed to happen for me to see my parents again finally.

My head becomes light. Lighter than it had been the past few weeks.

"Morana, your horns." Enver's eyes go wide.

I reach atop my head. The horns are shrinking or retreating back into my head. It doesn't hurt. The tingling goes through my head. I feel the tips of the horns as they disappear into my body. Gone, as if they were never there,

"What just happened?" Enver asks.

For a moment, I have no words. The horns were nothing but a burden to me. Now, they are gone. A sense of peace washes over me. Tears burst through my eyelids.

"I think I've finally accepted who I am."

CHAPTER TWENTY- NINE

The gloomy castle brings nothing but sadness to my heart all over again. Here, I wait for my fate, and I accept it, and now fate has brought me back to the one place I sought to never lay eyes on again.

Enver and I agreed he wouldn't take me to the castle. He didn't want to see me throw my life away, to sacrifice myself. He begged me to leave, but nothing he said would ever change my mind. This is what I have to do. To put an end to this brewing war.

The guards run towards me with their spears and swords drawn. I raise my hands. Showing them that I come here willingly. That I bring only myself. "I am here to turn myself into King Alaric," I say firmly.

An elemental takes my hands and binds them behind me. His sharp fingernails dig into my skin. The heavy chains are enchanted. Its only purpose is to suppress my magic, not because they think I may be violent.

We walk along the same hallway on the day of my trial, if you can even call it that. Everything is the same. Nothing is left untouched. What I once thought beautiful is a reminder of who caused this war. The man I will face in a few moments.

"When the guards awoke me from my slumber, I thought I was still dreaming. The girl who caused so much trouble." King Alaric clenches the arms of the chair. "Lovely to see you again, Morana of the *night realm*." The evil king laughs.

"I'm here to offer you a deal." My voice echoes off the tall ceiling.

Don't let them take my pride as their prize.

King Alaric sits up straight. His queen next to him does the same.

"I offer myself to you. Leave Tenebris and its citizens untouched and take me as your prisoner."

King Alaric laughs. Queen Inina frowns. Her shoulder slumps forward.

"I will take Astrid's place. You should no longer have any business tampering with the border."

The King and his men laugh in unison. Mocking me for what now seems like a reckless decision.

"Stupid girl, do you think *I* would listen to you? You are a daemon. Your kind is frowned upon here. I should take your head for even stepping foot in this territory. I thought I got rid of you."

His wicked smile never leaves his face. Queen Inina senses something is wrong with him. Like he's gone mad.

"I have no use for you. I'd rather burn Tenebris from the inside out. I would love to see your entire species burn."

So much hatred. I can't help but feel that was the same hatred I went through. Angry at everything and everyone. Being reckless and feeling absolutely helpless in every situation.

"Please, Your Highness." I drop to my knees. I'm embarrassed to show any ounce of respect toward this man. I'm desperate to save Tenebris. "Do with me what you will, but please leave Tenebris alone."

King Alaric's mouth drops. He knows I'm being serious. I'm not leaving till he takes me.

"If you so wish, traitor." He strokes his beard. "Take the girls' place. Making a spectacle of your death might be something I can stomach."

He laughs, and the guards take me by both of my wrists and haul me down the hallway.

We go down and down. It's cold and musty. The air is too thick to breathe. I try to take deep breaths as they take me to the cell. I don't know why I'm nervous. This is what I want. I came here to save Tenebris.

They push me into the cell. I catch my balance before hitting the wet ground. The lock echoes off the stone walls.

A single-lit lantern lights the hallway. Not enough to allow me to see thoroughly.

I find a corner in which the ground is dry. I wrap my dress around me. Luckily, they left me with my cloak. It's cold down here, and I can't summon fire to warm myself.

This is what I want.

To save Tenebris.

My eyes flutter open as I try to move. My neck sears with pain as each muscle glides against my bones. I fell asleep sitting up. My breath is slightly visible from the dropping temperature.

Footsteps sound down the hallway. I've lost all sense of time. I've been so tired I could have slept for hours, even days. I'm too exhausted to put up a fight anymore.

The King himself stands on the other side of the iron bars. Looking down at me with those beady eyes.

"What brings you here?" I breathe. "Is it my time already?"

The King grabs the Iron bars as if trying to pry them apart. He miserably fails.

"Hush, Morana. It's me, Nesrin."

I sit up straight, trying to process what I just heard.

"I took the King's body. I don't have much time till Queen Inina wakes up."

I crawl to her, legs and body aching. She crouches to my level. It's eerie to look into the eyes of the king. Upon looking deeper, his eyes are white. All color is gone from it. The king is not here.

"Why are you here?" I ask.

"When Sora told me you left, I couldn't believe it." She says, looking both ways down the hallway. "Morana, what were you thinking?"

She reaches to touch me. I gently take my hand away. I don't want to touch the king's skin. It's not Nesrin's body.

"I'm doing this to save Tenebris. Hopefully, he will uphold his end of the deal. Although I have my suspicions that he won't."

Nesrin sighs. "Where are your horns?"

"Enough about that. Is Sora okay? What about Astrid?"

Nesrin grips the iron bars tighter. Being in the King's body must be uncomfortable for her. I can't imagine taking over someone's body.

"Astrid is fine. Sora is fine too." Nesrin chuckles. "He and Xanthe kissed for the first time."

I smile at the thought of Sora finding someone he can share his life with. Someone he can truly love. From the depths of my heart, I am so happy for him. I remind myself that I am here to protect Tenebris. So, Sora and everyone I care for can live a peaceful life.

"I don't have much time, Morana." She looks both ways again. "You must know that Queen Davina is preparing for war. She is tearing herself apart for this. For you."

I shake my head. "Tell her to back down. No one else can get hurt or die."

I sit in a puddle of water, unable to hold myself up anymore. The water is seeping into my dress. I'm too tired to do anything about it.

"She isn't being reasonable."

"Neither is Bellamy," Nesrin adds.

Hearing his name, Seeing him in my head. The anger is no longer there. I expected the fire within me to rise, but it didn't even spark. Maybe it's from coming to peace with myself. The thought of him, though, also saddens me. I shouldn't have lashed out as I did. I regret it so much.

"I have to go, Morana. I'm running out of energy. I can't leave the King's body here."

I nod tiredly.

"I'll try to see you soon. But please, don't do anything reckless as you already have. You have many people who want you back in Tenebris."

Before I can say anything, she takes the King's body back down the hallway and to the King's bedroom. I hope she gets there safely. No one can see the king leave the dungeon. People would ask questions. And no doubt, the King would quickly blame his blank memories on me.

I remain on the cold stone floor. Wishing Nesrin would come back, even if she was in the King's body. Just knowing she's there would help me tremendously.

CHAPTER THIRTY

BELLAMY

"What do you mean her horns are gone?"

Nesrin hunches over the desk, just as upset as I am. I can't be mad at her, though. She had only done what I asked of her. Without her, we couldn't have had direct contact with Morana. We wouldn't have known if she was still alive.

"I'm telling you, they are gone. There's no scar even to prove she had them in the first place." Nesrin huffs.

What could this mean? Surely, she hasn't lost her daemon gifts. That isn't so easy to do. It's almost impossible. Binding her with enchanted chains could suppress her magic, but those horns are physical. I'll be damned if they cut them from her head. I'll be damned if they hurt her in any way.

Ever since gaining her horns, she hated them. She believed she was ugly. She blamed all her problems on those horns. I wish I could see her face to face to prove to her that she isn't what the horns made her. She is so much more than that. All the more reason to fight to bring her back.

"I will contact Kiveha immediately. We need all the reinforcements we can get." I turn to Davina and

Lazarus. "Will you ready your men and women willing to fight?"

Davina nods her head along with Lazarus. I've never seen them more anxious to start a war than now.

"Certainly. We can prepare the armadas as well. We will use every able citizen who is willing to fight. We can't go down so easily." Lazarus says.

I wish they'd have been this driven before it got this bad. I wish they had this same willingness when Astrid was gone. It makes me wonder if Astrid believes they don't love her equally as Sora and Morana.

"Xanthe, I need you to meet at the north base as soon as possible. Make sure the generals there know what to plan for. We need every weapon we can get our hands on. Ready the arsenals."

Xanthe nods and gives one last look to Sora. He touches Sora's hand as he leaves. I wish they had left their love life outside these doors. I can't let emotions get in the way of this war. I also have to be careful not to bring my emotions into this. If this isn't done correctly. We will lose, and Morana will never step foot in Tenebris again. At least alive, she won't.

"I hope you know what you are doing."

We turn to Astrid, who has barely spoken a word since returning to Tenebris. We all had thought she lost her mind in Rhemus. Maybe it was all a trick. She probably knows more than she's putting off.

Davina gasps at Astrid's surprising response.

"Rhemus is many things, but one thing they are not is fair. I'm sure you know this. Especially Sora." The room grows quiet. "I've seen what they can do and how they can hurt people. You are going about this all wrong."

I contemplate letting Astrid speak, but Davina and Lazarus seem more than happy to hear her say more than a few words. Words that actually make sense. She stands hesitantly in front of the many judgmental men.

"They have weapons like ours, but what they have that we don't are elementals. They wield the elements that surround us. Once they turn sixteen, they are taken to the Hesai Islands for vigorous training. Deadly training. Those who survive are anything but weak."

She takes a breath. Unsure if she should continue. I nod my head.

"The elementals are cruel. They can conjure hurricanes and earthquakes at the snap of a finger. It can hail, and the ground can be opened up, revealing the magma-filled earth. One thing you must not do is underestimate them.

"Alongside those who wield physical weapons, the elementals are also used to torture criminals. I was one of them."

Davina gasps. Astrid winces.

"You need an army of more than just weapons. You need magic and long-range fighters. Everything you thought about Rhemus isn't true. They will go to any lengths to destroy those who think differently."

She sits down, and Davina places a hand on Astrid's shoulder. Astrid remains neutral.

"Okay, so we have the succubus, witches, and dybbuks who wield magic," I add.

"No. Not good enough. Their magic will not compare to those who control the elements. The dybbuks and succubus can do their magic from afar, but they will quickly become outnumbered. So many bodies but so little to possess them." Astrid argues.

My eyes go wide at her attitude, just like Morana's.

No. Stop. Don't say her name.

"I suppose releasing the wyverns and bats would be useless?" I ask.

"They would if you think they'd be strong enough to withstand any natural disaster."

I sigh. "Lady Astrid, I mean no disrespect, but you have been gone for many years. You know nothing of Tenebris and its abilities. You know what the King has told you and what you have seen. There are much worse things than earthquakes and rain."

Lazarus's eyes widened. "Bellamy. Excuse me?"

"I'm only being honest. Can you expect her to know our world when she's only lived in it for a few short years at a young age? Don't be so ignorant, your majesty. If you want Kiveha's help. You will follow what I say."

The words flow out of my mouth before I can think, but I let it happen. There is truth to my words. Years ago, Tenebris had begged Kiveha for an alliance to form against Rhemus. Kiveha was initially very reluctant, but after much debate, and a blood contract, it was agreed that Kiveha would help Tenebris when the time called for it. This is the time.

"I think you are forgetting whose kingdom you are in, Bellamy." Lazarus coughs.

I turn to Lazarus and look him dead in the eye. "Must I remind you of the blood contract, your majesty? Astrid is tied to me as I am to her. If you want to keep this alliance and your daughter alive, then I suggest you let me take control."

Lazarus sits down in defeat.

Of course, I would never hurt Astrid, let alone kill her. But if her life ended, I can't help but think, maybe I'd have a chance with Morana. The one I'd die to be with. I can never let Davina know that. I can't let *anyone* know that.

I finish the final preparations for the armies to head out. Word has been sent to Kiveha, and we expect their company soon. All of their light and dark creatures come together to fight off the one cruel kingdom. We must get Morana back, and we must kill King Alaric.

CHAPTER THIRTY- ONE

MORANA

I fell asleep to the sound of water dripping. It was almost peaceful. Laying on the small slab of stone was never comfortable. Still, I was able to focus on the continuous sound, just enough to put me into a meditative state long enough to forget where I am.

In that state, I see many things. Orna and Kai are the first ones to show their faces. I ask if they are okay, but I have not received a response. They smile as their faces fade to black.

Raisel's glittering light follows her in my vision. Her blonde hair travels behind her like a river of gold. Such a sweet and pure soul, all ruined by me and for what I am. What I did.

Bellamy.

What can I say about him? He shows his face too. That anger I felt on the night of my birthday never showed. Instead, I focus on those feelings I have for him. The comforting warmness of his touch, despite his cold blood. The sparkle that fills his black eyes. And reflects everything I hate myself to be. If only I had told him sooner. If only I had never told him at all.

Soon enough, a trickle of sunlight beams in through the small window hole above me. The birds chirp in the morning light, reminding me of what once was and will always be. Rhemus will always be my hell.

A guard quickly passes my cell and drops by a tray of food. If I can even call it that. The bread, slightly warm, with a hint of moisture, fruit, but all the bad parts of it, and a single copper cup of water from the East lake. No one dared to touch it. But if I am to survive any longer, this food will have to keep me alive.

After choking down the rotted food, a different guard from earlier comes to unlock the gate. The iron keys rattle against each other, and my anxiety rises to the top of my throat. I swallow to keep it down.

I stand in the corner, keeping my hands where they are easily visible. I can't let him think I'd attack anyone. The way he fumbles with the keys suggests he is afraid. I don't know whether he's scared of me or scared of what King Alaric would do to him if he doesn't obey.

"Where are you taking me?" I ask as he grabs my wrists and tugs me along. This answers my question from earlier. If he was scared of me, he wouldn't have come at me so easily. Or touched my skin.

He turns his head as if to say something but continues down the dungeon path. The winding hallways seem never-ending. This uncertainty is constant. Every corner is a mystery.

We come to a door, and a woman meets me. A maid, to be exact. She doesn't look me in the eyes but looks at everything I am wearing, judging me for how dirty I've become in my time in the cell.

"He wants her cleaned up and a change of clothes." The guard says.

"It will take some time, but I'll figure it out." The maid nods.

"Make it quick. The King has asked for her as soon as possible."

The guard unchains my cuffs and hands the key over to the maid. She quickly takes the key and slides it into her pocket.

"You may be free now, girl, but there are guards at every corner of this castle. Don't think about running."

I keep my head down. In this situation, it's better to keep quiet. My life is in their hands.

The maid takes me through winding hallways and hidden doors. No one is in sight. No other servants or maids. They want to keep me well hidden.

She takes me to a bathroom much like the one I had in Tenebris. The tub is pure gold. The steam from the water rises above it. She begins to undress me without notice. Garments are being ripped off, and my hair is getting caught in the clasps on my dress. I make no fuss about it.

Naked and completely vulnerable, she leads me into the tub. The water is almost too hot for my skin, but I quickly get used to it. She scrubs my skin vigorously to the point where my skin is red. The same goes for my hair. She gets irritated with the length of my hair. I wish I had cut it off long ago.

She leaves me in the tub briefly before returning with a dress in her hand. I lift myself from the tub, and the maid jumps. I step out and stand there, waiting for her to make the next move.

She takes a towel and dries me. "What is going on?" I ask.

She ignores me.

"Please tell me what is going on. Is the King going to kill me?"

The maid sighs. "I don't know what the king has planned."

I stand at the end of a dark tunnel. Light glows at the end of it. Perhaps I am being led to my death, and the bright light is the unwelcoming light of the Inferno. That is where my fate lies. That is my forever home. I might as well accept it now.

The guards usher me along, arms chained behind my back. No one gives me an ounce of acknowledgment. Not a single glance is given my way. Gliding down this hallway, I am nothing more than an empty soul.

My eyes adjust to the light. I haven't seen real sunlight like this for many weeks now. Everything came alive when the stars lit up the sky.

Don't forget the sun. Don't. Forget.

I know what is happening now as they take me up wooden stairs to a platform that centers the castle. I wonder what they will do to me. Publicly humiliate me. Hang me or burn me. Whatever it is, it will be an eternal death. I can't die.

As I approach the platform, I notice King Alaric and Queen Inina sitting in their glorified thrones. Their eyes follow mine as I walk up the steps.

Every step feels like my soul is leaving this plane as I'm passing to the other side of the veil.

The village folk stand quietly around the platform. The King has decided to make his plan a spectacle for all to see. I see familiar faces left and right. Faces I grew up with. Faces that are now against me. None of them look worried for me, but I suspected that.

The guards unchain my hands but leave the cuffs on. They push me to my knees. The wood chips scrape into my knees underneath this thin dress. They take each hand and chain it to a rope that leads up to a pole on both sides of me. Both arms are completely in the air. Both arms are restrained from making any movements.

The King stands and starts to the platform. The villagers talk in hushed tones. As the King makes his entrance, the crowd bows in unison.

"On this fine day, my people, I give you, Morana, the traitor." The crowd cheers to his wicked words. "Morana, the liar." More cheering. "Morana, the murderer."

He basks in the villagers' praise. I keep my head down, slightly looking up from my eyelashes.

"Morana has decided to come back to our glorious nation of Rhemus. Why do you ask? She has taken the place of her sister, you see? Morana came to me and begged for her family's safety. In turn, she became my prisoner."

I wish I could tune it all out.

"She comes from a nation of liars, manipulators, and impure. Those creatures she's become friends with."

The crowd gasps.

"She's in love with a daemon. She is a harlot."
The crowd cheers.

He circles around me. Kneeling before me, he takes my face in his hands and makes me look into his sick and wicked eyes. No color to them. Only a spark of hatred lives inside him. If only I could see into his soul.

I spit in his face. The crowd gasps again. He wipes it from his face and continues like it never happens. His lips twitch.

"She's wicked. She spits fire, folks." He hands a handkerchief back to a guard. "Luckily, she can't hurt us here." He kneels to me again. "You are in my territory now."

King Alaric faces the stairs. Guards with arms full of spears enter. All the spears have handles like iron, but the point is not the same. It's white, faded to yellow. Stained red around the ends of it. All of them curved like the horns that were on my head.

Not good.

The King takes a spear into his hand. He grips it tightly, his hand turns white, and his knuckles show. He circles around me, but I can't see him.

Chills travel down my back.

"You all have been invited here today to be witness to this victory. We have the daemon. We have the girl that brought us so much grief with the loss of Draven of the East. We can avenge his death. Bring her forth."

A woman, young in age, walks up the stairs. Her shoulders slump forward, and her eyes meet everywhere but mine. Her fingers twiddle together. She meets King Alaric.

"I present to you, Heida of the East. She lost her dear husband in the hands of Morana, the traitor." He hands her the spear.

No. This cannot be happening.

"Are there any words you would like to say to Morana?" King Alaric asks.

Heida looks down at me—tears in her eyes. One tear drops before me. I wait for her to say something. She's speechless. No doubt she feels so much anger towards me. Does she know why Draven begged to be killed?

"You murdered my husband." Her voice shakes. "You whore." She slaps me with her free hand.

My skin stings. She kneels to me. Now I see her. She's beautiful. Her brown hair folds over her shoulder into a messy braid. Her eyes are blue, but like the color has been siphoned from them. It hurts me to look at her, but deep in the pit of my stomach, I know she's putting on an act.

"You should have gone to Tenebris. This should be you, Heida."

At the mention of her name, she steps back.

"Your husband begged me to kill him." I laugh. "I know about the deal Draven made with the King. To save you from being banished from Rhemus."

Her lower lip curls slightly. I can't wait to see what she has to say next.

"How do you know about that?"

I don't dare mention Enver. He showed me kindness upon my return. He led me to my parent's graves. I won't say his name.

"Daemons know everything." I smile. "The truth lingers on your tongue. You killed your child. You murdered it with a cold heart. Sliced its throat and left it for dead."

I don't know what comes over me. Something is speaking for me. I can't restrain it. The more I keep it from talking, the more pain I feel in my throat.

"You are the true traitor of Rhemus."

She lets out a sob, and as her scream rings through the air, the tip of the spear penetrates my stomach. Blood quickly runs down me as she takes the spear from my skin.

The pain is overwhelming. I laugh to fight the pain. Let her do it again. I want to see the same rage that showed when she killed her child.

Again, she stabs me, but this time with less fury. She's sobbing. The spear drops and leaves a loud bang throughout the courtyard. The villagers go silent. This isn't what anyone expect from this spectacle.

The guards haul her away. Her sobs become quieter as she disappears into the crowd. Where they take her, I haven't a clue.

"I guess she doesn't want to forgive you." King Alaric laughs. "Some crimes just can't be forgiven."

People form a line up the stairs, each with a spear in hand. What sick show does the King think he's putting on?

The next person steps up, veins popping out of his forehead. Stab after stab, each one becomes number than the last one. I won't let him break me. I won't let him have the satisfaction of killing me.

CHAPTER THIRTY- TWO

BELLAMY

I stand at the gate, waiting for their arrival. It feels like I haven't seen them for years. I'm frightened, to say the least. I want them to be proud of me. I want to show them that I am not useless. I've become stronger. I am fit to be king one day. And if I can't convince them that I'm worthy, I might as well be a bastard.

"Are they strict?" Sora asks.

I cross my arms. "Used to be when I was younger. Mother is nothing like Davina. I'd fear Queen Kenna over Davina any day."

That's why I'd never mouth off to my mother like I do Davina.

Sora tenses. I smile at his fear.

Horses emerge from over the hill. The black horse's tower, much as I remember. Every horse in Kiveha is abnormally tall. Despite their gentle nature, they used to scare me as a child.

"Just don't speak unless she speaks to you," I say.

The horses slow past us, and the carriage comes to a halt. Still, they use the same carriage they did when I was a child. Nothing has changed for them.

The tall, dark-haired woman emerges from the carriage.

"Good evening, Mother. Nice to see you." I hold my hand out for her. She gracefully takes it.

Her eyes roam the outskirts of the castle. Disgust consumes her face.

"Nice to see you as well, Bellamy. Surely, I thought this castle was bigger years ago."

"Nothing has changed, Mother."

She walks past me, and my father trails behind her. King Ronan. He still has dark eyebrows that make him look angry all the time. His beard is wild like his spirit, and red eyes that I fear so much.

"Father."

"Son. Good to see you." He grumbles. "Sorry, it is under terrible circumstances."

I look over, and my mother is leaning over a bush of flowers. She smells them, and that look of disgust runs over her face again. Nothing really satisfies her anymore. If it doesn't suit her likeness, she makes everyone suffer with her.

"I heard Astrid has returned. When may we see her?" She asks.

I stand still next to Sora, who has still yet to say one word. I'm glad he's at least followed that order.

"She is with Queen Davina at the moment. I can take you to her shortly."

Mother turns up her nose. "And who is this?" She points to Sora.

"This is Prince Sora. Astrid and Morana's brother. Morana's twin."

She nods. "Handsome." She comes to Sora.

"It's an honor to meet you, Queen Kenna." He bows slightly.

I tighten my fist, hoping Mother doesn't say anything rude as usual.

"I usually don't like meeting new people, but since you are Astrid's brother, I can't exactly ignore you, can I?"

I look at Sora and gently shake my head. He smiles and says nothing more. He walks behind us with his arms behind his back.

Mother and Father follow me into the castle. They mumble under their breath, but I chose to ignore their judgment. I was reluctant to invite them here, but we need to have them here for this plan to work. We are using the Kiveahan army. They have complete control over that.

I take them into the council room. Queen Davina and King Lazarus are already sitting and conversing with Councilman Hugo. Astrid is beside them, her head down and twiddling with her thumbs.

I clear my throat to gain their attention.

"My goodness." Queen Davina stands. "Sorry, we weren't at the gates to meet you. We are pleased to have you here in Tenebris, Queen Kenna, King Ronan."

Lazarus stands and shakes hands with King Ronan. They have always gotten along. It's Davina and my mother I am worried about. Once my mother heard that Astrid had been taken, their relationship was never the same. Mother has called Davina careless and many other names.

"Is this Astrid?" Mother asks. "She's grown into a beautiful woman. Don't you think, Bellamy?" She turns to me.

"Yes, of course." I nod.

"I can't wait to see you in your wedding dress. After this, we must make preparations." Mother smiles.

"If we even survive, Mother. We have more pressing issues than a wedding. Can we please continue discussing the plan?"

Mother sits down with anger plastered on her face. I don't care that I've angered her. I hate that she mentioned a wedding during a time like this. I know the blood contract is important to her, but I will do anything to prolong the wedding from happening.

"Your majesties." Councilman Hugo stands. "May we proceed?"

Everyone nods.

"Captain Garren has informed us that his platoons are heading to the border, all spread out in stations about five miles apart. The armadas are taking each shoreline from east to west."

Xanthe nods. "Kiveha's Captain has men and creatures alike on the way as we speak to merge with the other platoons."

I look to Nesrin, who seems terrified to speak. I nod to her. She stands and straightens her dress. My Mother is already giving her a nasty look.

"Your majesties, I have gathered all the succubi and incubi in a twenty-mile radius. When the signal is given, I myself will take King Alaric's mind and run him in a different direction. Preferably on the farthest coastline before running out of energy."

"I'm sorry, who is she?" My mother asks. Her voice scratching in the air like a banshee.

I sigh. "This is Nesrin. Bookkeeper and succubus. She has already met Morana in the King's castle. She is our inside person. However, she can only possess someone for so long. We can only use her at the right time."

"She is a nobody." Mother says. "You would be better off bombing the entire castle."

I steer my eyes to my mother. Her red eyes are glowing just as mine are.

"She is part of this plan. She's been beyond helpful the past few days. She is Morana's best friend."

Mother crosses her arms. "So we are starting a war because the princess is gone?" Mother scoffs. "Davina, can't you keep your children in place?"

The room goes silent. Davina tightens her jaw, and Lazarus lays his hand on hers to calm her. I bite my lip.

"Morana left on her own accord," Davina says.

"Did you drive her away? I guess Sora will be next, I assume. I'd keep Astrid close by for safe measure."

Davina rises from her chair. The table rumbles. She releases her wings. They tower over everyone at the table. Redness flares up in her eyes. This is not what should be happening.

"Keep my children's name out of your pathetic mouth." Davina huffs. "We are here because King Alaric is wreaking havoc on the entire continent. He has driven Morana to sacrifice herself for the sake of us and all of Tenebris. Although my child's decision may have been made out of anger, I can understand why she did it. You have no room to talk to my family like that in my own castle. Keep your mouth shut, or I will not hesitate to end this blood contract."

Her voice rings off the walls. Mother snickers in the corner. I had high hopes an argument wouldn't even have occurred, but I was very wrong.

"Go on." Mother growls.

I straighten the map in front of me. I'm scared to say another word. I would hate for this to break out in a fight between Davina and my mother.

"Sora, Nesrin, Xanthe, and I will head out after this meeting. Davina and Lazarus, will you be joining us at the front?"

Lazarus takes a deep breath. "We will be right behind you."

I nod and then turn to Mother and Father.

"Will you two be joining us at the front?"

Father nods quickly. Mother crosses her arms and slumps in her chair.

The council room fades to silence as everyone piles out and goes to their destinations. I let out the breath I'd been holding for the entire time of the meeting. I have never seen so much bickering coming from my mother. Then again, she is a daemon, just like me. She just hasn't gotten control of her emotions as I have. I can't blame her entirely, though. I left Kiveha when she begged me not to

CHAPTER THIRTY-THREE
BELLAMY

The sun is beginning to set—a mix of orange and blue smears across the sky. The stars fade into view. Almost to its highest peak, the moon traces the sky with its celestial energy.

This war has always been about releasing Tenebris from Rhemus, but my mind always wanders to the thought of saving Morana. She didn't have to do what she did. She made the decision without thinking clearly or consulting any of her friends. Perhaps that is what she wanted. She knew we would all be against her. If Sora had known better, he would have stopped her. If I were there, I would have never let her leave, even if she hates me.

Hate. She resents me, and it's entirely my fault. I've been thinking of ways to make it up to her, but nothing is good enough. Nothing is good enough for her pure soul.

I messed up badly. I should have told her about the blood contract when she asked questions. I often grew angry with Davina and Lazarus for keeping important information from her. All while I was holding another big secret from her. I am just as bad as the King and Queen. And I can't help myself for feeling like I should be where Morana is now.

I am still trying to gain Sora's trust. After he found out what I had done, I let him beat me. I deserved all of it, from one punch to the face and the other to my rib cage. I heeled quickly, but If I had found out some guy had done the same to my future daughter, I would react just the same.

"Queen Kenna is terrifying," Nesrin says.

I hoist my bag over my shoulder to keep it from slipping.

"I apologize for earlier. She is cruel in many ways. All the crueler because I haven't seen her or even bothered to write in forever. What she said about you isn't right."

"Don't apologize. I understand why you were so hesitant to bring them here."

I can't keep apologizing for my mother's behavior. I've done it for too long, even when I was a young child. I always came up with an excuse for why she acted the way she did. I even took the blame for many of her faults.

"King Ronan barely said a word. Does he usually do that?" Sora asks.

I hoist the slipping strap on my shoulder again. I'm growing irritated with it. I almost drag it.

"If you haven't already noticed, in kingdoms like ours, it is the women who rule. Women are the face of the crow. They say what goes. Everyone else is just there for support. That is what King Lazarus is there for. "

I set my eyes on the horizon. I can see the trees at the border.

"Women will always have the first say. That's why, Sora, I hope that Morana denies the throne and you become King. After all, you are with Xanthe. Maybe two kings ruling would be better than one daemon woman. They are always feistier." I laugh.

Sora blushes and laughs.

"Bold of you to think Xanthe and I will marry one day," Sora says.

"Why not? You are what love is. I've seen the way you two look at each other. It's almost disgusting."

The trees are still. Against the setting sun, they look like a picture in a book. Beautiful but eerie to see them so lifeless and still, even in this spring weather. The leaves hang in the air like they've been paralyzed by a witch. Like time has stopped.

The tents have been set up. I can only see so far in this growing dark. I hear the mumbling of voices, planning our next move. Bodies move back and forth, readying weapons of sorts.

Nesrin makes the cot in which she will lie when she takes over the king's mind. Guards will keep watch of the tent as this happens. We must get the King as far away from the action as possible.

Sora stands in the middle of the room, unsure of what to do next.

"First time going into battle?" I ask.

He smiles and shakes his head. "Not sure if you're being sarcastic or not, Prince. Honestly, I haven't a clue of what to expect."

I take out his sword from the scabbard. Recently sharpened to the exact point. Adorned in jewels from the kingdom's sword maker. It's a fine weapon to wield, but only if he has the stamina for it.

"Have you trained with this one lately?" I ask.

"Every moment I can, Xanthe and I —"

"Of course, you trained with Xanthe." I laugh. "I'm only kidding. He's a fine swordsman, along with his gargoyle abilities. On the other hand, he can withstand a dragon's weight. Are you capable of carrying and using this sword if your life depends on it? Morana's life as well."

He nods hesitantly.

"If there is one thing you can do, Sora is fly. I've seen your skills. So, take to the sky if you need to, but never leave a comrade behind. I've learned that the hard way myself."

I return the sword to Sora, who keeps it in the scabbard, tucking and clipping it to his belt.

"Let's bring in one more to watch over Nesrin. I won't be here when she goes to work so that she will need extra protection."

Sora exits the tent.

I watch Sora from the tent opening. Nesrin comes behind me.

"Are you sure this plan will work?" Nesrin asks.

"It has to." I unravel the map from my pack. "If King Alaric is where the action is, there is no telling what he will send for us. He is in complete control of the army. Most of their generals won't make a move without confronting him first."

Nesrin rubs her arms nervously. "I just want to get Morana back." She mumbles.

"And we will. You are the biggest help we have."

Everyone is here. This is the time that we have waited for. Revenge. We rescue Morana and take revenge on the cruel king. Our armies have trained for this very moment. Our kingdoms come together to rid this world of such hatred.

"Men, women, and creatures alike. Before we head into battle, I need to say some things."

I round the campfire, glancing at everyone's face before the battle.

My Mother and Father have joined us tonight. I'm glad they are able to see me in a position of power. No one has questioned it. I don't want to make this about me, but no other person seems qualified to take on such a respected and influential position.

"Tonight, Tenebris and Kiveha will come together as one country. To fight the evil that lurks just over those trees. For centuries, Tenebris has been oppressed. Its creatures and people were ruined by the people of Rhemus. All because of a wicked reign of Kings. We will end this King's reign today."

The crowd cheers around the fire. The energy pulses with the moon's energy. Together we become an unstoppable force.

"Women and children must be spared at all expense. For now, our presence is unknown to the King. We storm the castle and bring our Princess home. Once King Alaric is out of the castle, we will kill him."

I meet Nesrin's eyes in the light of the fire. She knows what I did to Morana. She knows that I regret everything. One thing that she knows for sure is that I will put my life on the line for Morana.

This war was predestined. For centuries people suffered at the hands of the Kings of Rhemus. Driven by hatred, each one destroys their own land, making their people suffer, brainwashing their people into thinking we are savages.

The people separate and head to their posts and ready for battle. Davina and Lazarus stand by. Mother and Father sit on the other side of the fire.

"Bellamy." King Lazarus ushers me over to him. "I know it may be too soon to thank you, but we wish to do that now for everything you have done. You have fought for us and fought for our daughters. We cannot thank you enough."

I cough. "I will do anything to protect innocent people, your majesties. I'm glad you have let me into your kingdom so t may call it my home too. We will meet again when this war is over."

CHAPTER THIRTY- FOUR

MORANA

Warmness surrounds me, comforting me. The sun, it's the sun, welcoming me. I can feel it. My vision is too blurry to see the light, but I know it's there.

I was beginning to wonder when I'd ever see the sun again. The sunlight was always the best in the flower fields. I'd spend all day with Raisel, basking in the light of the sun, without a care in the world. There was simply nothing in my life. I wish to see only Raisel and the never-ending sunlight one last time.

Only, this is not the sun. I am beginning to realize. Hot like fire, but not hot enough to burn me. I've felt this feeling before. It was on my hands when I grew angry. The same fire that devoured my hands all those times, lashing out at Davina and Lazarus and Bellamy. The same fire I used around Bellamy.

Surrounding me are the familiar flowers that Raisel would pick on our sun-basking days. Gardenias, roses, and hyacinths. Roses were Raisel's favorite. They look just as they had when we visited the last time. The last peaceful time.

A woman in white strides towards me. My legs have no energy to lift myself. I look down and realize the blood has disappeared, and the pain has gone. No trace of the blood remains.

Who is this beautiful woman? Has she come to take me to the Inferno? Looking around, this place doesn't feel real. It's dreamlike and hazy. Too comforting to be the Inferno.

"Morana." She calls me. Her voice is like that of a siren singing her song.

Her presence is calming. Pure light radiates off her like sun rays. I want to touch her. Not to make sure she's real but to feel the light that comes with her.

"Who are you?" I ask.

I have no energy to stand. I lean on one arm, but that is becoming difficult with how much my arm is shaking.

"It's an honor to meet you finally," she says. "I am Neera. I am the shadow that has been following you since you were born."

I squint my eyes. My vision is back. White hair flows behind her, longer than the wheat in the wheat fields. She has eyes that make me want to turn away, crystals like the ocean, and horns that remind me so much of myself.

"You know who I am?"

A trail of orange and blue flames follow her. Leaving the ground behind her black and burnt.

"I am the Infernal Creator. I am all that is darkness and all that is light. I have known you since you were a tiny seed in your mother's womb."

Impossible.

"Where am I?"

"Dear, you are in the Inferno."

I switch to my other arm to lean on. "How is that possible?"

"You are on the verge of passing. I am here to guide you to your afterlife. Wherever that may be, you may choose."

No.

I can't die. Daemons are nearly impossible to kill. No spear, no amount of poison could ever kill my kind. Our brimstone blood surely could never allow it.

If I am here, then where is my body? Perhaps King Alaric left me for dead on the platform. This has to be a dream. This is a dream.

"I am not ready to die." I stutter.

"You may not feel ready, dear, but I assure you, your subconscious knows what you do not. Your mind would not bring you here if you were not ready to enter your afterlife."

I came to Rhemus to make a deal with the King. I didn't make this decision so that I could die. I had to see to it myself that he would follow through with his end of the bargain. But I knew, in the back of my mind, he would go against it. That would be my own ignorance. That would be too easy. How could King Alaric have done it? How could he kill an unkillable creature?

"What about my brother, Sora, and Nesrin? How will they ever find me?"

Neera takes a rose from the ground. It bursts into blue flames with a white core. The ashes gracefully float to the ground. Sprinkling the flowers with a dusty gray color.

"Someone is wanting to speak with you, Morana."

From the ashes of the rose, a small person emerges from it. Golden hair and tiny fairy wings. I know those iridescent wings. Raisel.

"Raisel. How are you here?"

Her face lights up with a smile. I try to reach for her, but I am too weak. Instead, Neera holds her in front of me in her palm.

"It's so nice to see you again, Morana."

"I don't understand." I cry. "You shouldn't be here in the Inferno."

Raisel smiles. Lights flicker around her. "When I died, Neera was the one to meet me. She told me your death was very near. So, I chose to stay here till I could see you again. I couldn't leave you."

I never thought it would be possible, but my eyes fill with tears. So much so that I can feel their warmth running down my face. Perhaps this is real.

"I'm so sorry, Raisel." I sniff. "I didn't know King Alaric would go after you. I thought you would be safe. I'm sorry for everything. I'm sorry for killing Draven."

"Shhh." She comes to my shoulder. "You don't need to apologize. What's done is done."

I don't want to leave this moment. I have my best friend back. How can I fight for my life and fight to see Raisel ever again? I will never be able to choose a side. What kind of person would that make me if I did?

"Neera told me everything. She told me you have a brother." She smiles.

"I do. His name is Sora. He's just so amazing. I feel that I may have hurt him by leaving Tenebris. And now I can't apologize to him. I can't say goodbye. To anyone."

Raisel lifts off my shoulder and floats around me. I twiddle with the grass beneath. The hyacinth leaves fall between my fingers. Almost nothing is tangible. I can no longer feel anything, not even the warmth that welcomed me.

"What is going on?" I look at Neera. Her eyes widen.

"It seems you are needed on the plane of existence, child. Your time is, in fact, not now." She speaks in a low tone. The fire around her grows.

It isn't my time. Perhaps my physical body is waking up, fighting for everything I have left. This is it. I have to say my goodbyes now.

"Morana, what you are going back to is not what you remembered. War is ravaging the land. You must know that you and another who wields horns are the only ones who can save Tenebris."

Her voice travels off. Every second I am fading.

I look at Raisel. She is still smiling. She is at peace. She isn't worried that I won't see her for many more years.

"Raisel, I can't wait to see you in the afterlife."

"I'll be waiting."

I'm fading. The picture of Neera becomes harder to concentrate on. Neera looks to Raisel in her hand and lifts her to eyes view. Raisel bursts into flames, and the ashes flow in the wind.

My throat strains to scream. I can't get to her. She's gone.

CHAPTER THIRTY- FIVE

Lightning strikes my chest. The remnants of it courses through my veins. Pressure fills the center of my chest. For a moment, I feel the distant beat of a heart that I once had.

An unfamiliar place surrounds me. This is not the castle, and this is definitely not the cold dungeon I thought to be my tomb.

"Oh my. She's back." a voice calls.

My vision is coming in clearer. People huddle around me. An unfamiliar face towers directly above me. I begin to tremble. This is not where I want to be. I cannot be here. I need to be with Raisel.

"Settle down, Child. We have you back now." Davina's voice calls.

"What is going on?" I stutter.

Davina's hands comb through my hair. She hushes me with soft tones. I try to lift up, but pain strikes through my body. The wound on my stomach hasn't healed. I realize now that I have more cuts and bruises on my arms. My entire body stings with an unshaken rage.

"Morana, can you hear me?"

Sora looks down at me with big eyes. Sweat rolls down his face. I've never seen him so frantic before. His pupils are big, like he had been through a nightmare.

"Will someone tell me what is going on?" I stutter as the pain strikes me again.

The tent opens. Another familiar face fills the room.

"Is she alive?" Bellamy asks. "Did it work?"

"Bellamy found you. He found your lifeless body on the platform in the courtyard. He was able to bring you back by flying. He had no other way to avoid the battle."

Bellamy saved me. He found me and saved me. Brought me back to whatever place this is. I don't know if I should be angry or happy. I want to embrace him, but memories of my birthday come flooding back. I can see the regret in his eyes. The hurt consumes him.

"They left you to die, Morana," Bellamy says. His voice is shaking. He's trying so hard to slow his breathing. "They stabbed you hundreds of times. Do you know what the medics found inside your stomach? It's a miracle your alive."

I relax my body.

"They found traces of daemon bone inside you. Daemon bones are like poison to other daemons. Once penetrated with one, it is a sure death."

"Then how am I here?"

Bellamy looks to the floor. Guards enter carrying a white sheet and laying it on the floor.

"We had to find a witch who could bring you back. She sacrificed herself for you."

"Necromancy," I whisper.

Bellamy nods. "It was the only way."

A life for a life.

Bellamy leans closer to me. Blood stains his face and hands. His eyes are just the same as they were the day of my birthday. Filled with so much regret now, I see how hurt he is. My reckless love for him makes me want to forgive him, but it's just too late for that.

"You were on the brink of death when I found you. You were so quiet. I thought—we thought we lost you."

I push back on the cot to a sitting position. Davina helps me. The pain sears through me like hot coal. I notice I'm still in the same dress the maid had put me in. The blood has all but dried. The blood has turned cold. The blood clings to my skin.

"I was in the Inferno." I breathe. "I saw Raisel."

Everyone looks at me as if they are seeing a ghost. I can't tell if they think I'm lying or not. I know what I saw.

"I saw Neera. The Infernal Creator."

Davina gasps. A single tear falls from her eye.

"She said that only those who wield horns can save Tenebris. But I don't know who else has horns."

A loud roar of a dragon echoes through the air. A war cry to warn those of the endless bloodshed to come. The tent opens, revealing my sister Astrid.

Without a word, she closes her eyes. Her forehead cracks, and blood oozes from it. Horns emerge from her head. Exactly like mine. Everyone thought she was lying when she claimed to have horns. We thought her mind was corrupt from the years spent in Rhemus, that she was spewing nonsense.

"I am the one Neera speaks of."

Davina reaches for Astrid and her horns. Gently she touches them. Tears stream down her face. Lazarus stands behind his wife, acknowledging the daemonic presence of their daughter.

"How did this happen?" Davina cries. "That means you —"

Astrid keeps a blank stare.

"I died."

Davina hugs Astrid with Lazarus behind her. The atmosphere in the room darkens. Never have I felt so much pain and sorrow in one room.

"King Alaric himself tortured me. It happened to be on a full moon. He thought I was dead." She breathes. "I thought I was dead."

She died alone. No one was by her side. The transformation must have been brutal for her. I can't imagine waking up and being an entirely new person with no one there by my side. I wasn't alone during my transformation. I had many people there to help me through it. She was utterly alone.

I stand from the cot. I push away helping hands. If Astrid and I are going to fight in this war, then I have to be able to fend for myself. I need to push through the pain and forget what my body has gone through.

I reach to my head where my horns were. I close my eyes as Astrid did. I let myself go. Releasing everything that burdens me, everything that keeps me from being who I am. I am releasing all that hinders me from achieving this victory.

My horns emerge from my head. The blood drips down my face, but it doesn't bother me. I welcome the blood and pain. Now I realize the horns were never a problem. They were given to me for this very moment.

"Astrid and I have to go. We need to kill the king." I say.

The tent opens once more, making the tent even more cramped than before—Nesrin strides in.

"Then you must know where I hid him."

CHAPTER THIRTY-SIX

I run to Nesrin and embrace her like I haven't seen her in years. I feel so much. I regret leaving her the way I did. She was my first friend in Tenebris, and I abandoned her because I was selfish. I thought I was doing something heroic. But now I know I cannot win this war on my own.

"I'm so happy you are back." She says and nuzzles into my neck. "What were you thinking? Leaving us like that?"

"I'm so sorry. Nothing I do can make it up to you."

She lifts from my neck. "Yes, you can. You can kill the King."

Killing King Alaric will end his reign and free the people from him. Once he is dead, we can offer those a home in Tenebris, only if they are willing to. I realize some may never change their minds and ways of living. I can try my best to convince those of his cruelty. They have been lied to for hundreds of years. We must show them we are willing to fight for them.

"Where is he?" I ask.

Nesrin goes over to the table in which a map of the continent lies. She smooths out the wrinkles and points to a spot near the east coast.

"Before the ambush started at the castle, I took over King Alaric's body and took him to the cove. I may have slipped him something to keep him out for a while."

Bellamy shoots Nesrin a look.

"That wasn't part of the plan." He scolds. "I like it, though."

Nesrin smiles devilishly.

"It won't keep him out long, though. He should be waking up soon. Once he does wake up, he will waste no time coming back to the castle. He will gather his troops to come to the border."

My body is in pain. The wound still isn't fully healed. If it doesn't heal fast, there could be irreparable damage. No more time can be wasted. Astrid and I have to leave now.

"Have you brought Nox?" I ask.

"Of course," Sora assures.

"Great, bring me something to change into." I touch the bloodied dress.

"You're not serious, are you? You're injured. You were so close to death. You can't leave." Davina argues.

"*Mother*, we are the only ones who can stop him."

She drops her arms to her side. The words slip from my mouth faster than I can think. A smile cracks from the corner of her mouth. I return the gesture.

It's uncertain how Astrid and I can stop the King, but we can figure it out together. We both are the ones to wield the horns of the Inferno. That in itself is a special gift that is rare for daemons to hold. Once we put our magic together, hopefully, something like a miracle happens.

Being back on Nox gives me a new feeling. A freedom I've never had. Perhaps it's because I'm running toward the danger and not running from it. Deep inside, I am scared. I don't know what we are getting ourselves into. I can't let that fear hinder us on our mission.

Bellamy and Sora fly beside us. In the distance, I can see the dragon's fire igniting the night sky. I didn't think there would be this much bloodshed. I look below. Warriors of every kind fight against each other to storm the castle and the King's forces.

"They've got their dragons on every side of the castle. There's no way to avoid them. Some are lurking in the shadows. Nox isn't exactly small enough to conceal himself. We've got your back, so just keep going."

"What about you and Sora?" I ask.

"It's our duty to get you to your destination in one piece. Not incinerated by a dragon, princess."

Bellamy continues in front of us, leaving Astrid and me again in perpetual silence.

"He hasn't stopped talking about you since you left." Astrid breaks the silence.

I contemplate replying to her.

"He adores you, Morana."

The pit in my stomach opens. I breathe in the night spring air. I trick myself into thinking I could smell flowers, but I could only smell fire and blood.

"Is this the big sister talk I've been waiting for?" I ask.

"I don't think you understand. Every plan he makes, every move he makes, is all driven by you. He hasn't made one wrong decision yet. He loves *you*."

As much as I would like to hear those words from Bellamy himself, hearing them from my sister makes everything so real. I can't deny what he did to me, though. It still hurts. He lied in the worst way. Perhaps he thought he would save me the heartbreak, but he never planned for when I actually fell for him.

"I don't think you should be saying such things, given that you are engaged to him."

Astrid tightens her knees on my hips.

"I do not love him. He is a stranger to me. I don't remember much from our childhood. The blood contract means nothing to me."

My lips part if they want to say something, but I choke on my breath. I can't say anything. I don't want to ruin this relationship with her. As a child, I would have done anything to have a sister or even a brother. Now I have both, and I want to preserve it for as long as I can.

The sound of a sword sliding against the scabbard ring beside us. Astrid grabs around my waist, and Nox pulls back. A giant red dragon blows its fire in the night sky.

"You go on. We will catch up," Bellamy says.

Without hesitation, I guide Nox to the trees, the lowest we can go to conceal ourselves in the shadows. Nox's wings make the wind stir around us.

The dragon's screech echoes through the air. I want to turn back and help them. I don't know if Sora and Bellamy will be able to fend off the dragon and make it out alive. I pray they make it out alive.

Astrid points to the landing site. Slowly, we descend from the sky, keeping an eye out for any lurking creatures in the dark. I prepare my sword. I will not be blindsided in this realm.

Astrid looks around, and then at the map she holds before her.

"Nesrin said she left him in the cove right down there." She points. "First, we must check there. Keep yourself guarded, though. He could have already woken up."

"What is our plan once we find King Alaric?"

I scan the area for wanderers and keep my sword at the ready. I've never fought in hand-to-hand combat before, let alone with a sword. I'm not prepared in the slightest. On the other hand, Astrid has no weapons on her, maybe a dagger, but she's relying just on her magic to protect herself. If only I hadn't wasted time crying and feeling sorry for myself, then I could have tested the ability of my powers. My only option in battle is to run from it with a portal.

I never realized how similar we look until now. When we found her, she was nothing but skin and bones. Her hair faded to a dark gray. After feeding herself and becoming stronger, I notice we have the same hair and the same eyes. Our complexions are nearly the same.

"How old were you when you transformed?" I ask.

She avoids my eyes. "I was twenty. At least King Alaric was nice enough to let me become a woman before killing me."

I leave the subject alone. We have more pressing matters to attend to. Although I'd like to know more about her time in the castle, I'd rather kill the king now and talk later in the peacefulness of our own home.

"Right over there." She says.

I follow behind her, keeping my distance.

We listen carefully for any movement. The crashing of the waves makes it difficult to hear anything in the echoey cave. My night vision turns on. I see nothing but rocks, seashells, and occasional crabs peeking behind boulders.

"Perhaps he's woken up and returned to the castle," I say. "We are too late."

"I don't think that's the case," Astrid says. "I can sense another soul lingering."

CHAPTER THIRTY- SEVEN

Rising doom fills my stomach. Astrid is right. I can feel another's presence here. I don't know if it's King Alaric, but it's someone who does not want us here. The atmosphere leaves an unpleasant taste in my mouth, a taste much like sulfur and blood. The negativity pushes us back.

"No one is in here," Astrid says.

We return the way we came, climbing over mossy rocks and avoiding the sharp edges. Careful not to slip from the ocean mist.

Astrid assists me over the boulder blocking our path.

"Glad to see the two of you have finally reunited."

A cold voice comes from the darkness of the trees.

"I thought I saw the last of you when I had the villagers give you what you deserved, Morana." He laughs.

"King Alaric."

Astrid and I stand shoulder to shoulder—sword by my side and a raging fist of fire in Astrid's.

"I have to hand it to that succubus. Smart of her to lead me here." King Alaric circles us.

I notice a spear in his hand. The same bloody spear they used to try to kill me. I don't know how he attained it so quickly. Nesrin would have been smart enough to lead him away without the spear in hand.

Dragon fire lights up the sky. Our eyes divert to it. Hoping that we can see a tiny glimpse of Sora and Bellamy, to know that they are still alive. I hear the distant clink of swords. How much longer can they hold up?

"Don't worry. Your precious boys are still alive. I thought they would have been dead by now."

I feel the warmth of Astrid's fire touch me. Not hot enough to burn me, but enough to tell me to drop the sword and use my magic. The blade will only be a barrier in this final battle.

I'm trying to let go. Those thoughts that once caused me to lose control no longer bring forth the fire within me. This time, after coming to peace with myself, I can finally manifest the fire without losing myself. I can be who I want to be. I am in complete control.

"Astrid, I see you have finally gained your horns," he laughs.

"I've always had them. I have more control over them now."

King Alaric glances around as if someone is watching. He doesn't look like himself. His head twitches. He's not the collected King he once was.

"King Alaric, you stand no chance," I say.

I look at Astrid. She's planning something. I nudge her, but she doesn't budge. Her mind is set on something. I wish she would hurry and tell me.

"For many years now, I have done my research on creatures like you. You are the one who stands no chance."

The ground rumbles beneath us. With one hand, I cling to Astrid's wrist. Both of us are trying to gain our balance. The trees rustle together, making the trees fall and bend—the earth beneath us cracks. It sounds as if a thunderstorm is upon us, but there is not a cloud in sight.

"Fools. All of you." He says.

Sora and Bellamy land next to us. I catch a glimpse of their faces in the moonlight. Bloody, and part of Sora's face is burned. Both he and Bellamy are gasping for breath. Their wings are still intact, thankfully.

"There's a reason why almost no daemons are left with horns. I am the one who ended their existence."

King Alaric's body cracks and twists. Bones sprout from his body and point to a sharp edge. They come from his shoulders and arms, hands and legs. Not an inch of his body is left untouched. A monster from the depths of the earth. A beast that I did not plan for.

"What the hell is going on?" Sora shouts.

King Alaric's eyes turn bright red, like that of a glowing ruby. And horns. He grows horns from his head. Just like mine and Astrid's, but much bigger. Thicker and ragged.

As we head into battle, we realize that we may not come out alive. Every move we make must be thought out carefully. But we have no time to linger and form a plan.

"He's not a daemon, is he?" I shout.

"Impossible. He's human." Astrid replies.

None of it is true. He was never human. That's how he's become so powerful. He's kept these secrets for many years now. His sole plan is to kill all who threaten him. Daemons are his only threat.

"He is using his body as a weapon. Those are daemon bones."

He made all of Rhemus believe he was human. He manipulated their minds into thinking daemons and other night creatures were to blame. He is one of us, and he's using that to his advantage. This is truly what wicked kings do.

Crow wings spring from his back, bigger than Sora's or Bellamy's. They tower feet above him. I've never seen feathers so long and sharp, like feathers of iron.

We never could have prepared for this in any way. No one knew of this deadly secret. I don't know how we can defeat him without risking our lives. One puncture from those horns and Astrid and I are surely dead, and this time, we won't be able to be revived.

Sora and Bellamy break off to the left and right. Astrid and I stay standing in the middle.

"Morana, you've got this. Give it your all. Use all the magic inside you. Don't let him win." Astrid says before running off to the side, flames burning brighter than I've ever seen.

I may have the gift of flames, but I do have another advantage. I can use the portals. King Alaric will never know our next move.

"Bellamy, over here," I shout.

Bellamy searches for me in the rubble of the dirt. King Alaric watches us with his red eyes. Bellamy lands next to me, grabbing my wrist, making sure we don't get separated.

"What do you have in mind?" He asks.

We cover our heads from the falling tree limbs. It's hard to think when everything is flying in the air.

"I need you to grab that spear in his hand. It's the only thing that will kill another daemon."

He looks at King Alaric, and an unsure look spreads across his face.

"Are you mad? I can't get close enough to him without being impaled myself. His entire body is made of Daemon bone."

"I can use my portals to get you behind him. You can take the spear, and I'll bring you back here where we can assess further."

We look over to Astrid and Sora. Astrid blasts the tree limbs away with her flames, and Sora uses his sword in mid-air. They can't hold on much longer without our help.

"Grab onto me. He won't see us coming." I say.

He loops his arm around mine, keeping his grip extra tight. I bite my thumb. Bellamy gasps as I let the blood drip onto the ground, and the golden portal opens. The golden hue ignites Bellamy's war-ridden face.

"Jump!"

Together we jump through the portal. We swim through sun rays and beautiful peace for a short moment before standing directly behind King Alaric. He doesn't notice us until Bellamy's hand wraps around the spear. King Alaric kicks Bellamy in the face and knocks him back. Before King Alaric drives the spear through him, I manage to grab Bellamy and pull him into the next portal.

I take us to a spot behind the bushes. Bellamy holds his nose. The blood is dripping. He remains unfazed.

"Are you alright?" I panic.

"I'm fine. I couldn't grab it. He's too fast."

I help Bellamy to his feet. I've lost my sword somewhere along the way. Bellamy still has it on his hip and a dagger on the other. I grab the blade. He doesn't notice.

"He needs a distraction," Bellamy says. The blood is gone from his face. "He knows our plan now. He will keep himself guarded."

Bellamy is right.

I signal for Astrid on the other side of King Alaric. Sora remains hitting targets of debris and rubble.

She teleports over to us, using the same golden portals as I. For a moment, I am surprised and happy we share the same gift. I can tell she doesn't like using it, though. She sways back and forth. I've used the portals more than she has.

"We need you to distract King Alaric while we grab the spear," I suggest.

She turns to King Alaric. The full moon shines down on him. The elements bend to his will, circle in the air, and destroy the land he fought to create.

"Got it. But you have to make this fast."

Astrid runs to the opening charging full force with her magic. She forms a firewall with her hands, disintegrating everything in its path. She is much stronger than I ever thought her to be.

Bellamy assumes positions with his arm locked around mine. The blood drips to the ground, and the portal opens. We jump through, hoping this time we make it.

Astrid strikes King Alaric in one blow, causing him to lose balance and control of the spear. Bellamy reaches for the spear and quickly pulls it into the portal before it closes.

CHAPTER THIRTY- EIGHT

The one weapon that will surely kill me lies in the hands of Bellamy now. His hands grip tight around the spear, fearing it may fall from our grasp and we may be right back at the beginning. It would be an end to our fate.

I think of how I could kill King Alaric with this weapon. Should I impale him from the back or through his chest? So he can look me in the eye and see my hatred for him. I should have Astrid do the honor of killing him since she is the one who had to endure many years of torture at the hands of his wickedness.

"What is the plan now? We have the spear. Bellamy says.

I snap from my trance. I watch the flying debris. King Alaric hasn't taken a direct hit on any of us. He is waiting for something. He would have already struck us with his magic or the bones jutting from his body if he wasn't.

"He knows we have the weapon. We must be careful now. He will be expecting us." I pant.

He still stands in the middle of the open area. Trees surround us for miles. I don't know how far the castle is. The shore isn't far. We could lure him to the caves, but that may be easier said than actually putting it into action.

A giant tree trunk comes flying in the air. Feet before it hits us, Bellamy pushes the spears into my hands, turns around, and slices through the tree swiftly. The tree scattered around us. Luckily Bellamy has fast reflexes.

Sora lands next to us. "Is everyone still in one piece?"

"For now," I say. "Wait. Where is Astrid?"

I panic as I see her standing face-to-face with King Alaric. Her hands and his are aflame, but his fire is blue. The hotter the fire, the stronger the daemon. Astrid can't fight him on her own.

"Astrid, what are you doing? Get out of there." I yell.

She doesn't hear me, or at least it seems like she can't hear me. Her gaze blazes over King Alaric with so much hatred it could set the world on fire. I feel it too. That same hatred. It ignites a part of me I have never felt. As much as I want to face him, I am scared, and it hurts to admit that to myself.

"What does she think she is doing?" Sora shouts.

Before our eyes, a circle of flames encompasses them into a small arena. Closing them both in. I can see it, the invisible force field. It glistens like oil meets water. He's trapping her in there with him. So he can finish her off.

"We have to find a way in. There is no way we can all get through now." Bellamy pants.

I stare at the force field one more time. It clicks.

"I can get in," I whisper. "He knows Astrid, and I have the gift of portals. He wants me to teleport inside."

Sora lowers his head. "He wants this battle between you three."

My stomach sinks. I keep telling myself it isn't true. He had this planned all along. After many days of thinking and going over every possibility, this scenario never popped into my mind. Perhaps it did. I just never wanted to speak it into existence.

"Give me the spear," I demand.

Bellamy's eyes widen. "Are you mad? You're walking into the lion's den by doing that. There has to be another way."

I breathe and let it all out. "Bellamy, this will not end without a fight. You and Sora, get our people out of Rhemus. We can handle this."

Bellamy takes my hand, and I quickly pull it away. Sora senses hostility.

"You have been a guest to Tenebris. You have done all you can for this kingdom. As the princess of Tenebris, I command you to retreat back to Tenebris, along with every man and soldier fighting this war."

I choke on the air and let out a breath. Letting out that old air never felt so good. Letting myself go had never felt so freeing.

Bellamy flies up, and Sora stares at me. "I'm staying, Morana. You can't make me go."

I turn to face King Alaric and Astrid. I turn my chin to my shoulder, not quite making contact with Sora. "You're right. I can't make you leave, so stay out of this fight."

He takes my hand before I can walk away. My eyes meet him.

"If you die, I die with you. And I want your eyes to be the last I see before my death."

Chills run down my spine. I turn before tears can run down my cheeks. I wait for it to happen, but the tears are stuck. I want to cry, but I'm filled with so much adrenaline. I'm ready to fight even if this is truly my end.

I reopen the cut on my finger to open the portal. I keep my eyes on Astrid as I step through it. For a slight second, I close my eyes, picturing Sora's face/

I reopen my eyes, and I am met with the darkened eyes of the King. Astrid stands next to me.

"I hope you have said your goodbyes, Morana. You will never see your brother again."

I look at my sister. Tears stain her eyes. She's just as scared as I am. Up until now, I had never seen her show much emotion. There is an unsettling look in her eye. I feel guilty for this even happening.

"When this is all over. Will you take me bat riding?" Astrid asks.

"I'd like nothing more, Sister."

King Alaric lunges for Astrid, but she quickly dodges his attack. She trips over her dress but catches herself just before hitting the ground. I circle him, but he keeps one on me in his peripheral vision. He can't possibly watch the two of us in unison.

Astrid's fire blazes in her hand. It travels along her entire arm, making both arms one big flaming weapon. The flames extend like the wings of a phoenix.

I send a fireball to King Alaric's back with my open arm. He dodges the hit in one swift move.

"If you'd let go of that spear, you'd have more of a fighting chance." King Alaric growls.

"No chance."

King Alaric makes his blows of blue fire toward Astrid. She increases her firepower and conjures a firewall bigger than the trees above us. How can she possibly be this powerful?

I'd risk my life if I tried that move on the next attack. I've never practiced using my infernal magic. I don't feel confident I'd make it out alive. I instantly regret not training for this sooner. I am out of my skill level.

King Alaric whips fire beneath my feet. The blue fire burns my skin. I don't know how it can be. My fire doesn't even burn me. But this fire is the hottest I've ever felt. I fall to the ground, and he returns to Astrid.

Astrid and King Alaric are close in their distance. Their attacks are made only from a few feet. Astrid can barely keep up. She's losing energy quickly. I don't even know my own limits. I feel so useless.

King Alaric catches her and kicks her to the ground. Before I can reach Astrid, he has the daemon bone from his arm through her stomach. The other end reaches out and drips with blood.

"Astrid. No!" I scream.

I race to King Alaric and drive the spear between his shoulder blades. He winces. I hold the spear in place, waiting for him to make any more movements.

He takes the daemon bone from Astrid, and she topples over to the ground.

"Finally, Morana. You have finally proven what a wicked little girl you have become." He mumbles.

I twist the spear, and more blood pours from his back. I push it in further, ensuring to get every last part of him. I let my hatred pour into him, leaving no room for kindness. This man must die.

I pull the spear from him, and he falls to his knees. I circle to face him. Astrid is holding her stomach, still alive but barely holding on. I can't leave until I know he's dead. I have to see the light vanish from his eyes.

"Morana, just kill him. We have to go." Sora shouts.

The force field lifts. His magic is fading quickly.

"You will die with the weapon you tried to end me with. People like you have no room to exist in this kingdom. Have fun in the Inferno, you bastard."

I take the tip of the spear and slice open his throat. Blood pours over his chest. The daemon bone disappears from his body as he reaches to cover his throat as if he could stop the bleeding.

His body goes limp in his pool of blood. Staring at his lifeless body fuels me with so much power that I can feel it in my veins, going straight to my heart. Before this moment, I would have been terrified of ending one's life, but he is the only exception.

Sora races next to me and kneels to Astrid.

"Can you stand?" He asks.

I turn to her. She's pale. Much paler than she had been before. I'm worried she may not make it since being pierced by a daemon bone. Her fate is not well.

Sora and I lift her from the ground. She holds her stomach. Her hand is now covered in her own blood. I listen for her faint breaths.

"We have to make it back to camp now." I pant. "We have to get her back to Davina."

I don't ask Astrid to make a portal. She must preserve every ounce of magic left within her to stay alive.

I open the cut on my finger and let the blood drip to the ground. All connected, we walk through the portal. I feel no pain for a moment, and I hope the same for Astrid, as she is much worse than Sora and me.

We have to make it back in time.

We land before the row of tents. Warriors of every rank swarm us with unsettling looks.

"Princess, we must get you to a medic." A gargoyle says.

Astrid pushes them away. I can't understand why she doesn't want to see a medic. She has only minutes left before she leaves us for good.

"I can't. One more thing must be done." She mumbles. She is barely able to breathe.

"Nonsense," I say. "Someone get Davina."

People scurry to find Davina and Lazarus.

"Sister, I have one more thing to do. I need you and Sora to help me with it." She winces and breathes in. "Take me to the border now."

Sora and I exchange looks. Whatever this is, it must be important for her. She is driven and will not take no for an answer. I can't let her spend her last moments doing something without a purpose.

I nod, and we begin to walk into the trees. Our nostrils fill with the scent of pine and ash. I can see the border from here. It's so close. I hold tight to Astrid, hoping she doesn't fall into our arms.

From left and right, people run over the border, escaping the war that still plays on in the kingdom of Rhemus. Swords clash, and roars of fire fill the nighttime sky. Flaming arrows cross the sky like shooting stars. This isn't the Sea of Lights

"We must close them off. Rhemus shall no longer harm its people. Whoever does not make it shall be confined to this treacherous filth."

She kneels to the ground. Sora and I follow. She places her hands on the ground and digs her hands into the dirt.

"Feel it. Feel the infernal power in the dirt, in the roots. Break them all."

She's trying to separate the two kingdoms. Lands shall no longer touch, and the grounds shall be free.

I can feel it. The power she speaks of. Sora does, too; by the way, he looks so natural. We follow Astrid.

The ground behind breaks, causing a rumbling sound on all sides. It shakes with more vigor than what King Alaric did. I push more energy into the earth. I feel it flowing out of me as If I am becoming one with nature.

People run for their lives. They leap over the cracks that are only growing in size. I begin to doubt we can pull this off. Astrid's lap is encased in blood. She can't hold on much longer.

The earth breaks before us. I look down into the massive hole as water fills it. Water from the ocean. Once again, I am met with my demise. I stare into it, this time hoping that I will not die here.

A wave comes between the two lands, separating the two kingdoms. Our magic is pushing away Rhemus.

The water crashing muffles the sounds of the crying citizens. I look at them, feeling some regret. They wanted out but are now banished to live in a broken kingdom.

I look over, and Astrid is laying on the ground.

"Astrid," I call out.

Sora brings his ear to her chest. I watch him closely for any signs that she might still be alive. She can't be dead. She's come too far for this to be her fate. I promised I'd take her bat riding.

Sora lifts back up, face remaining neutral. His eyes look down. He brushes the hair away from Astrid's face. Those dark eyes meet mine again. He need not say a word, for I know what has happened.

I shake my head. "No." I stand. "She was just alive. No." I scream. "No!"

I kneel to her and rest my hands on her chest, trying to feel any warmth left in her. Her chest does not rise and fall. Her skin has turned white like all the blood has been drained from her. My tears cover her face, and I wipe each one away. Thinking the wetness will bother her.

"She can't be dead," I mutter. My throat burns.

I look down at my hands resting on her chest. My knuckles are black with ash from the fire. If only this fire could have saved her.

"We have to get her back to camp. The others will know what to do."

I throw the spear into the nearest tree. I can barely think with all the waves crashing alongside the cliff. The grayness and vastness of the waves send chills down my spine.

"We didn't have enough time together." I cry.

"Morana. She was my sister too."

We have both lost someone who barely had the chance to know. We only knew she existed once we made it to Tenebris. The only memory of her is when we found her in the dungeon. Her mind was too corrupted for us to even form a bond. If only we had found her sooner.

CHAPTER THIRTY-NINE

I keep my eyes on the wet ground, avoiding all eye contact with those of the Tenebrisean army. If I look into their eyes, I fear they will think I have failed as their princess to save Astrid. I fought alongside her. I did not let her go down alone. I was there till the very last breath.

The last drops of the spring rain drop onto my shoulder. I wished it would have rained more to wash away the blood from Astrid. I don't know how to bring her back to camp looking like this. Bloody and broken. Still and dead.

I breathe, keeping my breath steady. Almost there. Then everyone and all of Tenebris will know their future queen has perished.

I continue to keep my eyes down.

Sora and I lift Astrid's limp body to the bed. People begin to swarm her. Pushing and poking her body in hopes that she would gasp for air and be with us again. I can't look them in the face when they realize she is dead.

"My daughter," Davina screams. Lazarus hoovers over her, tears falling from his face. "My precious daughter."

Her cries fill the small tent. I want to back out, but I have to see how this plays out. Will Davina blame me for the death of her firstborn?

Davina caresses Astrid's body. Touching her fingers, counting each one like she's still a tiny babe. She flattens her hair to fix its tangles. Davina looks at her stomach. A bloody hole open to the world. There was no fixing this. The poison of the daemon blood was just too much. Exhausting her magic brought death closer to her.

"Morana. Sora." She cries.

With no emotion in my voice, I say, "The king is dead. I killed him. But not before he struck Astrid with daemon bone."

Davina hustles to me with Lazarus behind her. She embraces me with her warmth. Lazarus does the same to Sora. Sora and I look at each other, trying to figure out what to do. This reaction is different from what we expected.

I wrap my arms around Davina. Waves of emotion wash over me like the oceans that separate the kingdoms. I don't want her to let go. Even after everything that led to this, I can't let her go.

"I'm so sorry." I cry. "I tried to save her. I just wasn't quick enough."

Davina hugs me tighter. Lazarus pats Sora on the shoulder as they exchange looks of defeat.

"Son, you did well. You fight like a true warrior." That is all Lazarus has to say.

The tent opens, and for a moment, I want to shout at anyone who dares to enter.

Bellamy.

His eyes fall on Astrid, but not in the way I thought he would. His dark eyes leave no emotion. He looks at me and goes back to Astrid. I can't tell what he's feeling. I can't ask him in front of everyone.

"Morana has killed King Alaric," Davina says. "Daemon bone. She used too much of her magic to save Tenebris."

Bellamy nods.

"Are you both alright?" He asks Sora and me.

Sora nods.

"I tried to save her, Bellamy," I mumble.

I sound like I am trying to save him from hurt. Like everything was my fault. He was bound to marry Astrid, and now that deal has been broken. I can't imagine what that could mean for the two kingdoms. I fear his mother and father may blame me.

Bellamy strides over to me. "You are a warrior of Tenebris. You saved your kingdom. This is what war does. It kills, and it spares. We are all dealing with death."

I look into his eyes. I feel the warmth spinning in my stomach. I can tell his words are genuine. It strikes me odd that he wouldn't be more distraught by Astrid's death. He was so serious about marrying her. He said it was for his kingdom. Now that Astrid is dead, what does that mean for Kiveha?

Bellamy turns to the others. Davina wipes her tears with a worn handkerchief.

"We have much to deal with now. We have rounded up all of the citizens of Rhemus who escaped before the land separation. We must assess them all and keep track of everyone who entered. We have to ensure there is no risk of letting them stay here."

I look at Astrid. Regret fills me.

"There are more matters that must be taken care of before we let the citizens of Rhemus into the city."

All eyes shoot to me.

"We must have a proper burial for Astrid. We cannot let her body rot in this place."

Lazarus nods. "Agreed. We will keep them here until after the burial. We will keep guards here at all times."

Silence falls over the room. We acknowledge Astrid's beauty before covering her body with a thin white sheet. The blood begins to seep through, making the sheet no longer pure white. Her body becomes a ghost with a reminder of the past soaked in it.

Commotion rises outside the tent and breaks us of our trance. Sora leaves the tent in a hurry. Soon after he comes back in, his body is tense with frustration. He breathes heavily.

"Queen Inina requests your presence." He looks at Davina.

Davina's eyes turn wide, and her eyebrows furrow. How could Queen Inina have made it over the border? I thought she would have been dead the moment the warriors invaded the castle.

"Bring her in," Davina says.

Two gargoyles bring in Queen Inina, bound in chains behind her back. She's calm, but her red eyes state otherwise.

As she enters, her eyes fall on the white sheet in the center of the tent. A blanket in the shape of a woman she once knew—a person who was once her prisoner.

"Is that…Astrid. Is that her?" She begins to weep. We all look at each other, wondering why she would be crying. She married a man so cruel. Surely, she knew what tortuous things he did to Astrid. Surely she was in on it. We all believed her to be of the same wickedness as King Alaric.

"What is your business here?" Davina demands.

The gargoyles step away from Queen Inina but still remain close to her. Queen Inina stands still, eyeing the white sheet and back to Davina.

"Your majesty," She starts. "I come here not as a queen. Please, hear my plea."

Davina's eyes flash red.

"Have you come here to gloat about the death of my child?"

"Quite the opposite, your majesty."

With elegance, Queen Inina rests her shoulders. She makes it known that she is not in her own territory. She must respect ours if we are to listen to her.

Davina nods hesitantly.

"When Astrid crossed the border, no one wanted anything to do with her. She was so small and helpless. She was extremely confused. She cried every night looking for you. Unfortunately, Alaric and I could never conceive, so he permitted me to treat her as my own."

Queen Inina breathes. Davina looks paler than usual. She sits in the nearest chair, hands folded in her lap.

"We mostly kept her confined to the castle, and only a few maids and guards were allowed into the inside. If word got out that we were housing the enemy, it wouldn't have been good for us.

"I made sure she ate. I sang to her every day. Read books to her at night. I even taught her to play a few instruments. She was well beyond cared for. She was essentially my responsibility. King Alaric forbade me to take her outside in fear of someone seeing her.

"She was eighteen when I let her experience the greatness of the outdoors. She had grown to be just like us. Even King Alaric was getting used to having her around, but he never fully trusted her because of where she came from and the blood that runs through her."

Lazarus sits next to Davina, taking her hands in his.

"One night, we decided to let her out. No one was about, and the courtyard was clear. Word must have gotten out about her, and suddenly, an arrow was sent straight into her back."

"She died that night of the full moon. I was sure that we had lost her. We took her inside the infirmary. There was nothing they could do for her. She was gone. That is until minutes later, as they were taking her body away, her head began to sprout horns, just like yours, Morana."

I feel the weight of the horns on my head. It makes sense now that Astrid said she had horns.

She was able to hide them somehow when I first met her. Perhaps all the years she was confined helped her realize her true self. She came to terms with her destiny. That's how she hid her horns so easily.

"My daughter died and became a daemon in your kingdom." Davina cries. "And you kept her? I thought you hated creatures like us."

"King Alaric hated creatures like you." Queen Inina cuts in. "I still loved Astrid. I still cared for her. I think you forgot, Davina, that I did not marry King Alaric for love. I married him because I was forced to by my own unruly parents. What King Alaric believes in has nothing to do with me. I did not know that King Alaric was a daemon himself until your warriors came across the border."

The room falls silent save for Davina's cries. I want to cry with her, but I'm so angry that I can't conjure any tears. I can feel the heat boiling in my veins.

"When her powers began to come forth, King Alaric said she posed a risk to us all. She could no longer be outside her room with her horns. He had her tortured. I tried to stop him, but my strength never matched his. He eventually put her in the dungeon so life in the castle could return to normal."

I walk to Queen Inina and look her in the eyes. Her lips quiver.

"I saw her every day. She eventually shut me out." She cries. "He broke her horns." Her cries become heavy.

I embrace her for a moment. Then, I close my eyes to avoid seeing anyone else staring at me. My actions may be considered crazy, but I can feel her regret. I sense the love she has for Astrid. She's been more honest with me than Davina ever did in the beginning.

"What are you doing?" Queen Inina asks.

"Thank you," I whisper. "Thank you for caring for my sister."

Davina stands and lifts her hand from Lazarus' hand. He stands behind her. Davina strides over to Queen Inina. Her face is tense and wrought with despair.

Davina clears her throat. "I'm not particularly fond of what happened." Davina takes a breath. "But I must thank you for your compassion. Had you none, I may have gone a lifetime without seeing my daughter again."

Sora and I exchange glances. Bellamy is left staring at Astrid's dead body. By the look in his eyes, he's yet to process her death fully. Just as all of us are.

"King Alaric was a madman. I tried countless times to leave his kingdom, but I, too, was a prisoner. I'd be ruined if I left. I was scared of disappointing my own family. I now realize that I should have done the right thing and brought her back to you."

"Unchain her," Davina demands. "She will not be a prisoner of *this* kingdom."

Queen Inina rubs her wrists. "With your permission, I would like to take refuge in your beautiful city of Drafanel. Even when she was little, Astrid told me of its beauty."

Davina and Lazarus look at each other, talking in their own language.

"Permission granted."

It surprises me that Davina has so easily let her go. Even though she was married to King Alaric, she had no part to play in his wicked games. A game in which everyone involuntarily played. Rhemus was a prison.

Inina is escorted out of the tent. Complete silence rings in all of our ears. The events that have played out seem almost like a dream. A nightmare even. I have to keep myself grounded in this reality. If I were to wake up one day and find myself back in Rhemus, I don't know what I'd do.

The smell of corpses and fire lingers in the air. And I wonder when the scent will ever leave Tenebris. Or will it serve as a reminder of the power Sora and I hold? A reminder which I can never forget. It will always haunt me till the end. If there ever is an end.

CHAPTER FORTY

The clinking of the utensils echoes through the dining room. It's an unbearable ring. I've spent enough days in this dining room alone with Davina and Lazarus. Although they mean well, I desperately need out of this hell.

Sora will be home in a few days. He's been gone for almost a month now. He seems to be having the time of his life in the letters he writes us. I always look forward to reading them.

He spends most of the time with Xanthe, but he's been learning so much. Apparently, he's mastered the sword, a bow and arrow, and many other weapons I still have yet to learn about. The King has taken him to the military base in Kiveha. That has been the highlight of his visit there.

"Do you think he's engaged to Xanthe now?" I ask.

Lazarus drops his fork. Davina smiles with her chin turned down.

"I suppose. It's still too early to say. They have only been together for a short time." Davina says. "Are you so eager to be queen one day?"

I take a sip of my wine. I knew she would say such a thing. Although Sora is the oldest of us two, the women are always in line to become Queen. I don't know how such a rule came to be, but I'll gladly take the throne one day. That will be hundreds of years from now.

The door creaks open. "Your majesties, I apologize for intruding. There is an urgent message from Prince Sora."

The messenger carries the letter to Davina, but I hold my hand out to demand the letter be given to me. The messenger hesitates once he sees Davina bow her head.

The messenger leaves in a hurry.

I open the seal, eager to hear from Sora.

"I wonder what could be so urgent," Lazarus says. "Perhaps he's chosen to stay longer than planned."

The letter rips open. I know from this handwriting that it is not Sora's. I look to the bottom. It's Bellamy's.

"Go on. Read it, dear." Davina urges.

"Oh gods," I whisper.

Lazarus and Davina's faces tense.

"I apologize if you were expecting Sora to write back. This urgent message is for King Lazarus, Queen Davina, and Princess Morana. Please send any willing person to Kiveha to aid us. Sora has gone missing. We do not expect he is dead, but we have been searching for him to no avail. By the time you get this letter, it will have been two days since his disappearance. Please send help."